BLOOD BROTHERS

A Selection of Recent Titles by Patricia Hall

The Kate O'Donnell Series

DEAD BEAT *
DEATH TRAP *
DRESSED TO KILL *
BLOOD BROTHERS *

The Ackroyd and Thackeray Series

SINS OF THE FATHERS
DEATH IN A FAR COUNTRY
BY DEATH DIVIDED
DEVIL'S GAME

* available from Severn House

BLOOD BROTHERS

Patricia Hall

CRÈME de la CRIME

This first world edition published 2013
in Great Britain and the USA by
Crème de la Crime, an imprint of
SEVERN HOUSE PUBLISHERS LTD of
19 Cedar Road, Sutton, Surrey, England, SM2 5DA.

British Library Cataloguing in Publication Data

Hall, Patricia, 1940- author.
  Blood brothers. – (A Kate O'Donnell mystery; 4)
  1. O'Donnell, Kate (Fictitious character)–Fiction.
  2. Women photographers–England–Liverpool–Fiction.
  3. London (England)–Social conditions–20th century–
  Fiction. 4. Detective and mystery stories
  I. Title II. Series
  823.9'14-dc23

ISBN-13: 978-1-78029-061-4 (cased)

All Severn House titles are printed on acid-free paper.

Severn House Publishers support the Forest Stewardship Council™ [FSC™],
the leading international forest certification organisation. All our titles that
are printed on FSC certified paper carry the FSC logo.

Typeset by Palimpsest Book Production Ltd.,
Falkirk, Stirlingshire, Scotland.
Printed and bound in Great Britain by
TJ International, Padstow, Cornwall.

ONE

Detective sergeant Harry Barnard looked in distaste at his Italian shoes which, after only a couple of minutes on the building site, were caked in yellowish London clay.

'You can't lend me a pair of gumboots, can you?' he asked the site foreman in hard hat and mud-caked boots himself who stood beside him at the top of an excavation which looked more like the beginnings of a mining operation than the early stages of a controversial skyscraper, which would eventually dominate the southern end of Tottenham Court Road in the West End of London.

'I'd've thought you'd come better feckin' prepared,' the foreman said in an Irish brogue. 'I told you on the phone it was likely dumped in the feckin' pit last night. It wasn't far under the surface. Someone would have noticed if it had been there longer.'

'Yes, well, you didn't actually say it was definitely a body, did you?' Barnard snapped, his irritation increased by the bitter north wind which seemed to swirl around the building site with malevolent intent. 'Just a suspicious parcel. Could have been anything.'

'To be sure, that's all it looked like when the excavator brought it up. Whoever dumped it was unlucky. They must have known we were due to pour concrete today. It was only because some eejit surveyor got the depth wrong that we had to keep digging this morning. If everything had gone to plan it'd have disappeared beneath the foundations with thirty-two storeys to go up on top of it. It'd never have been found till twenty sixty-three, if this damn tower lasts a hundred years. Come on then, will ye? You'll be needing a close-up.'

The builder nodded towards the cabin at the top of the excavation where he kitted Barnard out with a pair of wellingtons several sizes too large for him into which the sergeant carefully tucked the trousers of his suit before being led down the treacherously muddy slope which gave access to the bottom of the excavation. The builder grabbed his arm as he skidded on the shining wet clay before they plodded through the mud to where a uniformed policeman was standing guard. Close by, the excavator driver was leaning against the side of his machine smoking and did no more than wave the detective towards what looked like a pile of rags lying near to the business end of the machine. Barnard stepped carefully across the sticky clay to take a closer look but even from a distance he had little doubt that the bundle contained human remains.

'You actually scooped it up?' he asked the driver, who nodded. 'You didn't see it at first?'

'Nah, I didn't, mate,' the driver replied. 'Not that it's that unusual in London, though it's usually bones you find. A skull now and again. But this is new. That wrapping's not rotted, just a bit torn up by the scoop. It looks fresh.'

'Thanks be to God for that,' the foreman said. 'If you get lumbered with Romans or feckin' plague victims everything stops to let the feckin' archaeologists in for weeks at a time.'

Barnard nodded, wondering how many unidentified bones on building sites were quietly reburied to save time and money. He sighed and peered more closely at the package, which was stained with clay and also something browner. He poked gently with his foot where the sacking cover had been damaged and was not surprised when a stickier, redder patch oozed through on to the toe of his wellington boot. 'You're going to have to stop work for today at least,' he said to the foreman. 'I need to get forensics down here while we open it up. And the murder team. It hardly looks like a natural death, does it?'

The foreman scowled and glanced up to where the buildings in Oxford Street and Tottenham Court Road hemmed them in. 'I swear it'll be a miracle if this feckin' building gets up on time,' he said. 'It's a bloody stupid place to put it, right on the road junction and with the tube station underneath.'

Barnard shrugged. His only interest in the building boom which was sweeping the parts of London ravaged by German bombers, was focused on the armies of labourers who had been drafted in from all over the world to work on the new sites. Some of them would know where the concrete was being poured this morning and if this was indeed a body conveniently dumped where it could easily have disappeared forever within hours, he would need to know exactly who knew and who they might have passed that information to.

He clambered out of the pit with the foreman, closely followed by the excavator driver, all of them slipping and sliding on the shiny wet surface.

'Keep everyone out of there,' Barnard said. 'I'll report back to my boss and we'll be back very soon. It's more than likely we have a murder here. And we'll need an up-to-date list of the people working on the site. Either one of them dumped it, or maybe they told someone the concrete was supposed to be coming today. I reckon we'll need to talk to them all before we're done.'

The foreman's face dropped. 'I'll see what I can do,' he muttered. 'But a lot of the labourers are casuals – you know? On the lump. Here today and gone tomorrow.'

'And no tax paid?' Barnard snapped. 'Well, if that really is a murder victim, and it looks like it, I'll want to know about everyone who's been here recently. It's too convenient for them not to have known it was going to be set in stone within hours. I don't buy that as a coincidence. And don't let anyone touch anything down there, please. We'll be back sharpish.'

After he had laboriously cleaned the mud off his shoes, Barnard reported back to DCI Keith Jackson, who sat behind his meticulously tidy desk, drumming his fingers on his clean blotter.

'It's not been there long, guv,' Barnard said. 'And it's a good size, certainly not a child or even a small adult. It's twenty feet below ground level and I guess it would have taken at least two people to get it there. I doubt it was just chucked in. There'd be too much risk of it bursting open. And the excavator driver said it was actually buried beneath the level they were working at yesterday, covered by sodden wet soil. It wasn't very deep but he swears he didn't see it before he scooped it up. There are six or seven concrete lorries lined up outside ready to fill the foundations but the foreman says they were required to dig a bit deeper this morning, unexpectedly. But for that, whoever's down there would never have been found.'

'You're quite sure it's a body?'

Barnard wondered for a moment if his years of experience counted for anything with this meticulous boss. 'There are signs of what looks like blood,' Barnard said carefully. 'I've not touched it at all, of course, but I don't think there's any doubt.'

Jackson nodded slightly wearily, avoiding Barnard's eye. He was a taciturn Scot who generally showed little emotion but today Barnard wondered why he was exceptionally disinclined to engage. 'Very well, sergeant,' he said. 'We'll get a murder team down there, and forensics. I expect the developers are totting up the cost of every minute we're going to delay them already, so we'd better get a move on.' He glanced at Barnard's still smeared shoes with the glimmer of a smile. 'Muddy down there, is it?'

'Gum boot territory, guv,' Barnard said hiding a grimace. He was known, and mocked, around the nick as a snappy dresser, an Italian suit and Liberty tie man, but Jackson too was never to be seen without an immaculate dark suit and highly polished shoes. Neither of them, Barnard thought, would enjoy the imminent prospect of watching a body unpacked in a sea of mud.

Standing later in the deep pit where Harry Hyams already controversial Centre Point tower would eventually rise, DCI Jackson stood fastidiously on duckboards beside Harry Barnard watching as forensic officers unwrapped the sacking parcel close by. It did not take long to satisfy themselves that inside the sacking lay human remains but nothing had prepared any of them for the horror which unfolded and to a man they flinched.

'Jesus,' Barnard said softly, while the DCI's face blanched as they surveyed what could only be said to be the remnants of a man.

'Pathologist?' Jackson snapped, taking a deep breath before he spoke.

'On his way, guv,' Barnard said. 'He's going to have his work cut out. You might chop someone up to get them into a package but some of that happened before the poor sod died. Fingers and toes? What's that for, for Christ's sake?'

'The amusement of some psycho, maybe,' Jackson said grimly. 'Or a warning to others?'

'Buried under tons of concrete and thirty-two storeys?' Barnard asked sceptically. In his experience most psychopaths relished the exposure of their handiwork. 'But the state his face is in? That has to have been done to stop anyone recognizing him, surely. In the unlikely event he was found too soon, before he went under the concrete.'

'I'm sure if someone wanted people to know what had happened to that poor beggar it could be arranged,' Jackson said. 'There are people in this city quite capable of that. You know only too well there are.'

Knowing exactly what connections of his had prompted that barb, Barnard turned away scowling. 'There are also people who know that without a body we'd find it difficult to launch a murder investigation,' he offered. He glanced over Jackson's shoulder.

'Here's the doc,' he said, his voice neutral as he indicated a figure descending warily, with the help of a uniformed officer, into the pit they were standing in and picking his way along the duckboards the police had put in place but which were already beginning to sink into the mud. 'Not someone I know,' he added quietly. 'Dr Lockwood's on leave, they said. This is Dr Jaffa.'

'I hope he knows what he's at,' Jackson muttered, but in spite of his reservations he held out his hand to the muffled figure who approached and who flinched as much as the police had done when he saw what lay in its shroud of sacking.

'There will not be very much I can tell you here and now,' he said, peering at the bloodied mess which had been a human being. 'I will need him – it appears to be him – on the table. And if you need an identification I can tell you now, it will be difficult. His own mother would not recognize that.' Jaffa spoke precisely with only the faintest trace of an Indian intonation.

'Have you been in the country long, doctor?' Jackson asked with a hint of aggression. It was obvious that an Asian pathologist was not what he had been expecting or wanted.

'I trained at St Thomas's,' Jaffa said, his voice cold and his accent impeccably English. 'Some time ago.' Gingerly he approached the body and made a cursory examination. 'In this case it will be very difficult to give you any immediate information with any certainty,' he said. He was obviously not going to accommodate Jackson's obvious reservations about his competence. 'I would guess he has been dead for a day at least before he was dumped. There still seems to be uncongealed blood but the wetness of the ground might account for that. Most of the major knife incisions could have killed him or could have been inflicted after death. But in this condition I can't be sure. I can't even be sure all the parts are here. All I can say is that he appears to have been stripped. There is no sign of any clothing, just the sacking he was wrapped in. I'll arrange for him to be moved to the lab as soon as possible and report back as soon as I can.'

'Some of the damage may have been done by the excavator which dug him out of the mud,' Jackson said. 'We'll talk to the excavator driver and let you know exactly what happened.'

'That would be very helpful,' Jaffa said.

'Somewhere someone must have dumped his clothes,' Jackson said, turning back to Barnard.

'Or burnt them, guv.' the sergeant suggested.

'Why bother if they obviously never expected him to be found,' Jackson countered.

'Well, judging by the state of him they'd be covered in blood. But I suppose they might have identified him in some way. But even if they did it'll be like looking for a needle in a haystack. He could have been brought here from just about anywhere in London. Or even further away.'

'He was dumped by someone who found out exactly what was going on at this site,' Jackson said sharply. 'I want every person working here interviewed to find out if anyone has been asking questions about when the concrete was going to be poured. That's the only lead we have. Let's get on with it.'

Kate O'Donnell sat at her desk at Ken Fellows' photographic agency in the heart of Soho feeding new film into her precious Voigtlander camera and feeling surplus to requirements. Her boss, she knew, had flown in the face of convention by taking a woman on as a photographer but she could tell he still felt uncomfortable when he assigned jobs to his crew. Some, he evidently thought, though never admitted, were not suitable tasks for a woman, and especially perhaps, a woman as young and attractive as Kate with her dark curly hair smoothed precariously flat, her sparkling blue eyes and slim figure. This morning the assignments had all gone to the men on duty: a serious accident in the East End, a fire raging at a factory at Park Royal where the London Fire Brigade feared an explosion, and a secondment to one of the national papers whose picture editor needed some extra help.

Kate's own recent foray into the rag trade, which Ken had hoped would enable the agency to penetrate the women's magazine market, had ended in tears, and of the assignments on offer that day the one she most coveted this morning she knew she was the least likely to get. She yearned to put her foot over the threshold of one of the national newspapers which lined Fleet Street like impregnable fortresses on either side, with their provincial acolytes' London offices squeezed into the narrow gaps and elderly offices in between. But Ken had merely raised an eyebrow when she had mentioned that ambition.

'I've never heard of a woman photographer on a national paper,' he had said. 'Or a provincial one, come to that. There was too much heavy kit to lug about while they were still using plate cameras. They're on the way out of course but I don't see that anything's going to change soon. The unions are very strong and very stroppy. The printers certainly wouldn't like it. Even the lady hacks get a barracking when they get too close to the Linotype machines.'

'But it might change now,' Kate had insisted, waving her thirty-five mm at him, the small, fast item which was changing the face of photography. 'With the smaller cameras?'

'Maybe,' Ken had said. 'I shouldn't hold your breath. I've seen no sign of it.' He looked thoughtful for a moment and then seemed to come to a decision, though with some uncertainty in his eyes. 'As it happens I'm due to have a drink with the crime reporter from the *Globe* some time soon. He's an old mate from when I was a Fleet Street photographer myself. Come with me for a quick bevvy and he can fill you in on what goes on down there these days. I've been away from it

too long. Maybe things are changing. Perhaps next time they
want someone to fill in, cover for a holiday or something, I
could put your name up. If they don't like the idea they can
always say no.'

Kate's heart missed a beat and she tried to keep any trace
of excitement out of her eyes. 'Great,' she said. 'Let's do that.
I hate sitting here doing nothing.'

Kate had spent most of the unproductive day flipping idly
through the morning papers, desultorily bringing her files of
photographs up to date, and then reading the early editions of
the evening papers which had been dropped off at the agency,
but her mind was not on them. There was another problem
which was keeping her awake in the small hours, and its name
was Harry Barnard, the Soho cop who had charmed her the
very first time she had met him and into whose bed she had
eventually been lured. But the relationship flared and spluttered
out again at intervals and Kate was never sure that she wanted
it to survive. And nor, she thought, was Harry. Neither of us,
she had confided sadly to her flatmate Tess after being stood
up one more time, really wanted to be pinned down.

At the end of the afternoon, when the flurry of photographers
on assignment had come back to the office and developed their
pictures, and most of them had gone home, Kate waited for
Ken Fellows to clear his own desk. At last he finished and
nodded in her direction.

'Get your coat on girl,' he said. 'It's fixed. I'll buy you a
G and T at the French pub and you can have a chat with Carter.'

They walked together through the early evening lull as the
West End workers straggled home and before the evening's
revellers poured in to the pubs and clubs, restaurants and clip
joints which lined the narrow streets of Soho. Pushing open
the door of the French pub's bar, Fellows glanced round and
raised a hand in greeting to a burly, red-faced man in a green
tweed three piece suit which did nothing to hide his expansive
belly, sitting on his own at a corner table with a half empty
glass of Scotch in front of him. He was younger than Ken,
Kate thought, but seemed to be deliberately cultivating an
old-fashioned look. She held back as the two men shook hands.

'It's been a long time,' he said. 'Carter, this is my newest recruit, Kate O'Donnell. Kate – Carter Price, crime supremo at the *Globe*, a very old mate of mine and a Fleet Street star.'

'Hello, my dear,' Price said with an enthusiasm which surprised Kate. 'It's surprising we haven't bumped into each other before,' he said. 'I've picked up on some of your adventures for my rag. You seem to believe in living dangerously.'

'Not really,' Kate said. 'Most of what's happened to me has been purely accidental.'

Price raised an eyebrow at that but did not comment.

'Well, sit down, darling, and tell me all about it. What can I get you to drink?'

It was late when Kate got back to the flat she shared with Tess Farrell, her head spinning from the combination of one G and T too many and from listening to the endless stories from Fleet Street the two men regaled her with.

'Kate fancies her chances as a snapper for one of the papers,' Ken had said as the evening progressed, his voice becoming slightly slurred. 'I told her that's not on.'

Price laughed loudly, attracting attention around the now crowded bar. 'They'd eat you for breakfast, petal,' he said.

'I'd like to see them try,' Kate had snapped, filled with alcoholic bravado. 'You forget I come from Liverpool.'

'Ah, that's where that accent comes from. I should have known now these bands are ruling the roost,' Price said. 'Knew them, did you? The Beatles.'

'I was at art college with John Lennon,' Kate said sharply.

'Were you now?' Price had said. 'Well, I tell you what. I'll set up a meeting with the picture editor at the *Globe* and give you a tour round the old Lubianka. How about that?'

'And what did your boss say to that,' Tess asked as they sipped coffee in front of the gas fire when Kate got home.

'I think he was a bit miffed, but he couldn't really say anything, could he? After all he'd introduced me to Carter Price in the first place. It's only a visit anyway. From what they said I shouldn't think anything will come of it.'

'I wouldn't be too sure,' Tess said, laughing. 'On recent form you seem to be able to talk your way into just about anything you want.'

*   *   *

After a gruelling afternoon working through the paperwork at the Centre Point site and supervising interviews with all the labourers who were there and making a note of those who weren't, to be followed up later, Harry Barnard called it a day as the winter light faded. He signed off at the nick after telling DCI Jackson that nothing of significance had emerged, and made his way to his red Ford Capri in search of a final interview which he did not intend to tell anyone else about.

He drove through the City, where the streets were already emptying, and east towards Whitechapel where he parked outside the unobtrusive entrance to a gym in a side-street, checking his doors carefully, although he had little doubt that the safety of the car, his pride and joy, was more or less guaranteed anywhere so close to Ray Robertson's property. He went inside and found even this early in the evening there were a couple of lads sparring in the ring, and more using the training equipment around the bleak hall.

'Is he in?' he asked the older man in grubby singlet and shorts who was watching the sweating pair in the ring carefully and shouting out advice as the slighter of the two began to flag.

'In the office, on the phone,' the trainer replied with barely a glance at Barnard, who had trained here himself when he left school, encouraged by Robertson to believe he had potential in the ring. He had known Ray since he and the two Robertson brothers had been evacuated together in the early days of the war, but their paths had diverged when Barnard went to grammar school and the other two boys had followed their family's criminal traditions. But there were bonds that were never truly broken when Barnard put on a police uniform and as a detective there were occasions when the old links proved useful. Barnard came to the gym much less often now to help out the next generation of East End lads, black now as well as white, who saw the ring as a way out of dead-end jobs or crime. Followed by the monotonous thud of leather on flesh and the rattle of skipping feet, he made his way to Ray Robertson's tiny office in the far corner of the hall, knocked and stuck his head round the door to be beckoned in with the wave of a cigar as Robertson ended his call.

'Harry my boy, nice to see you. Have you come for a workout or is this just a social call?'

'To pick your brains, Ray, as it goes,' Barnard said, taking the only other chair in the cluttered room and accepting Robertson's offer of a cigar which he tucked carefully into his top pocket for later. 'We had something very nasty turn up this afternoon. It was too late for the evening papers but it'll be all over the rags in the morning. With your contacts I thought you might have heard a whisper.'

Robertson's smile faded slightly. 'You'd better tell me all about it, Flash,' Robertson said and drew deeply on his cigar, thickening the air in the tiny space into a fog. 'So far as I know everything's quiet at the moment on the West End front, which I assume is what we're talking about as you were on the spot.'

'The big building site at Tottenham Court Road, the one there's been all the fuss about. Someone made mincemeat of some poor beggar and dumped him there, obviously expecting him to disappear under tons of concrete today if everything had gone according to plan. With brother Georgie safely locked up awaiting trial I couldn't think of another psycho who might fit the bill.'

Robertson leaned back in his chair, eyes narrowed. 'Can't say I've picked anything up of that sort,' he said. 'What makes you think it's not some loony tune like Jack the Ripper?'

'Random killers don't usually go to that amount of trouble to hide their victims,' Barnard said. 'Someone put a lot of thought into this poor beggar's disposal. It was sheer accident that he didn't disappear as planned. The contractors had a sudden change of plan and put an excavator back into the foundations. We're waiting for the post-mortem report. That should tell us how he died.'

'I'll keep my ears open,' Robertson said. 'But I can't say I've heard a whisper so far.'

And with that, Harry Barnard thought, he would obviously have to be content.

TWO

Assistant Commissioner John Amis, in full uniform, stood at the window of his Scotland Yard office gazing pensively across the Embankment at the turbulent River Thames in flood. He was a tall man, heavy but not obese in spite of his confinement to a desk job which, after army service which had not ended until after the Korean War, he occasionally chafed against. But at least, he thought, there was the prospect of some action ahead. He tidied the top of his desk, glanced into one or two drawers, one containing a heavy and strictly illicit old service revolver, before locking them and putting the keys in his pocket. He picked up his uniform cap and made his way through the Victorian building which had long ago become inconvenient and overcrowded for a modern police force. Perhaps soon the long promised new building would materialize on the site which had been selected near Victoria Station.

The AC's objective was a small unit dedicated to the protection of witnesses which he knew would not be looking forward to his visit. He burst into the office without warning causing the three plain clothes officers working inside to jump to their feet in alarm.

'Sir?' the senior sergeant said, his face blanching slightly. Amis had lost none of his military certainties and could spread dread amongst his subordinates who had been known to be demoted and sent to the farthest reaches of suburban London after crossing the assistant commissioner in some entirely unexpected and often minor way.

'Your bloody Scotsman,' Amis snapped. 'Have you found him yet?'

'No sir,' the sergeant said. 'We've got the local nick in Reading searching. Best bet is that he's gone AWOL looking for a drink. He was strictly rationed at the safe house.'

'And what has his nursemaid got to say for himself?'

'Not a lot, sir. He checked that he was asleep before midnight and then went to bed himself. Heard nothing untoward during the night but by morning the bird had flown, the back door unlocked and left open. No sign of a break-in, apparently. They're still looking.'

'Any evidence someone's got to him?' Amis asked.

'None at all, sir,' the sergeant tried to sound reassuring. 'It's not as if he had any connection with the accused. He just happened to be in the right place at the right time, as far as we were concerned. An independent witness.'

'I remember the circumstances,' Amis snapped. 'It's a great pity that there's only one defendant, not two. I've never been totally convinced that DCI Venables drowned. Why has no body ever been found, I wonder? There's still enough crooks on our side of the fence in Soho to make the whole situation suspect. Has anyone from there been asking questions? Ted Venables must still have mates over there. Most of them are as bent as a three-pound note.'

'Sir,' the sergeant said non-committally. It was not that he did not agree with Amis's assessment but he knew as well as he did that efforts to clean up CID in the square mile of Soho had constantly run into the sand. 'Venables must be out of it, one way or another. He's probably abroad if he's still alive. He'll keep his head well down. If anyone's got to our witness it would be Robertson's own mates, most likely his brother Ray. But there's no sign of that, according to the local CID in Berkshire. Nobody reported loitering near the safe house. They reckon he's wandered off on his own, looking for booze, most likely, and they'll have him back as quick as you like.'

'I certainly hope so,' Amis said irritably. 'I'll be having another look at the other aspects of that case shortly. In the meantime, find that bloody Scotsman. And check up on the other witnesses. We don't want the case falling apart before it's even got to court. Keep me in touch with developments.'

'Do you want us to have words with anyone connected? Ray Robertson maybe?'

'Not yet,' Amis said. 'We'll keep the whole thing under wraps for now. But if he doesn't turn up soon we'll have to turn up the heat in Soho. I'm not going to end up with egg on my face over this one. It took long enough to pin that bastard down, and we still haven't got a handle on his brother. We'll have him too before we're finished.'

'Sir,' the three officers chorused, glad to have escaped a more serious dressing down. But they knew even better than Amis that if their witness had really disappeared, the case he was involved in would be seriously weakened when it reached the Old Bailey. And if Georgie Robertson got off that would do none of their careers any good.

DS Harry Barnard disliked post-mortem examinations and he guessed that DCI Jackson, with his fastidious personality, disliked them even more. He was not surprised then when the senior officer made his excuses and left the mortuary even before the bodily remains had been completely disentangled from their sodden, muddy and bloody packing.

'How soon can you let me have a report?' Jackson asked Dr Jaffa as he opened the door, not bothering to disguise the relief on his face at finding a credible excuse to depart – an upcoming visit from Assistant Commissioner Amis from Scotland Yard. Barnard had raised a sceptical eyebrow at that but said nothing. But on past form, Jackson would add little to the proceedings except some heavy breathing.

'A preliminary report later today,' Jaffa said. 'Unless something unexpected occurs. Of course, there will be tests that take longer, toxicology and so on.'

Barnard, wrapped in a green surgical gown, leaned with what he hoped was nonchalance against the wall near the head of the table as the doctor began to rearrange what looked like little more than a pile of meat into something that more closely resembled a human body. The head was easily identifiable as a skull and as Jaffa placed it gently at the top of his operating space Barnard took the opportunity to study it carefully. Beneath the coating of grime and blood and several vicious wounds which he guessed where inflicted by a heavy weapon it was just about possible to discern the face of an elderly man, with traces of facial stubble and strands of wispy red hair clinging to the skull. A slightly red aquiline nose survived beneath smears of mud and the shattered lips were drawn back over a depleted set of yellowing teeth. But the flesh was bruised and cut and had been bleeding heavily and it would have taken the victim's mother to identify him with any certainty, Barnard thought.

'He looks like nothing so much as a tramp,' he said to Jaffa, puzzled. His own expectation, which he had not shared with anyone, was that this was a gangland killing but the emaciated body which was beginning to emerge from the macabre jigsaw puzzle on the table looked nothing like he anticipated. London gangsters generally were much better fed than this human wreck. He watched as the doctor, his face impassive, meticulously counted out severed fingers and toes and placed them beside what was left of hands and arms. What worried him most was that he had a suspicion that the face, battered as it was, looked vaguely familiar.

'Whoever did this took pleasure in it,' the doctor said curtly. 'But the body is not as old as I thought. Taking account of the fact that it has been wrapped and protected from the outside temperature since it was dumped, I think he was killed in the last twenty-four hours. Not more than that.'

'So it was carefully planned,' Barnard said. 'They're unlikely to have been able to suss out the possibilities of the building site very quickly. They must have found the burial site and then killed the victim.'

Jaffa nodded non-committally, his dark eyes giving nothing away. 'I assume nothing,' he said. 'I look only for scientific evidence.' But as the dismembered body gradually took shape and he recorded his comments, the doctor began to look puzzled as he studied the torso. 'There is no obvious defining cause of death,' he said. 'No major stab wound entering any major organs. It is possible that if a knife was used he simply bled to death. He looks in poor physical condition generally. He would not have much resistance.' Delicately he picked up the skull and turned it over. 'Ah, here we have it. Look.'

Swallowing his distaste, Barnard studied the traces of matted red hair, but could see little of significance until Jaffa pulled strands away from a small dark indentation.

'A bullet entered here,' he said. 'Downward into the brain. 'The neck and jaw are so damaged by the ragged post-mortem dissection that the exit wound is invisible. Or it may be that there wasn't one. That the bullet simply lodged in the jaw or spine. If it's there, I'll find it. I promise you that.'

Barnard gritted his teeth and swallowed hard but kept watching as the serious part of the examination began and the doctor opened up the torso on the table and removed the internal organs. He could see that Jaffa was paying particular attention to the jaw and neck and eventually he gave a grunt of satisfaction and removed something from the severed head with forceps.

'There you are,' he said. 'The bullet they finished him off with, lodged against the vertebrae in the neck. It never left the body. What do they call it: the *coup de grace*?'

'Something like that,' Barnard muttered. 'Can I take that back to the nick? Forensics are quite good at matching bullets to guns these days. We may find a match.'

Jaffa washed the small piece of metal under a tap before Barnard could protest and placed it in the evidence bag which Barnard handed him. 'I wish you luck,' he said.

To her surprise, Kate O'Donnell received a call from Carter Price at the office the next day. She had not really imagined that he was serious when he had talked in his cups of introducing her to his colleagues at the *Globe*.

'I've fixed it with Ken to let you go early this evening, petal. I'll give you a tour of the old Lubianka, as it's not so fondly known, the proprietor doing a good impersonation of Genghis Khan most of the time. When he comes on the phone the editor and news editor jump to attention, believe me. Anyway, you can see us gearing up for the first edition print run, and I thought then we could have an early dinner. Would that suit you?'

Surprised, Kate glanced towards Ken Fellows' office door but it was firmly closed. 'Are you sure that's OK with Ken?' she asked, hesitating as much because she was not sure that this was what she wanted as because she only half believed Price. She wondered why Price was so keen to follow up on a casual acquaintance and what she had thought was an equally casual promise so soon, and why Ken was going along with it so readily. She hoped it wasn't just a way of tempting her into bed.

'I'd like the tour, but I've got a dinner date already,' she lied, keen to keep an escape route open. If Price thought she had anything more than a professional interest in him, she thought it was best to disillusion him now rather than later. Listening to the two older men chat in the French pub had been interesting enough but underneath Price's friendly facade she could see a self-obsession which was not very attractive. If he thought he could charm her out of her tree, she thought, he had another think coming.

'Come down to the *Globe* at four,' he said. 'I'm at the Old Bailey earlier but I should be back in the office by then. I may have a short piece to knock off but it won't take long. Ask for me at reception and I'll come down and fetch you. OK?'

'Fine,' Kate said. 'I'll be there.' She put the phone down and stood looking at the receiver for a minute, wondering what she had let herself in for. Still unsure, she knocked on Ken Fellows' office door and put her head round.

Her boss was hunched over contact prints and looked reluctant to talk.

'Are you happy for me to go early?' she asked. 'I thought you wanted me to try to get a photo shoot with the Rolling Stones. I haven't made contact yet.'

'Leave that till tomorrow,' Fellows said. 'I thought you wanted to have a look at the national papers. You should grab the chance while it's there. Carter seems to have taken a shine to you, but I shouldn't get your hopes of a job up. I doubt very much that's going to happen.'

'I'll go then,' Kate said, unable to tell from Fellows' tone whether he was pleased at the thought of her leaving or not. She wrapped herself up in her winter coat and bright red scarf and set off through Leicester Square and along the Strand to Fleet Street instead of picking up a bus, as much to think through her feelings as to clear her head. By the time she got to the *Globe,* a tall and slightly intimidating fortress of dark glass and steel, rather incongruous amongst the Victorian buildings close by, her eyes were sparkling and her cheeks flushed by the chilly breeze which funnelled down the narrow main artery of the newspaper industry. She had decided to enjoy the trip but keep Carter Price firmly at bay. He was not, with his deliberately old-fashioned look and self-obsession, someone she wanted to get to know better, as the saying went.

She pushed through the revolving door and stood uncertainly for a moment in the glittering reception area of the *Globe,* one of the most famous, if not best respected newspapers in the country. A uniformed man at the main desk raised an eyebrow in her direction and she marched across the shiny floor and asked for Price.

'I'll see if he's free, dear,' he said. 'Is he expecting you?'

She nodded and he raised an eyebrow and made the call.

'Sit over there, pet,' the man said waving at armchairs on the far side of the lobby. 'He says he'll be down in five minutes.'

In fact Price was much longer than that, and when he arrived, in shirtsleeves and mustard coloured waistcoat, he looked slightly red-faced and flustered, his greying hair dishevelled across his brow like some romantic poet interrupted in mid-sonnet.

'Sorry, petal, something came up. But it's fine now. Let's get on, shall we, and then maybe we'll have time for a quickie in the Cheshire Cheese before you go off on your date. Someone dishy, is he? Lucky fellow.'

Kate barely had time to nod before she was hustled into the lift and deposited on a floor where the clatter of teleprinters and typewriters provided a constant backdrop to the hum of conversation and an occasional shout of 'Copy', which evidently summoned a young lad to take sheets of smudged typewritten paper away.

'This is the newsroom,' Price said. 'We're coming up against deadline so it's busy.' He dodged out of the way of a boy dashing past with a sheaf of paper in his hand. 'These are the copy boys,' Price said. 'When a piece is finished the reporter gives it to him and he takes it to the Linotype operators, to be set in metal type, a black – that's a carbon copy – goes to the news-desk and one on to the reporter's spike for reference.'

'Spike?' Kate asked. 'What's that?'

'Exactly what it sounds like,' Price said. 'Look on that desk.' He waved at a long metal spike on a heavy wooden base with a pile of paperwork impaled on it. 'There've been a few acci-dents with those bloody things,' he said laughing. 'If you jam your copy too hard you can put the spike through your hand. Come on, I'll show you how the paper's printed later but first I'll introduce you to the picture editor. That's where your boss

Ken used to work before he set up his own agency. Bill Kenyon, our picture man, will remember him, I'm sure.'

Slightly bemused, Kate followed him across the busy newsroom where few of the reporters, including, she noticed, a couple of women, so much as glanced in her direction. He led her to a glassed off area where she instantly felt more at home. There were only a couple of photographers in evidence, both of them middle-aged men who looked distinctly harassed, but there were many cameras lying about, some of them the heavy glass plate machines which were rapidly going out of use. There was the usual jumble of contact sheets and glossy black and white prints she was used to at the agency and all the lights over the row of darkroom doors were glowing red. At the end of the room a heavy, sandy-haired man in shirtsleeves was studying pictures at his desk, tossing some on to a pile of what looked like rejected shots and keeping a small number spread out in front of him. He glanced up at Carter Price and Kate only briefly before returning to his task.

'Bill, old man,' Price said heartily. 'This is Kate O'Donnell. She's with Ken Fellows' agency and I'm just giving her a quick tour round the old place. I thought you might like to meet a lady snapper. Ken reckons she's pretty good.'

Kenyon looked up at that and waved a hand in Kate's direction, with a look which while not downright scornful she still did not find the least bit encouraging. 'Scraping the bottom of the barrel, is he?' Kenyon asked with a faint sneer. 'I told him it wasn't easy to run an agency.'

Kate flushed and would have retorted angrily if Price had not jumped in quickly.

'Oh, I don't think so,' he said. 'That's not right at all. Ken thinks very highly of Kate.'

Kenyon glanced up and shrugged. 'A woman wouldn't cut it here,' he said. 'You'd get trampled underfoot, darling. It's cutthroat enough in here, and out there, in the real world, it's a bloody jungle.' He turned back to his pictures with a dismissive expression and Price shrugged while Kate swallowed down an angry retort which she knew would be a waste of breath.

'Come on, pet,' Price said. 'I'll show you the Linotype machines and the case room – that's where they fit the metal type into pages. And I'll take you down to see the presses. They won't start rolling till later, when the first edition goes. Then you really feel the building shake. But there'll only be blokes around down there. That's certainly somewhere you won't see a woman working. The printers' unions wouldn't have it for a moment. They don't even like women walking through their space.'

'It'll happen eventually,' Kate muttered, her face stormy. 'They'll run out of excuses in the end.'

For half an hour she trailed after Price as he led her into the business end of the printers' domain, noisy, hot and reeking of oily ink and hot metal, conscious of the hostile looks which were occasionally flashed in her direction by the blue-overalled operatives who were producing the next morning's paper. This, she thought, was a citadel which would not easily be breached.

'The Linotype men are only doing what you do with a typewriter,' she whispered to Price at one point, gazing at the clattering machines slotting type into place.

'God, don't let them hear you say that,' Price said, laughing. 'They earn three or four times what a typist does – and more. Why do you think they're so aggressive about keeping women well away from printing? It'd drop wages through the floor if the bosses could employ girls.'

'It'll change,' Kate said flatly.

'It'll take a century,' Price said equally flatly. 'Come on. Let's go and have that drink I promised you before you start a riot – or, even worse, a strike.'

Price led the way back into the newsroom and his desk where he flicked through piles of papers for a moment before being approached by a young woman with a tray loaded up with small brown envelopes. She handed one to Price who signed for it.

'Pay day,' Price said. 'Newspapers have so many workers on weekly cash pay that they pay the journalists the same way. The union's trying to get us cheques but they've not managed it yet.'

He pocketed the envelope casually and they made their way out of the looming glass building, past the conveyor belts which carried the printed papers from the presses to be bundled up with string before delivery, and through massive doors on the ground floor which led into a narrow alley where dozens of *Globe* vans were parked and groups of men stood or sat about, some of them playing cards, and smoking and gossiping. Price said nothing until they had turned a corner and were making their way back to Fleet Street.

'It's an old-fashioned industry,' he said quietly at last. 'And the print unions run the production side. Jobs pass from father to son, have done for generations. There's corruption in there, everyone's sure of it, but the management can't do a thing about it because if the beggars choose to stop the presses one night a whole day's work becomes a dead loss. No one can sell yesterday's newspaper.' He sounded bitter and Kate guessed that a crime reporter worth his salt might not be best pleased by crime in his own backyard. He led her to a pub in another alley just off the main road, settled her at a corner table, bought her a gin and tonic and himself a pint of beer, and slumped into the seat opposite her with a sigh as he unbuttoned his waistcoat to reveal straining shirt buttons beneath.

'So,' he said. 'I've let you pick my brains. Have I shown you how impossible some of your ambitions are?'

'Maybe,' Kate said, sipping her drink thoughtfully. 'But there's always a first time. Ken had never had a woman on the books till he took me on. And he seems happy enough with me now. Even the other photographers seem to be getting used to the idea slowly.'

'It's easy for Ken to stick his neck out,' Price said. 'He's his own boss and doesn't have the print unions to contend with. No one cares tuppence who took the pictures that come in from agencies like Ken's. Though even there I think you'll have a struggle to get to the top.'

'We'll see,' Kate said with more optimism than she really felt. 'No one thought women could fly warplanes till they found they needed them to do it during the war. My mam knew someone who went off and did it. You never know what you can do until you try.'

'Anyway, never mind all that,' Price said dismissively. 'Now I want to pick your brains about some of your more interesting friends. A little *quid pro quo.*'

Kate raised an eyebrow at that. It wasn't quite the *quid pro quo* she had been half expecting. 'What interesting friends?'

'For starters, what do you know about Ray Robertson and his brother Georgie?'

Kate's eyes widened in astonishment. 'How do you know that I know anything about them,' she asked, her mouth slightly dry.

'Darling, I'm a crime reporter. I followed your brother's case. And the nasty business in Notting Hill. And your dealings with the crazy Russian woman. I also know you're having a fling with that dodgy copper, Harry Barnard – though from what I'm picking up from Scotland Yard, the vice squad is going to get a very thorough going over shortly from Assistant Commissioner Amis. A new broom Soho cops will need to watch out for. And, as it goes, I happen to know you've met Ray Robertson more than once.'

'Is that why you came to Ken? To suss me out for your story rather than my pictures?'

'Not at all,' he said quickly. 'I need a photographer and Bill Kenyon's being coy about giving me one. These investigations take time and persistence and he can't spare the manpower, he says. It's a bonus I got you, with your interesting contacts. So tell me about Ray Robertson.'

'I met him at one of his boxing galas,' Kate said defensively. 'Ken sent me to take pictures of it, for heaven's sake. I had to get all dolled up in my best frock.'

Price smiled wolfishly. 'I bet you'd never been to anything quite like that before. I suppose there are places where being a woman with a camera could be quite an advantage. And what about Georgie? Did you meet him too?'

'Only that once,' Kate said, not disguising her distaste. 'He made a pass at me.'

'Did he now? I don't expect your friend Flash Harry thought much of that, did he? Was he there? Or is he too junior to be asked to Ray and Georgie's parties?'

'He was there,' Kate admitted. 'If you know so much you must know he and Ray are old friends from when they were scallies together somewhere in the East End. But there were other policemen there too.'

'Of course there were,' Price said with a smile. 'The Robertsons both know which side their bread is buttered in Soho. But

Georgie was always a bit of a loose cannon as I hear it and bloody dangerous with it. Not just violent but a bit twisted.'

'You seem to be forgetting that Harry Barnard was responsible for arresting Georgie Robertson,' Kate snapped. 'He hates him. Even though he's known him as well as Ray since they were kids together, he says he's always hated Georgie. He says he's a psychopath.'

'I wouldn't argue with that,' Price said. 'By rights they'd hang him for what he got up to with kids, but we're too namby-pamby for that now. It wasn't just the *Globe* who argued to keep the rope, you know. The whole country thought Parliament was crazy. And your Harry Barnard may have arrested Robertson, but just maybe, from what I hear, he could have quietly let DCI Venables get away. They never found his body, you know. Missing believed drowned is as far as that ever got. I wonder if he really did drown or whether he had enough mates in the Force to see him safe, the bent looking after the bent, as it were. Scotland Yard doesn't seem totally convinced he's dead.'

'Harry wouldn't do anything like that,' Kate said, draining her drink and pulling on her coat. 'I think I need to go now.'

'So it's Harry you're meeting is it, petal? You're quite sure about him, are you? I never had him down as the marrying kind. And I'm damn sure he's much too close to Ray Robertson for a copper. It's one thing to take the odd backhander. We all know that goes on in Soho with the vice squad. But to be in bed with one of London's biggest gangsters is something else. Especially when as far as I hear it, that someone's working pretty hard to get his brother out of jail.'

'Are you sure about that,' Kate asked, her expression icy now. 'Harry doesn't talk about his work all the time. But I got the impression Ray Robertson was quite happy to have his brother off the scene. He's a nasty bit of work and has become a liability to Ray I think. Anyway I didn't come here to have my brains picked like this. Thanks for the drink, Carter. And the tour. And for your information. If you and Ken cooked this up to put me off Fleet Street, you've pretty well succeeded.'

THREE

K ate walked thoughtfully back to the underground at Holborn and fought her way through the rush hour crowds to Shepherd's Bush. She had lied to Carter Price about a dinner date. In fact her flatmate Tess had promised to cook supper. But she would, she thought, as she straphung on the Bakerloo line, call Harry Barnard later and give him the gist of what Price had talked about in the pub. It was obvious that the reporter was picking up a lot of confidential information, probably from Scotland Yard itself, and she guessed that Harry would be very interested in a lot of what he had said.

She had not seen the sergeant for a couple of weeks and she had come away from the last visit to his smart but curiously sterile flat with a feeling that perhaps his interest in her was waning. And the longer she waited for him to ring, the more uncertain she became that she actually wanted him to. He was not the type to settle down, she was sure, and she herself didn't long for domesticity. In her experience of teeming Catholic Liverpool around Scotland Road, babies followed marriage with an inevitability and frequency which alarmed her. But she had at last escaped the clutches of all-enveloping families and censorious priests. She was enjoying her freedom too much now to get involved in another family for years yet. And so far Harry's promise that he was 'taking precautions' had proved trustworthy.

'Come on, la,' Tess pressed her later over sausages and mash. 'Tell us all about this fella from the *Globe*. Is he after what they're all after or what?'

Kate grinned. 'Oh, I expect so. Liverpool, London, aren't they all the same? I'm sure he'd grab anything that was offered. Anyway I don't fancy him so there aren't likely to be any offers. He's middle aged and podgy and far too full of himself.'

'So why did you bother to meet him then?'

'Oh, I think Ken set it all up to put me off the idea of working for the newspapers. I don't think either of them believe newspaper photography is a suitable job for a woman.'

'You think Ken doesn't want to lose you now?' Tess looked slightly sceptical. 'After all the fuss he made about taking on a woman himself? He wasn't exactly keen, was he?'

'Well, maybe he's changed his mind,' Kate said. 'I work hard enough for him and I've produced some good pictures for him, one way and another.'

'At a price,' Tess said, looking sombre, and Kate knew she was thinking of the risks Kate had taken along the way that had involved her friend's safety as well as her own.

'I'm sorry you got involved in all that,' she said quietly. 'Anyway, hanging on to me is the only reason I can think of for him to make sure I saw all the downside of Fleet Street. And if that's what it was, Carter Price easily proved Ken's point. If all the picture editors are like the one at the *Globe* I'll never get a foot in the door.'

Tess looked at her friend quizzically. 'But you still think maybe they're not? You're still an optimist?'

'Of course I am, la. You never know till you try, do you?' Kate said with a grin. 'Anyway I'm quite content with Ken at the moment. He seems happy to send me on most assignments that come up. Even the blokes are learning to live with me. They take me to the pub for lunch now and again, though I can't keep up with their intake of booze and they regard it as a mortal insult if I offer to buy a round. But I'm very nearly one of the team, though I'll never be one of the boys.'

'It's taken a while,' Tess said doubtfully. 'At least in teaching we get the jobs, but as far as I can see we don't get the top ones. Still, not to worry. I'll probably meet some nice Catholic boy and have lots of kids. That would please my mam.'

'I read somewhere that some woman in America has written a book complaining that housewives are all going slowly barmy, shut up at home with the kids and the new washing machine,' Kate said.

'I suppose it's the washing machine that's doing it,' Tess said, laughing. 'Our mothers didn't have them, did they? Just a dolly tub and a mangle and the housework took all day.

Anyway, I'm not rushing into anything just yet. I like my job, too, you know.'

They both jumped slightly as the phone rang, a new acquisition which, after a long wait for a connection, had pushed long treks downstairs to the payphone in the hall into history.

Kate got up and picked up and was, as always, slightly surprised to hear Harry Barnard's voice. 'Hello stranger,' she said tentatively.

'Sorry,' Barnard said. 'I've been a bit busy. Have you eaten?'

'Just finished,' Kate said, feeling the slight surge of excitement that Harry always engendered and feeling equally irritated that he could still have that effect, and that he probably knew it.

'A drink then? I'm still in town. I can drive down to Shepherd's Bush in ten minutes. I'll pick you up at the flat?'

'Yes, fine,' Kate said, picking up an urgency in his voice which she did not quite understand. 'I'll powder my nose.'

Tess raised an eyebrow quizzically as her friend got up and picked up her handbag. 'The master calls?'

'It's not like that,' Kate said irritably, but she wondered if it was.

Barnard was as good as his word. He sounded the horn impatiently as he drove up to pick her up outside the flat, revving his engine loudly as she came down the steps of the tall Victorian house. He whisked her down to Hammersmith at speed to a riverside pub which was bright and welcoming enough to relax Kate slightly. He bought a gin and tonic for her and a Scotch for himself and leaned over to kiss her cheek after he had put the drinks on the table.

'Sorry it's been a while sweetie. I've been a bit busy,' he said.

'I'm glad you called,' Kate said, her expression sober. 'I was going to call you.' She hesitated for a moment and sipped her drink slowly, considering just how much to tell him. 'Something a bit odd happened earlier that I wanted to tell you about, though I'm not quite sure where to start.'

Barnard raised a quizzical eyebrow. 'The beginning maybe,' he said.

'I met this reporter from the *Globe*, Carter Price, and he started asking me some very odd questions when he took me for a drink earlier. He's a friend of Ken's and he offered to show me round the *Globe* and introduce me to the picture editor, a man called Bill Kenyon.'

'But there was more to it than that?' Barnard asked, with unexpected certainty. 'I know Carter Price. He's a bastard, always got his nose poking into something he shouldn't have and certainly not the man to do anything just out of the goodness of his heart. There's a payback in there somewhere, isn't there?'

'It seems like it,' Kate said and told Barnard, hesitantly, how Price had quizzed her about what she knew of Ray and Georgie Robertson and had described Harry himself as a 'dodgy' Soho cop.

Barnard's face darkened as he listened. 'He even said he's heard about a plan at Scotland Yard to sort out the vice squad. How on earth does he find out things like that? Did you know about that?'

'Well, not in so many words, no, I didn't, but there is some sort of a purge being planned,' Barnard said. 'There's a new assistant commissioner making his presence felt. You have to understand, a lot of these nosy hacks more or less live in the Scotland Yard press room. It's a toss up who's helping who. They pick up all sorts of stuff they shouldn't, some of it official, some of it not. And if they're masons, they meet more senior people at some lodge or other, either the one they belong to or one they visit for meals. There's plenty of cops in the masons and they're all willing to scratch each other's backs even if the back they scratch belongs to a reporter. Favours are taken and given. I've never gone in for that nonsense myself but maybe that's a mistake. They look after their own, these people. It's certainly the way to get promotion in some nicks.'

'What do they do, masons?' Kate asked. 'My lot were all Catholics and they're not allowed to join, but you hear some funny stories about men in pinnies and strange rituals.'

'It's a secret society,' Barnard said. 'And a powerful one, especially in the police force. And there's much more to it than pinnies and rituals. Did your reporter let on who's planning to sort out the vice squad?'

'No, he was picking my brains but I didn't get much of a chance to pick his. He wasn't giving much away, apart from how I'd never make it in Fleet Street as a photographer. He was all smiles and sympathy when he was showing me round the offices but his attitude changed when we went for a drink. That was when I realized he wasn't just doing Ken a favour taking me on a sightseeing tour. There was much more to it than that.'

'I bet there was,' Barnard said. 'I told you. He's a ruthless beggar.'

'He did seem to know a lot about the cases you and I have been involved in. He did say he thought you might have helped Ted Venables get away. That he might not be dead . . .'

'Jesus Christ,' Barnard said. 'If they believe that at the Yard they'll want my head on a platter. They found Venables' boat – you know that – but they never found a body. I guess that still rankles at the Yard. They've always been convinced that they should have been in on that case, that they could have wrapped it up better than we did. They don't forgive or forget.'

'Surely if he got away, someone would have heard. People don't just disappear off the face of the earth.'

'Maybe, maybe not,' Barnard said gloomily. 'I wouldn't be so sure about that. Some of the bad guys seem to be getting quite good at spiriting themselves away. Anyway, while he's missing anyone can spin any sort of rumour about him can't they? I'm a sitting duck if someone's looking to take pot shots in my direction.'

'Why would they want to do that?' Kate asked. 'Is it because Ray Robertson's a friend of yours.'

'It's partly that, I suppose. But they should have learned by now that unless you keep close to some of the bad guys you never find out what's going on. And we do find out what's going on and generally we keep Soho under control. We don't have gun battles in the streets like they do in New York and Chicago.'

'But maybe they think you get too close,' Kate said tentatively.

'Which is why right now it's not the gangsters I'm worried about,' Barnard said. 'It's the cops. This new assistant commissioner at the Yard is supposed to be cleaning the whole of CID up, but I expect the vice squad is top of his list for that. My DCI's seeing him tomorrow. And there's a new murder case which I think just might involve a witness who's supposed to be holed up waiting for Georgie Robertson's trial. We don't have a definite ID and the DCI said we would have heard if he'd gone missing, but I'm not so sure about that. You remember the old tramp who was a witness against Georgie and the rest, don't you? Hamish Macdonald, he was called. It was just a passing thought when I saw the body on the building site. I've no real evidence it was him. I'll just have to wait and see. But if it is, there'll be all hell let loose around the whole Robertson clan. Who got to a witness and how? One way and another I'll be in the firing line too. One way or another I reckon I might be up the creek.'

Kate put her hand over his. 'I'm sorry,' she said.

Assistant Commissioner John Amis arrived at the nick in full fig the next morning and swept into DCI Keith Jackson's office without ceremony. The Scotsman got to his feet quickly and stiffened to attention.

'Good morning, sir,' he said. 'Can I get you anything – tea, coffee, something stronger?' Jackson's face was flushed although if he had been drinking there was no sign of it on his breath.

Amis sniffed suspiciously and waved away his offer with undisguised contempt. 'Your department is a disgrace, Jackson,' he said. 'And it's about time something drastic was done about it.'

'Sir,' Jackson said, wooden-faced and glassy-eyed, sinking back behind his desk, appearing to visibly shrink as the AC sat down opposite him. 'Since I've been here efforts have been made,' Jackson said defensively. 'You know we've tightened up on contacts with informants, payments for information, prosecutions for gross indecency, after-hours drinking, soliciting . . .'

'Not enough, not soon enough, not great enough efforts, in fact, as far as I can see, completely ineffective,' Amis came back hard. 'You've still got detectives roaming the streets day and night running their own protection rackets, consorting with known criminals as they please. It's getting the whole

Metropolitan Police Force a bad name.' Amis swivelled angrily
in his chair and banged a file on to the desk in front of him
while Jackson subsided back into his seat with what sounded
more like a sob than a sigh.

'It's going to take time, sir,' he said. 'Soho is like a hundred
year old cesspit that needs draining, but we have made a
modest start. I'm concentrating on the homosexual pubs and
clubs this month. I want them closed down . . .'

'That's a minor issue,' Amis snarled. 'The rest of it's
entrenched, isn't it, run by men making a fortune out of vice
and racketeering? You've had time enough to make an impact
since the scandal a year ago and nothing's happened. So as
from now things are going to change. We have a target. It's
perfectly obvious that Barnard is still thick with the Robertson
clan and Ray Robertson seems to be pushing the boat out with
Reg Smith, who runs just about everything south of the river.
We've got no intelligence on what they're planning, although
I'm sure Sergeant Barnard could give us chapter and verse if
he chose. But he doesn't choose. So I'm going to give you
some extra help, with the specific brief of pinning Barnard to
the floor. I want him out. If possible I want him in the dock
with Ray Robertson. It's where he should have been years
ago. He's a disgrace.'

'But with Georgie about to go down . . .' Jackson ventured.
'That's the worst of them out of the way. I'd begun to think
we were making progress even in that area.'

For a second Amis seemed to hesitate but then changed
his mind. 'Not with Smith involved,' he said. 'If he's thinking
of linking up with Ray Robertson they'll have an army at
their beck and call. Things can only get much worse. You'll
concentrate on Robertson and I'll get our boys south of the
river to put pressure on Smith.'

'So this extra help?' Jackson asked, his voice slightly
strangled. 'Who have you got in mind?'

'DS Vic Copeland,' Amis said. 'He's perfect for the task.
He's had army training. He's on the square, so he can be
trusted. He blotted his copybook, according to the City of
London, but he's very happy to transfer to the Met and start
with a clean slate. He can start straight away. But I don't want

you getting him bogged down in trivial stuff. His brief is to watch Barnard, find out what's going on with him and Robertson, and report back. I want a weekly report, at least.'

'Copeland?' Jackson looked even paler. 'His reputation . . . He was lucky not to be charged with manslaughter after that case in Smithfield.'

'He cuts corners, I wouldn't deny that. But he cuts them in the right direction, not like the bloody vice squad. Copeland was trained in a hard school. But isn't that what you need? Nothing else has worked in Soho. It's time to come down hard. He's the man for the job. He'll report to you, of course, but he'll report to me too. I want results this time. No more pussyfooting around. I want Barnard out and if possible alongside Ray Robertson, in the dock where he belongs, with his blasted brother.'

'Sir,' Jackson said faintly.

'This discussion goes no further than these four walls of course,' Amis said getting to his feet. 'If you want a private word you can invite me to your lodge, away from prying eyes. We can even invite Copeland as a guest if we need a chat away from the job. Anything else of interest I should know about?'

'A very odd murder,' Jackson said, his voice slightly strangled. 'Someone tried to dump a body on that huge building site at Tottenham Court Road, the one there was all the fuss in the newspapers about. They obviously hoped he was going to disappear under tons of concrete but a digger turned him up before it was poured. Could be a victim of one of the gangs but we've no ID yet. I'll keep you informed.'

Amis got to his feet and tucked his uniform cap under his arm. 'I'll have a look round while I'm here,' he said. 'Good for the troops to see the top brass occasionally. Keeps them on their toes.' He gave Jackson the thin smile of a hungry tiger. 'I'll let you know when Copeland will be arriving in CID. Arrange a briefing tomorrow, will you, and I'll give them a taste of what it's going to be like here in future. Nine in the morning will be fine.'

DCI Jackson stood by the window of his office looking down into the car park. He waited until he saw the assistant commissioner get into his car and be driven out into the busy

West End traffic, and then waited again until his summons for DS Harry Barnard was answered. He failed to wave the sergeant into a seat and stood for a minute by the window looking at him stony-faced.

'Did you see the assistant commissioner?' he asked eventually.

'He did a walk round CID,' Barnard said. 'He didn't speak to me.'

'He's sending us reinforcements in the shape of DS Vic Copeland. Do you know him?'

Barnard could not disguise his surprise and he knew it was tinged with horror, which he hoped Jackson could not see. 'I've never met him,' he said. 'As I hear it he's lucky to still be in the Force. He's well known as a bit of a thug.'

'AC Amis wants Soho cleaned up and he seems to think Copeland is the man to help us do it. The City force is very happy to transfer him over. Want to be rid of him, no doubt, and his little embarrassment in Smithfield. So we're stuck with him. I want you to show him around when he arrives. He can't have ever worked in the West End before, and certainly not in Soho.'

'He'll go down a storm with the tarts and the queers,' Barnard muttered. 'They'll all know about the deaths in custody, and there's much more, so I'm told. He's the sort of man who talks more with his fists than his mouth. A good thumping first and then the questions. And another good thumping if the answers aren't the right ones. The courts are beginning to catch on and turf his cases out.'

'Mr Amis is coming back for a nine o'clock briefing in the morning so be there. I thought I'd suggest then that you were the best person to take Copeland round,' Jackson said sharply. 'You know where all the bodies are buried. So don't complain you weren't warned.'

'Talking of bodies, did Mr Amis say he was missing a witness in the Georgie Robertson case? I could be mistaken about the corpse from Centre Point. One tramp looks much like another, especially in that state. But he had a look of our man except that he's supposed to be tucked away somewhere in a safe house.'

'He didn't mention anything to do with the George Robertson case,' Jackson said. 'He seemed much more concerned about what his brother Ray is up to, especially as he seems to be having meetings with Reg Smith. Did you know about that?'

'I'd heard a few rumours but I didn't think it was serious. They've been at daggers drawn for years. Every now and again it goes off but so far we've had no serious casualties. I can't imagine they're going to get together after all this time.' Although allowing for Ray Robertson's fantasies of outdoing the Great Train robbers perhaps the idea was not so far fetched. Barnard knew him well enough to know that a heist on that scale was beyond Ray Robertson's competence, but Reg Smith was another matter entirely.

'See what you can find out,' Jackson said. 'I don't like intelligence coming from the Yard when we should have picked it up ourselves.'

'Right,' Barnard said. 'So when's he arriving then, Bruiser Copeland? I think CID should be told.'

'You'll be told tomorrow,' Jackson snapped. 'I suppose he might even get here tomorrow. The AC seemed to be in a hurry. You can pass it on quietly so no one can complain CID wasn't warned beforehand. I'm not best pleased to have him here, believe me. He'll bring nothing but trouble, you can be sure of that, for me as well as you. So keep an eye on him, sergeant. I don't want any dead bodies in my cells, d'ye understand?'

'Yes, guv,' Barnard said soberly. 'I'll see what I can do.'

FOUR

When Kate O'Donnell arrived at work the next day, she was surprised to see the heavyweight figure of Carter Price weaving through the cluttered photographers' desks to Ken Fellows' office, tapping on the door and being welcomed inside. All that could be heard for the next half hour was the steady drone of voices, and she was even more surprised to see Fellows eventually open his door and beckon her inside.

'Kate,' he said as she squeezed into the limited space available without getting too close to Price. 'We've got an assignment for you that's a bit unusual.'

'What's that?' Kate asked, looking uncertain. The last unusual excursion she had taken for the agency was a secondment into the fashion industry which had not ended well.

'Perhaps you'd better explain,' Fellows said to Price, and Kate wondered why he too seemed unusually hesitant. Something, she thought, was up, and it was not a thought she welcomed.

'I need some pictures taken,' Price said with a heartiness which did not ring quite true. 'And for now I want them taken outside my office set-up. You met our picture editor, Bill Kenyon. For some reason he's never got a photographer free when I want one, especially when I want to do some digging around. Research I suppose you could call it. He'll send a man down to the Bailey or the High Court at the drop of a hat but anything a bit more offbeat and he's suddenly too short-staffed. I think there's more to it than that, but of course I can't prove it. So I thought I'd look for a bit of freelance talent I could hire on my exes. No one ever queries them.' He gave Kate the smile of a grizzly bear about to land a salmon.

'Naturally I thought of you,' he went on. 'I want to go down south of the river this week and some snaps would be really useful. I could go on my own but a couple in some of the pubs I want to visit will look much more innocent than a nosy bloke on his own. We'd just look like tourists out for a jaunt on the wild side. Something like that.'

'Is this to do with what we were talking about the other night?' Kate asked, her voice full of suspicion. 'You were talking about Ray Robertson and his brother. I really don't want to get involved with them. You know why.'

'No, no, this is nothing to do with his mob. This is strictly south of the river, Reg Smith's territory. There's no love lost there.'

Still unsure, Kate glanced at Ken Fellows. 'Is this official with you?' she said. 'Part of the job.'

'Of course,' Fellows said airily, although Kate could see he was not entirely comfortable with the idea.

'As far as you're concerned it'll just be an evening out, with a few quiet pictures taken when I tell you,' Price said. 'A little bird tells me there's something going on down there, something to put the train robbers' noses out of joint. A big job but without the stupid mistakes Reynolds and that gang made. But it's only a rumour I want to check out. Nothing heavy.'

Kate couldn't help feeling that Price was trying to convince himself as much as her. 'How do you come to hear rumours like that?' she asked.

Price smiled and tapped the side of his nose. 'That's more than you need to know, petal,' he said. 'Crime reporters have their own contacts, you know? Their own sources of information. Will Saturday night suit you?'

'You can have a day off in return,' Fellows said, though he sounded grudging.

Price must be paying him something substantial to justify this, Kate thought. She nodded. 'OK,' she said. 'It's out of the office, at least, and it sounds interesting. Why not?'

'Right, you make the arrangements with Kate,' Fellows said to Price dismissively. 'Now bugger off and let me get on with the rest of the day.'

Kate followed Price out into the main office, from which most of the photographers had already set off on the day's assignments. She herself was due at a fashion show in the West End, but Price put a hand on her arm before she could collect her coat.

'This is a private arrangement between me and you and Ken,' he said quietly. 'Don't go telling anyone about it. You know who I mean?'

'Why is your picture editor being so difficult about it?' she asked.

'I don't know for sure,' Price said. 'There's wheels within wheels in Fleet Street. A lot of the printers and some of the hacks live in south-east London, where there's also a lot of crime. I sometimes think there are connections there. It's a very tight world, jobs get handed on from father to son, there's supposed to be a whole lot of men on the payroll who don't actually exist – Mickey Mouse and Tommy Steele are favourites. The unions are powerful and connive with it all. But that's something people like me have to leave well alone. I think I'm safe enough looking at what Reg Smith is up to, but if Reg Smith down in Peckham turns out to have a best mate working at the *Globe,* I'm stuffed. The story will never run.'

Kate shivered, trying to push her misgivings aside. 'Just this once, then,' she said. 'If I don't feel safe I'll say no next time. I've had a bit too much excitement in this job already. I think I prefer a quiet life.'

'You're a doll,' Price said. 'You'll be fine, I promise. Give me your phone number and I'll call you when I've got something set up.'

DS Harry Barnard, in his usual smart Italian suit but an unusually sober dark tie, had taken his place in the conference room early, choosing a seat centrally placed but towards the back of the chairs set out that morning for the entire complement of CID officers who served the West End. The room filled up quickly but the conversation was muted as if the men had gathered for a wake. The news that they were apparently under surveillance themselves had flashed around CID in record time and the name Copeland had raised hackles in the pubs after work. As the clock ticked relentlessly up to nine, the murmuring was reduced to a sullen silence.

Assistant Commissioner John Amis arrived dead on time, led in by a stony-faced DCI Keith Jackson and followed by a broad-shouldered heavyweight wearing a leather jacket over his suit and a look of subdued triumph barely concealed by a bland smile. But the eyes were watchful, small and set deep, beneath a thatch of dark hair cut very short, and the lips thin, the lines around them deeply entrenched. DS Vic Copeland looked like trouble, Barnard thought, but he had so far come up with no feasible strategy to dodge Jackson's plan to make them a team.

'Good morning, gentlemen,' Amis said, prompting more than one hastily concealed smirk from a group which was seldom thought of – or thought of itself – in those terms. 'Let's be under no illusions,' Amis went on. 'The commissioner himself has authorized this meeting and the measures I have been asked to take to tackle what we see as a crisis in public confidence over policing in this division. The law-abiding residents of Soho – and I am assured there are some – are quite clear that it is increasingly difficult to distinguish between lawbreakers and law enforcers in their area particularly.' None of the assembled officers dared to voice even a murmur of dissent at that, although the funereal faces of many of them dropped another couple of notches into outright discontent. Undoubtedly able to feel the chilly atmosphere Amis raised his voice a fraction as Jackson scowled at his detectives.

'It can't go on,' Amis said. 'It is perfectly evident to the public, and even more damagingly, to members of the Press, that Soho has become lawless. It is obviously in the hands of criminal gangsters who run prostitution and protection and extortion rackets, and equally obvious that some of you are in the pockets of these gangsters and others of you are being paid to turn a blind eye by petty offenders and perverts and to ignore the complaints of innocent business people. You are bringing the entire Force into disrepute and it has got to stop.'

There was an uneasy shuffling amongst the detectives which was quelled by icy looks from both senior officers.

Amis held up his hand. 'DCI Jackson has been instructed to refer any wrongdoing which comes to light straight to me at the Yard,' he said. 'And to help him in his task of uncovering illegality, I have seconded DS Copeland, late of the City of London force, to CID here. He will work with the team in the normal way but will be required to report back regularly to

Mr Jackson if – or more likely when – he becomes aware of any misconduct. And by that I mean even the smallest infringement of the rules.'

DS Robbie Mason, heavyweight, red-faced, stalwart of the Police Federation, and near enough to retirement to be the least intimidated by the assistant commissioner amongst those present, waved a hand in the air and lumbered to his feet. 'With respect sir,' he growled, 'you seem to be working from an assumption that everyone here is guilty of something, regardless of evidence to that effect.'

There was a murmur of agreement from those around him, and AC Amis's face darkened. 'Disciplinary matters will be dealt with in the usual way,' he said. 'But nobody here should make any mistake. I expect there to be far more of them than there have been in the recent past. Far more.' And if anyone in the room did not entirely believe John Amis's determination the vigorous nods of agreement from DCI Jackson and DS Copeland should have left them in no doubt of the seriousness of the situation. Amis glanced at his watch and made to pick up his uniform cap and gloves but before he could stand up Harry Barnard put up his hand and stood up in his turn.

'Could I ask one question, sir, about an ongoing case?' Amis looked as if he would refuse but Barnard went on quickly. 'The witnesses in the case against Georgie Robertson,' he said. 'Are they all present and correct, sir? No one's gone AWOL?'

'Of course not, sergeant,' Amis snapped. 'What makes you ask that?'

'Just that I saw someone who looked very like one of them, sir,' Barnard said airily, trying to bury his anxiety about one very young witness in Georgie's case. 'He was found in very unfortunate circumstances. But if you have them all safe there's no problem, is there?'

'You arrested Robertson, didn't you, sergeant?'

'Yes sir, and I'd very much like to see him put away,' Barnard said.

DCI Jackson, who had looked embarrassed during this exchange, stood up. 'If there are no more questions I will see Mr Amis out,' Jackson said, making it pretty clear by his stony expression that no more would be taken. 'Barnard, I'll see you in my office in ten minutes.'

DS Copeland did not follow the detectives back to the CID office where a torrent of grumbles immediately erupted, but made his exit with the senior officers.

Barnard slumped in his chair without, for once, taking off his jacket and hanging it up carefully.

'You're going to have to watch it,' Robbie Mason muttered, leaning confidentially over the back of his chair, taking care not to be overheard in the general hubbub. 'I always thought you were too pally with Ray Robertson. It'll come back to haunt you mate, if that bastard Copeland gets his teeth into it.'

'Yeah, yeah,' Barnard said. 'I can't undo the fact that I grew up with the Robertson brothers, can I? But you're right. I'll steer clear of Ray for a bit. I know it makes sense.'

'You're not the only one who's going to have to make changes while Copeland's around. Let's just hope he's not here for long.'

Barnard glanced at his watch. 'I'd better go and see what Jackson wants,' he said. 'Thanks for the advice, Robbie. Believe me, I'm listening.' And as if to prove it, there was less spring in Barnard's step than usual as he made his way to Jackson's office and knocked on the door. To his surprise it was opened by DS Vic Copeland whose eyes were as stony as his welcoming smile was wide.

'Come in, come in,' he said and waved to one of the two chairs ranged in front of the desk of a definitely unsmiling DCI Jackson.

'Sit down, both of you,' Jackson said. He steepled his hands in front of his face. 'You both heard what Mr Amis said,' he said. 'I don't need to repeat any of it except to say that things have got to change. Barnard, I want you to work closely with Sergeant Copeland until he learns his way around the manor. Take him around with you for the rest of the week, introduce him to your contacts, show him the premises of particular interest. There's plenty of those, God knows. Point him in the direction of the toms, the pimps and the perverts, the petty thieves and the conmen. Make sure he knows who's a likely source of information on the Maltese and Ray Robertson's mob.'

'Sounds like quite an education,' Copeland said. 'I'm looking forward to it. I gather you know Robertson quite well yourself, Harry.' He smirked.

'I happened to grow up in the same neck of the woods as they did,' Barnard said. 'Same school to start with. We were evacuated to a farm together for a while. After that we went our separate ways.'

'No one's ever pinned the older brother down, have they?' Copeland pressed on. 'Funny, that.'

Barnard scowled but said nothing. Any differences of opinion he was going to have with Copeland, and he had no doubt there would be a few, would not be aired in front of the DCI.

'Find Sergeant Copeland a desk, Barnard, and fill him in on current cases.'

'Are we any nearer an ID for the body on the building site, guv?' Barnard asked.

'I've heard nothing more from forensics,' Jackson said. 'We'll chase them later in the day if nothing comes back. In the meantime, introduce Sergeant Copeland to the rest of CID and then to the manor. I'm sure he'll be a great help to us all.'

You lying bastard, Barnard thought as he closed the door on an anxious looking DCI. You're stuck between a rock and a hard place and I'm not sure whether I can drag you out or you'll drag me down with you.

Kate had agreed to meet Harry Barnard at the Blue Lagoon coffee bar after work and had half agreed to go out for a meal with him afterwards. But she was on her second cappuccino, and checking her watch every couple of minutes, before he arrived a good half hour after he had promised.

'Sorry, sorry, a bad day,' he said, pushing his hat to the back of his head and making no effort to take his coat off. 'Do you want to stay here or go somewhere different? After the day I've had I'd like a change of scene. Soho's losing its charm.'

Reckoning she had little choice, Kate pulled her coat off the back of her chair, and stood up. 'Have you got the car,' she asked, failing to react to his attempt to kiss her.

'Parked just outside,' Barnard said, waving at the red Capri, visible through the steamy windows, with its wheels on the pavement and a taxi driver irately trying to squeeze through the narrow gap which remained. He put an arm round her shoulder and ushered her outside, held the car door open for her and ignored the angry hooting of another driver trying to inch past. He swung into the driving seat and glanced at her briefly.

'I love you when you get mad,' he said, and raised a faint smile. 'Come on, I'll take you to a very nice Italian I know in Charlotte Street, far enough from the nick and all its works for no one to see us. Will that suit?'

Kate nodded. 'Are all men as impossible as you?' she asked, but had to be satisfied with an only marginally shamefaced grin in reply as he weaved the car through the narrow streets of Soho to cross Oxford Street and park eventually outside a bustling restaurant, on a corner which looked as if it was serving food on at least three floors of a tall building.

'This place is supposed to be authentic Neapolitan,' he said. 'Their speciality is pizza. Have you ever had pizza?' Kate shook her head and Barnard laughed. 'It's another world up there in the north, isn't it? No wonder all these Liverpool bands head down south as quickly as they can.'

Kate pulled a wry face but did not have the heart to argue.

He quickly locked the car and led her into the restaurant where they were soon seated in a small alcove away from the window and faced with a menu listing eighteen different varieties of the mysterious pizza which Kate studied in wonderment. She watched a waiter carrying plates to a neighbouring table.

'Is that it?' she asked.

'It's like a pastry base, a bit like bread, and then they put all these different toppings on top. You just choose what you like best,' Barnard explained.

After they had painstakingly ordered their toppings and Barnard had poured her a glass of wine out of a raffia-encased bottle, Kate waited for a moment before picking up her glass, saying nothing.

'So how was your visit to the *Globe*?' Barnard asked at last.

Kate shrugged. 'Interesting, but the picture editor wasn't

interested in me. I was a woman – or a girl, as he would put it. But I did get something out of it. I'm going to work with Carter Price taking some pictures he wants on his own account. Ken has agreed I can help him. It will be good experience.'

'With that fat creep?' Barnard said. 'I wouldn't trust him further than I could throw him.'

'That's because you don't like crime reporters,' Kate said. 'Anyway it's only a temporary arrangement. He's doing some investigating that he doesn't want the picture desk to know about until he's got a bit further with it. It shouldn't take long.'

Barnard took a long swig of his wine and lit a cigarette, looking stormy and Kate offered her sweetest smile.

'Come on. I work for Ken, not you. It'll be OK. So, stop all this avoiding the issue. Tell me what's going on with you and why you were late.'

'Ah, it's a long story,' Barnard said quietly. 'We've had a visit at the nick from the top brass who seem to think we're doing a lousy job, especially in Soho. So they've drafted in an extra detective sergeant who's supposed to be keeping an eye out for infringements of the rules. The problem is he's a bit of a thug with a reputation for bending the rules himself. My job this afternoon was to give him a guided tour round my patch. I can't say many of my contacts greeted him with much enthusiasm. I think his reputation had travelled ahead of him. It's hardly surprising. He was all over the *Globe* and the rest not long ago.'

'What has he been up to?' Kate asked.

'He's a bit free with his fists. If a suspect won't talk he likes to help him to see it our way with a bit more than a few slaps. He worked for the City of London police, so I've not met him personally before, but there was one case where he was lucky not to end up in the dock himself. A suspect died in his cell after a session with Copeland. Somehow they got a verdict of misadventure at the inquest and nothing more was done about it but I'm sure that's why he's moved on to the Met. I reckon he was pushed out and the Yard were fool enough to take him on. When I took him round it was obvious some of my contacts knew who he was and they weren't best pleased. He's trouble.'

'Won't he be useful in this murder case?' Kate asked. 'Didn't you say you thought it was a gangster killing?'

'Maybe,' Barnard said, moving his wine glass as the waiter arrived with two enormous pizzas which Kate gazed at in amazement.

'We'll be here all night,' she said and ignored Barnard's shake of the head. He had, she guessed, different plans. 'So why only maybe?' she asked.

'I told you. It's a long story, going back to Georgie Robertson's case. I've got a nasty feeling about the body we found on the building site. I think it might be one of the witnesses who's supposed to be kept safe for the trial. You remember the old tramp at the church? It's almost impossible to be sure, the state the body's in, but I think it could be him. In which case I'm worried about the rest of them, especially the young lad, Jimmy.'

'Jimmy?' Kate sighed. Even the mention of the boy's name cast her back to some of her darkest days. She chewed thoughtfully on a slice of pizza.

'What about your friend Ray?' she asked. 'Could he be trying to get his brother out?'

Barnard stared at her in disbelief. 'Ray was very keen back then to get his brother inside,' he said. 'He reckoned he was a liability. But at the moment I need to keep away from Ray. With Copeland breathing down my neck he's the last person I want to be seen with for a bit.'

'Seems to me you're in a bind,' Kate said.

'Seems to me, you're probably right,' Barnard said gloomily.

FIVE

Carter Price picked Kate up after work the next day, opening the door of a black Citroën DS with a flourish and ushering her inside.

'Very nice,' she said as she snuggled down as he got back into the driving seat.

'Not mine,' Price said dismissively. 'It's best if the bad guys don't see my car too often.'

Kate raised an eyebrow at that and wondered just how bad these bad guys were. 'Where are we going?' Kate asked, as she settled herself into her seat. She knew very little about cars but knew that this one was something special.

'Just a little recce south of the river,' Price said, swinging the big car effortlessly around Piccadilly Circus and into the Strand with a motion Kate had not encountered before and was not sure she liked. 'I know where Reg Smith and his mates drink regularly and I'd like to just watch and see who he's talking to. We won't go inside. If you take snaps of the people going in and out while Smith is inside we'll get some idea of what's going on. Surveillance, the cops call it, but I get the feeling that there's not much of it going on in Bermondsey these days. I guess he's got the local nick pretty well sewn up.'

'Won't anyone recognize you,' Kate asked uneasily as they crossed Waterloo Bridge and headed south down heavily congested main roads.

'They might but they won't see us if we stay in the car, petal,' Price said reassuringly.

'Or could they recognize the car anyway? It's not exactly anonymous, is it?'

'I told you, it's not mine. I borrowed it. If we come down here again we'll use a different one. Bermondsey and Rotherhithe are funny old places. They're cut off from the rest of south London by the railway going up to London Bridge.

People don't move in and out much, though it took a hammering during the war. Reg Smith was born there, I think, and must still have lots of friends round and about, though I hear he's living in some big house near Blackheath now. Quite smart, that area. But I told you. This is just surveillance. We'll slide in quietly and park outside his favourite pub for a while and then slide out again. I'm not stupid enough to go head to head with Reg Smith. That's a sure way to end up at the bottom of the Thames.'

'Or dumped on a building site,' Kate said with a shudder, thinking of the body Harry Barnard was investigating.

'Yeah,' Price agreed. 'According to the Yard they haven't identified that poor beggar yet. You haven't heard anything different from your buddy Sergeant Barnard have you?' Kate shook her head. She knew that Harry would not thank her for passing anything on to Carter Price, especially fears that witnesses in a major case were being interfered with. And the same went for telling Harry what Price was up to. She was going to have to be very careful juggling these two men and she wondered whether this assignment had been a good idea.

Price took a right turn at a major junction and eventually crossed a bridge above multiple tracks where the rackety commuter trains which ran south of the river to the Kent suburbs were speeding in both directions. He then took a left, past a park and street after street of small brick houses, some of them still lying derelict as an obvious result of bombing.

'East London took a hammering during the blitz, both banks of the Thames,' Price said. 'The Surrey docks are over that way.' He waved a hand vaguely to the right. 'And on the other bank is Wapping and the Isle of Dogs. I was in my teens and I can remember the fires burning day after day. But the docks are in big trouble these days. Shipping is moving out further down the river and the dockers are a bolshie lot. It'll all be dead and gone soon.'

'I know about dockers,' Kate said, hackles rising. 'Don't forget I come from Liverpool. We got hammered by the Germans too, you know. It wasn't just you lot in London.' The car was stuffy and Kate opened a window. 'What's that awful smell?' she asked.

Price sniffed. 'Tannery,' he said. 'This was the leather district for years. They used to put the dirty stuff down here south of the river, away from the posher areas. But it's all dying out now, just like the docks. There's not much going on in that trade. I think there's only one tannery left but it still makes a dreadful pong. There's a biscuit factory down here too. You sometimes get a nicer class of whiff from that. But with the docks in trouble this whole area's going to fall apart soon. Shipping will move to Tilbury and no one will know what to do with all the redundant water round here. It's no wonder they put up with gangsters like Smith. If there's not much else going on crime might look like a good bet.'

'My grandfather came over from Ireland and worked in the docks,' Kate said. 'It doesn't seem possible they could close.'

'It's more than possible, it's highly likely,' Price said dismissively. 'Just look at this area and the things that have gone, and not just because of the Blitz.' He waved at a substantial Victorian building on the right. 'The Leather and Hide Exchange. How's that for a Victorian relic. Dickens had Bill Sykes meet a nasty end round here, too. It was a notorious slum in his time.'

'You know a lot about it,' Kate said.

'I was brought up not far away in Deptford. I've always been interested in local history.'

He turned into a short street at the end of which Kate could glimpse the river.

'Here we are, the Angel,' Price said, pulling into the kerb at a T junction and opposite a solid four-square London pub which appeared to back on to the river bank itself. 'If we sit quietly here for a bit no one will notice us and we can see who comes and goes. Is the light good enough for you to take some snaps?'

'I doubt it,' Kate said, peering through the deepening evening gloom. 'If you want good shots I need daylight. If I use flash someone will certainly notice.'

'Of course they bloody will,' Price said. 'I should have thought of that. I tell you what. We'll just wait a while to see who's coming and going. Then you can have a wander round with your unobtrusive little camera. At least you're not lumbered with one of those heavy beggars. You'll just look like a visitor gazing at the river. You can get to the embankment down the side of the pub there, look. Take a few shots while there's still a bit of light, and next time we'll try it in daylight. I know for a fact that Reg Smith is a Millwall fanatic and the stadium's just down the road. Just the right club for a bastard like him. The fans are all thugs. I reckon he'll meet up with his mates here on Saturday for a few bevvies before the match and we can catch him then. Be interesting to see who he goes to the match with. And we'll mosey down to Blackheath in daylight too and see what he gets up to at home. I'll check out his address.'

'Someone's coming,' Kate said quietly pointing at a big car which nosed past them and parked immediately outside the pub's main door. She felt rather than saw the tension as Price watched.

'That's Smith's car,' he said. 'And there's another Jag parked a bit further down, look. Something's going on.'

They watched in silence but could not see who the new arrival was. Eventually Price leaned across Kate and opened the passenger door. 'There you go. No one knows you, so you'll be quite safe. Have a little mosey round the back. No one will think it odd if you take a few shots of the river. We're not far from Tower Bridge. You'll see it on your left.'

'Can you get over the river from here?' Kate asked.

'Oh yes. There's a road tunnel just down the road in Rotherhithe and the first one which Brunel built is still there. It's part of the underground now. It's not completely cut off from the other side.'

Cautiously Kate got out of the car and walked down the side of the pub as Price had suggested and suddenly found herself facing a huge sweep of water which, even in the dusk, was still choppy with the wake from strings of barges chugging steadily in each direction. To the left she could make out the bright lights of Tower Bridge sweeping high over the water and opposite the much dimmer lights of Wapping and Shadwell. It was low tide and the unpleasant smell of Thames mud rose up from the beach beneath the embankment wall. The sight and smell of the working Thames made her catch her breath in a moment of nostalgia for her own home town. She hoped that Carter Price's pessimism about the future of the Mersey as well as the Thames was ill-founded, but she guessed it wasn't. She took several shots of the river and of the slightly decrepit old pub and then made her way back to the car.

'He's there,' Price said as she got in. 'It wasn't him in that first car which pulled up. But I saw him quite clearly getting out of a Bentley. It's parked over there, look.' He waved in the direction of a couple of large cars at the far side of the pub. You see? I was right. There's something big going on. We'll hang on until they go and then meet up again in daylight – Saturday before the match would be ideal if you can make it. And get some snaps of whoever he meets then if we can. Did you get anything useful round the back?'

'There's a veranda sort of thing facing the river,' Kate said. 'There were some people out there with drinks even though it's so cold. I thought that was a bit odd. I took some shots in that direction but I daren't use the flash. They would have noticed. The pictures will be very dark but they might just show something with the pub lights behind. I'll print them up tomorrow and you can have a look.'

'Good girl,' Price said, starting the engine and easing the car across the road and past the parked cars. 'Whoever's in there's not your usual Bermondsey punter, that's for sure. They don't drive around in Jags and Bentleys. And they don't hang about on chilly balconies unless they've something very private to discuss. Something's going on and if Reg Smith is involved you can be bloody sure that it's not going to be legal.'

Harry Barnard rang Kate at the office next morning and offered to take her for lunch.

'I'm pretty busy,' she said, looking at the contact prints from the previous night, which were on her desk. 'I could do coffee and a quick sandwich at the Blue Lagoon.'

Barnard groaned at the thought but then agreed. 'One o'clock then?'

'See you later, alligator,' Kate said absent-mindedly, but Barnard had already hung up. She turned back to her work, and when the rest of the staff went off for lunch at a pub, without inviting her to join them, she strolled through the crowds to the coffee bar where her aspiring actress friend Marie used to work. Barnard was there before her, his coat carefully hung with his hat nearby and a cup of steaming cappuccino in front of him.

'I could have done with something a bit stronger than this,' he said irritably as she slid into the seat opposite him. 'What would you like?'

The black girl who had taken over Marie's job when she decided to go back to Liverpool took their order and when she had finished Kate looked at Barnard quizzically.

'You don't look very pleased with life, la,' she said.

'I'm not,' Barnard said. 'I've got Vic Copeland dogging every step I take. And someone's told the DCI that you've been seen snooping around with Carter Price. He wants to know what Price is up to and I have to tell him something convincing. What do you suggest?'

'Just tell him the agency is doing some work for the *Globe*,' Kate said. 'It's nothing to do with you lot what Carter's investigating. I'm sure he'll tell you when there's anything to tell. Where am I supposed to have been snooping, anyway?'

'Oh just around Soho,' Barnard said, to Kate's relief. 'But someone recognized you both and thought it was odd even if Price does have a rep for liking women half his age. Are you sure it's just pictures he's after?'

Kate drew a sharp breath at that. 'I'm sure he'd like to get into my knickers if he got half a chance, but he's not going to get that is he,' Kate said tartly, hugely relieved, at least, that no one had seen her with Price south of the river. 'Don't tell me you're jealous, Harry Barnard? I didn't think we had that sort of relationship. Do we?'

Barnard glanced away and Kate grinned.

'It's a job,' she said. 'Nothing more or less. Tell me how, in my trade, I'm going to work at all if I don't work with blokes? There aren't any other women around. Nor likely to be any time soon, as far as I can see.'

'OK, OK, I get the message,' Barnard said. 'I suppose I'm a bit twitchy since this nasty murder.'

'Do they know who it was yet?' Kate asked.

'They say not,' Barnard said. 'And who am I to contradict in present circumstances. I'm trying to keep a low profile. And surely a whisper would have leaked from the Yard if one of their key witnesses had really gone missing. There'd be a row of mammoth proportions if it looked as if Georgie Robertson was going to get off the hook.'

'What worries me is that if one's gone there may be more,' Kate said. 'What about the young lad Jimmy? And the rest? If one of them has been killed surely someone will be trying to get them too.'

'They may be, but no one's going to tell me,' Barnard said gloomily. 'The Yard play this sort of thing very close to their chest. If I started asking questions they'd have me down as trying to get them out rather than making sure they're safe. That's just the sort of accusation they're looking to pin on me. I can't get involved.'

Kate took a bite of her somewhat limp and soggy egg sandwich and sighed.

'There is one thing you could do for me, sweetie,' Barnard said. 'Just a small favour. I daren't go anywhere near Ray Robertson at the moment, for obvious reasons, or even phone him. If the body really is who I think it is, they may have Ray's phone tapped. They still have him down as likely to try to try to get Georgie off somehow because he's his brother. They don't seem to realize the brothers are not exactly devoted, and haven't been for years. In fact they hate each other's guts. Do you think you could track Ray down at the Delilah – very discreetly – and ask him to call me at home from a number he's not connected with? I really need to suss out what he thinks is going on. And with Vic Copeland sitting on my tail it's almost impossible.'

'He's not following you now, is he?' Kate asked, glancing out of the steamy window anxiously.

'No, he went with the boss to some meeting at the Yard about the murder case. I wasn't invited. I'm seeing them when they get back.' It was obvious from his expression that this was not a prospect he was looking forward to.

'I'm not booked for anything special this afternoon,' Kate said. 'I could drop into the Delilah on my way home.'

'Great,' Barnard said. 'And not a word to that weasel from the *Globe* you're working with.'

'Of course not,' Kate said. 'Trust me.'

'When are you seeing him again?'

'Saturday,' Kate said. 'He wants some pictures of football fans.'

'Chelsea, I hope,' Barnard said with a grin. 'Though they're a dead loss this season.'

Kate finished her sandwich, feeling uneasy at the subterfuge she was being pushed into. 'I'll pass on your message to Ray,' she said.

Barnard pushed his chair away from the table explosively. 'Thanks, Katie. You're a doll.'

'Maybe,' she said.

It was mid-afternoon before DS Harry Barnard was summoned to the DCI's office, where he found Keith Jackson ramrod straight behind his immaculate desk as usual and DS Vic Copeland lounging in a chair opposite with a satisfied look on his heavy features. The DCI waved Barnard into another chair and steepled his hands in front of his face, his pale blue eyes more than usually chilly.

'We had a very productive meeting at the Yard,' he said. 'Information has come to hand that the liaison we suspected between Ray Robertson and Reg Smith is developing rapidly and that major criminal activity is planned. It seems that the murder we are investigating at Tottenham Court Road is intimately linked to what is going on between these criminal gangs, which is what I suspected all along. We don't have a formal identification yet but I am anticipating that very soon we'll pin down who that poor devil is and which of the gangs he either belonged to or annoyed in some way. But as another line of investigation AC Amis feels that it would be fruitful to use your long-standing relationship with Robertson, Sergeant Barnard, to uncover something of what he is planning with the south London gang.'

Barnard drew a sharp breath. 'I'm sure Robertson wouldn't confide in me if anything major was going down,' he said. 'It's not as if we're bosom buddies these days. We were kids together twenty years ago. Since then I've arrested his brother, for God's sake. And if Reg Smith is as ruthless as he's cracked up to be, he'll be watching his security like a hawk. If what you say is true about their plans I reckon I might be the next one to end up without my fingers and toes.' There was a guffaw from Copeland at that.

'Pull the other one, Harry boy,' he said. 'We all know you're still thick as thieves with Robertson. Always have been. What Mr Jackson fancies is you and me making use of that and doing this together. You go in and have a chat with him at the Delilah, wired up to eavesdrop, with me listening in and providing back-up if it all goes pear-shaped. What's wrong with that?' Barnard shrugged.

'We could try that, I suppose. But I think you're wasting your time. If he's really hitched up with Smith he won't be telling me anything about it.'

'We could bring him in for a little chat, then,' Copeland said, with a look of anticipation.

'We could, but he'd have heavyweight lawyers on the scene even before the interview room door closed,' Barnard objected. 'What the hell are we going to ask him on the basis of what we've got? Are you and Reg Smith planning another great train robbery? He'd laugh at us.'

The DCI drummed his fingers impatiently on his desk and scowled.

'Are we getting anywhere with chasing down the site workers from the murder scene?' Jackson snapped.

'Not as far as I know,' Barnard said. 'We've got six DCs working their way through the lists the contractors gave us. But nothing of interest has come up so far. I doubt it will, to be honest. If someone in there told the killers when the concrete was going to be poured he'll have made himself scarce by now.'

'What we really want to know is whether any of Robertson and Smith's people have disappeared,' Copeland said. 'If we pick up a few of their associates that should be easy enough to discover.'

'Not if they're scared they might be next,' Barnard said. 'If the Yard's got contacts in the gangs surely they could suss it out. It's certainly easier than trying to frighten one of the bosses. They're not likely to tell us anything. They'll laugh at us.'

'The Yard are working on it,' Jackson said. 'Meanwhile we are to pursue our own inquiries. So the two of you get an interview with Robertson. It can be on his own turf initially but make it clear we're not messing about on this one. We'll have him in if you feel we have to.' He flashed a glance at Copeland. 'Softly softly to start with,' he said. 'I'll listen to what you tape before we decide on the next step. Understood?'

Barnard nodded non-committally.

'Right guv, I'll get it set up,' Copeland said much more enthusiastically. 'We'll let you know when we're going in.'

SIX

Harry Barnard swung his favourite tweed swivel armchair disconsolately, sipping a glass of Scotch on the rocks without his usual enjoyment. Even his new Beatles record, which he had bought in Oxford Street on the way home and carefully placed on the radiogram's turntable immediately, failed to cheer him up, and every now and again he picked up the telephone receiver just to make sure that the dialling tone was still purring away. So far Ray Robertson had not called, although Kate O'Donnell, who had delivered his request after she finished work, had sworn that he had agreed to contact him when he called her at home.

He felt under siege. Between them DCI Jackson and DS Vic Copeland were constraining his movements around Soho and his strong desire to check out what he believed was the real identity of the body on the building site. He had left Copeland at the nick still finalizing the details of their eavesdropping equipment for tomorrow's date with Ray Robertson. He needed to talk to Ray before that but was entirely dependent on him to make contact. Edgy with frustration he wandered into his small kitchen and made himself a sandwich. It was not what he wanted for supper but he could not stray from his phone until he had heard from Ray.

After more than an hour of frustration the phone eventually rang and the familiar sound of a call box phone cranking into gear came a split second before Ray Robertson's irascible voice cut in.

'I don't know what I'm doing standing here in a smelly call box in the freezing cold,' he said. 'What the hell's going on, Flash? Why all the cloak and dagger stuff, for God's sake?'

'We need a meet, Ray,' Barnard said. 'Somewhere private where no one will recognize us. Believe me. This is important. Any suggestions?'

There was silence at the other end of the line and it took

some time for Robertson to cut through the crackle. 'Do you know where Fred Bettany lives?' he asked.

Barnard shifted uneasily. 'Somewhere in Hampstead,' he said cautiously. 'Not far from where I am?'

'Meet me there at nine,' Robertson cut in, dictating the address. 'I'll fix it with Fred and Shirley.' He hung up abruptly, leaving Barnard slightly breathless. He had no doubt that whatever the Bettanys' plans for the evening were they would now be put rapidly on hold. What Ray Robertson wanted Ray Robertson generally got. He just hoped that Shirley Bettany, his occasional lover, betrayed not a hint to either her husband or Ray that in these circumstances he himself would be a very unwelcome visitor to her family home.

Barnard parked outside Fred Bettany's house shortly before nine without the usual precautions when he was visiting Shirley. There were no other cars parked on the road where most of the large houses had ample drives for family parking, and he waited until Ray Robertson's Jag pulled up behind him.

'Come on,' Robertson said without bothering with a greeting. 'I've told Fred to take his missus out for a drink while we have a chat.' He rang the doorbell impatiently and Bettany, already in his coat, trilby in hand, opened it almost immediately. He flashed Barnard a look of inquiry before calling for his wife, who appeared on the stairs in a fur coat and hat with a tiny veil over her eyes. The pair were obviously not dropping into any old boozer, Barnard thought ruefully.

'Come in Ray,' Bettany said. 'Trouble?'

'Nothing to concern you, Fred,' Robertson said, holding the front door open so that Bettany and his wife had no choice but to exit.

Shirley avoided Barnard's eyes as he hurried past her, catching just a waft of an expensive perfume and the rustle of silk, as he went inside closely behind Robertson.

'Now then, Flash,' Robertson said, leading the way into the Bettanys' extensive sitting room at the front of the house and pulling the curtains closed. 'What the hell is going on?'

'I wish I knew,' Barnard said flinging himself into one of the soft armchairs, carefully avoiding the sofa where he and

Shirley had fairly recently dallied. 'Scotland Yard is calling the shots. They've put a DS called Vic Copeland into Soho, allegedly to clean up the nick.'

'Copeland? Isn't he the bastard who killed someone? He was a City of London cop then. Has he joined the Met?'

'Unfortunately yes,' Barnard said.

Robertson nodded slowly. 'Can't be good, can it? I heard he was lucky to get away with what he did. It was only because the casualty had a string of convictions as long as your arm that he swung it with the coroner. I didn't know the poor beggar personally but I know a few people who did. He was a harmless enough sneak thief, as it goes, no violence in him. Hardly likely to launch a ferocious attack on someone of Copeland's size, as alleged.' Robertson shrugged and glanced around the room enquiringly. 'Never mind. I think maybe we can treat ourselves to a glass of Fred's Scotch,' he said, making free with one of the well-filled decanters on a sideboard.

The two men tasted their drinks and nodded in satisfaction.

'So what's Copeland got on me? Or hoping to get on me?' Robertson asked.

'Nothing specific as far as I know. But he and the Yard seem to be convinced that the body that was found on the building site at Tottenham Court Road has connections with you, or the Maltese or even Reg Smith. They see it as a gangland execution of some sort – the poor bastard had no fingers and toes as if he'd been tortured for information or maybe just as an example to others. They're going to be looking very hard at what you're up to. And the rest. And I've a nasty feeling I'm on their list too, long term. In any event, Copeland's coming to see you tomorrow and I'm supposed to be coming with him. And I've no doubt that he's planning to record what we say.'

Robertson laughed. 'Just shows I was right not to link up with Smith,' he said thoughtfully. 'I'd more or less decided to give him a miss. I reckon you and Fred were right about him. He's trouble. Does Copeland know for sure me and Reg have had words?'

'Not as far as I know,' Barnard said. 'That's what he'll be wanting to know.'

'Right,' Robertson said.

'But what I want to know is whether you've heard any whispers about the digitless victim, who he is or why he might have been killed,' Barnard asked.

'None at all, Flash,' Robertson said. 'Not a dicky bird. You know I don't go in for that sort of thing. Not my scene. The Maltese can be vicious and so can Smith, but I've not heard so much as a whisper and I'll tell your mate Copeland that, don't you worry. What's your own take on it? You don't sound as if you go along with his theory.'

Barnard hesitated for a moment before he went on. He knew that his own suspicions as to the identity of the murder victim would concern Robertson far more than anything else and not for the reasons that Copeland might suspect. 'I saw the body,' he said. 'He was difficult to identify even after he'd been cleaned up a bit at the morgue. But he had a look of the old tramp who's a witness in Georgie's case. A crucial witness, as it goes.'

'You think someone's got to him and topped him?' Robertson asked, his face flushing a dangerous shade of pink.

'I can't get anyone to admit that any witness has gone AWOL, but if one has, there are people at the Yard who will put you top of the list of suspects. They've never really swallowed the idea that you were the main man when it came to wanting Georgie put away. They're convinced blood must be thicker than water.'

'So's my old ma,' Robertson said with feeling. 'But they don't realize what a psycho Georgie's become the last few years. I couldn't trust him an inch any more. You know he's always been a nutcase ever since he was a boy.'

'The cats,' Barnard said, thoughtfully.

'The cats,' Robertson agreed.

'You need to make all this pretty clear to Copeland when we come calling, as well as the fact that whoever the victim was he wasn't one of your associates. We need to cover both possibilities. But if I'm right – and no one believes me so far – who would have a reason for interfering with Georgie's trial? The only person I can think of is your ma.'

Robertson snorted in disbelief. 'She still thinks the sun

shines out of Georgie's bum, and I should be busting a gut to get him off,' he said. 'But she's an old woman now, Flash. There's no way she could be interfering with witnesses. Most of her and my dad's old mates are dead now, long gone. Who would she get to help her?'

'God knows,' Barnard said. 'I don't like any of this, believe me. Just thought I'd fill you in. Just in case. You know as well as I do that if I'm right there'll be more than one witness ready to drop out – even if no one comes calling to help them on their way. They'll be scared witless.'

'And I'm grateful, mate,' Robertson said, getting to his feet. 'But I think it's your imagination running away with you. And there's no reason I need to start cutting off fingers and toes for any other reason, though I can't speak for the Maltese or Reg Smith. Copeland may be right to think about them. Let's take it as it comes, shall we? But if you do find anything to prove someone's trying to mess with my brother's trial, let me know. That I can seriously do without.'

When Kate O'Donnell got to the picture agency next morning she found to her surprise that Carter Price was already ensconced with Ken Fellows in his office, the air thick with cigarette smoke which caught her breath when she opened the door on hearing her name hailed in raucous tones.

'You called?' she said, although she knew both men were impervious to her sarcasm, although she heard a chuckle from one of her colleagues in the busy photographers' room behind her.

'Come in, Kate, and shut the door,' Fellows said. 'Carter here would like to take you out with him this morning for a bit more snooping around. You haven't got anything else on, have you?'

Kate shook her head. 'Where are we going this time?' she asked Price.

'Another little trip south of the river. I think we'll take a look at Mr Smith's home territory. I hear he's moved up in the world since he left Bermondsey. Got himself a view of Blackheath which is a different neck of the woods altogether.'

'Fine, if that's OK with Ken,' Kate said.

Her boss nodded equably and Kate went back into the office to put a new roll of film into her camera and put her coat on again. Outside, Price ushered her into a much smaller car this time which was parked half on the pavement and causing a passing taxi driver to have a red-faced rant as he tried to squeeze past.

'Another borrowed car?' Kate asked.

'Yeah, sorry we can only run to an A40 this time, but it's pretty inconspicuous. No one will notice us in this if we do a couple of circuits of Smith's place.' He pulled into the centre of the road to allow Kate room to get into the passenger seat.

'Right,' he said. 'Blackheath it is.'

As far as Kate could see they took more or less the same route as they had taken to Bermondsey but did not pull off into docklands. The traffic was heavy but eventually they climbed a steep hill and emerged to find flat grassy open space on either side of them.

'Wat Tyler led his rebellion round here,' Price said. 'There's a road named after him somewhere.'

Kate looked bemused. 'You must be a Londoner born and bred,' she said, racking her brains and finding no trace of Wat Tyler.

'Oh yes,' Carter Price said. 'I was born in Deptford, remember, and you can't grow up there without being a bit fascinated by the local history. The Navy was on the doorstep in more ways than one. Anyway this is Blackheath and this is the road where Reg Smith has apparently taken root.' He took a right turn into a road of Victorian villas which immediately began to head downhill and parked unobtrusively behind a van. 'That's Smith's place,' he said, pointing to a tall stucco three-storey house with a far more substantial fence around it than most of the similar houses, and a sturdy wrought iron gate closing off parking space for several cars.

'There's his Bentley,' Price said. 'I reckon we're in luck. He seems to be at home.'

Kate leaned back in her seat and surveyed the scene. The road was tree-lined and quiet, dropping away from the heath. Some of the houses appeared to have been turned into flats but there was almost no sign of movement anywhere. 'What

if he stays in all day?' she asked. 'We could get pretty uncomfortable, and hungry, come to that.'

'Well they call this Blackheath but in fact this road runs
down to Lewisham, comes out quite near the station, so we're
close to amenities if we need them. Let's see how it goes,
shall we?' He turned off the engine and put an arm behind
her with one hand on her shoulder but she wriggled away.

'My pictures are what you've paid for,' she said tartly. 'Nothing
else.'

He shrugged and pulled a wry face but took his arm back
to his own side of the car.

Kate delved in her bag and pulled out some prints. 'These
are what I took outside the pub in Bermondsey. They're very
dark, which is what we expected, but this one which catches
the people on the terrace I thought you might be interested in.'

Price took the prints and studied the one she had placed on
top. 'I'll swear that's Smith, even just in silhouette,' he said.
'But this one here looks familiar too. The light from inside is
just catching his face. But I can't quite put a name to him.
I'm sure we'll do better in daylight, petal.'

DS Harry Barnard spent the morning with Vic Copeland doing
a quick survey of the bookshops which trod a delicate line
around the laws of pornography and obscenity in the narrow
streets of Soho.

'When did you last raid any of these places,' Copeland
asked. 'What they put on display is on the edge but what's in
the back rooms must be well over it. Do any of them specialize
in queer stuff? It seems to be a bit of an obsession with your
DCI?'

'There used to be one but the owner got stabbed when we
had that queer murder case. You remember?'

'Oh yes, I do remember. That's when you mislaid DCI
Venables, isn't it? You never know who to trust in this game,
do you? Anyway, let's save porn for another day. We can give
the God-fearing Mr Jackson a treat later. Let's work out a
strategy for tackling Ray Robertson this afternoon.'

Barnard glanced at his watch. 'I'm meeting someone for a
quick bevvy,' he said. 'I'll see you back at the nick at one

thirty. That gives us an hour to get down to the Delilah to see Robertson, no problem.'

Copeland shrugged and turned away. 'See you later then,' he said. 'Be good.'

As Copeland headed west to the nick, Barnard weaved his way through the narrow streets and alleys, crowded now with lunchtime visitors to the cafes and bars, until he reached a towering gothic church on the northern edge of his patch, with a crumbling vicarage next door. He rang the heavy doorbell and it was opened after a long wait by a cleric in a pale blue sweater whose face brightened when he saw who his visitor was.

'Harry,' said the Rev David Hamilton. 'What can I do for you? You're not bringing me more waifs and strays are you?'

'Not this time,' Barnard said. 'Can I have a word, though?'

'Of course,' Hamilton said. 'Come in.' And he led the way, with a pronounced limp, to his study overlooking the neglected looking churchyard at the back of the building and waved Barnard into a chair. 'What's your problem?' he asked.

'You've got your ear close to the ground,' Barnard said, offering the vicar a cigarette, which he waved away, and lighting his own. 'I need to pick your brains.'

'Feel free.'

'Do you remember the old tramp who saw more than he should have done when there was that unfortunate death here?'

'Hamish, wasn't he called? Very smelly, very Scottish. Wasn't inclined to listen to me. Yes, I remember him,' the vicar said.

'Have you seen him recently?'

David Hamilton looked puzzled. 'I thought he was being looked after until the trial,' he said. 'Has he run off? It's probably because you're not keeping him topped up with booze.'

'Probably,' Barnard said. 'I'm not sure about this but I thought I saw him recently and I was worried about his safety, that's all. Can you let me know if he crosses your path?'

'Of course,' Hamilton said. 'And what about the boy? What was his name? Jimmy? Is he still safe?'

'As far as I know, but I'll check up on that if I can,' Barnard said heavily. 'The Yard are handling the witnesses and no one's going to fill me in if I go asking about them. But I'll see what I can do.'

'I'll keep my eyes and ears open,' Hamilton said. 'There's a grapevine amongst the youngsters who turn up here looking for a bed. I don't know how they do it, but they know what's going on.'

'Thanks,' Barnard said. 'It may be nothing at all. He's probably quite safe and my bosses won't thank me for asking awkward questions. I'll give you my home phone number if you need to get in touch.' He wrote his number on a piece of paper Hamilton handed him. 'Or you can leave a message at the nick.'

'I thought things would get better once you'd pinned Georgie Robertson down,' Hamilton said without his normal cheerful optimism. 'But I've not seen much sign of it myself.'

'I think there are people trying to fill the vacuum,' Barnard said. 'Don't hesitate to call me if you hear anything, anything at all, about that case.'

'I won't,' Hamilton said, looking even more anxious. 'I'll keep my ears open, believe me.'

Barnard left the vicarage and made his way back to the centre of Soho where he caught the landlord of the queer pub just opening his doors. He did not look pleased to see Barnard and merely grunted when he asked for a sandwich to go with his pint at the bar.'

'We don't really do food,' he said.

'I'm sure you could make an exception if you want a quiet life,' Barnard said with a faint smile. 'We've got a new DS on board who's not nearly as tolerant as I am about poofters. You really don't want to meet him.'

He took his glass across the empty bar to a corner table which gave a good view of the main doors and the landlord quite quickly delivered a ham sandwich and a small pot of mustard and waved away the pound note which Barnard offered.

'On the house,' he said, and Barnard grinned.

He had finished his beer and his sandwich by the time anyone he wanted to talk to came into the now busy pub. But Vincent Beaufort was never difficult to spot even in the most crowded environment. He marched through the swing doors resplendent in a black slouch hat, a purple suit and a green and pink flowery shirt and tie combo which made even fashion-conscious Barnard flinch. His sharp-eyed glance round the bar soon singled out Barnard in his corner and his expansive smile at the assembled throng faded as Barnard crooked a finger and he inched his way towards him and took the empty seat opposite.

'Vinnie, you old poofter, long time no see,' Barnard said cheerily while Beaufort's face visibly blenched, showing up the two circles of rouge on his cheeks.

'What do you want?' he asked faintly. 'I've just spent two months at Her Majesty's pleasure in Wandsworth for chatting up a friend in a cottage. What the hell do you want now?'

'Yes, I heard about that,' Barnard said. 'Soliciting, was it? Nothing to do with me, Vinnie. You go putting yourself about in public lavs and uniform will have you. You know that.'

'So what now?'

'Just a quiet word,' Barnard said, lowering his voice. 'If you keep your eyes and ears open for me it may help next time you cross the line.'

'So what are you after,' Beaufort asked sulkily. 'I'll believe you're more give than bloody take when I see some evidence of it.'

'Fair enough,' Barnard said. 'It's only a theory I'm working on anyway. Nothing official. But if you hear any whispers about Georgie Robertson, and the witnesses at his upcoming trial, just tip me the wink, OK? You remember there was talk of him being your way inclined, don't you?'

'I never thought there was anything in that,' Beaufort said contemptuously. 'I have a nose for these things after all these years.'

'Doesn't matter,' Barnard said. 'Just let me know if you hear his name mentioned, or the name of anyone else involved in the case. D'you remember the old Scottish tramp who used to be around? You haven't seen him recently have you?'

'I haven't,' Beaufort said sharply. 'He's not my sort of person. Leaves a lot to be desired in the personal hygiene department.'

'Let me know if you do see him,' Barnard said. 'It's important. He's supposed to be being kept safe but I think he might have come to some harm.' He got up from the table and put

a hand on Beaufort's shoulder which from a distance might
have looked friendly but which was firm enough to make him
flinch. 'Don't be a stranger,' he said.

Beaufort turned away and did not reply.

By lunchtime Kate was hungry and in urgent need of a lava-
tory, as she told Carter Price in no uncertain terms for at least
the fifth time.

'All right, all right,' Price said eventually, starting up the
grumbling engine of the A40 and doing a three point turn
outside Reg Smith's wrought iron gates. 'We'll have a lunch
break.' The morning had not been entirely unproductive. Soon
after they arrived a small car had turned into the drive and a
middle-aged woman had opened the gates, driven inside and
closed them again behind her battered Ford.

'Cleaning woman,' Kate suggested.

'Probably,' Price had agreed. They had waited another hour
before anything else happened. Then a green Jag had driven
up fast, stopped outside the gates with a squeal of tyres and
repeated the opening and closing ritual. Kate had taken another
photograph and then glanced at her companion.

'Do you recognize him?' she asked.

'Someone with a driver,' Price said. 'I couldn't get a good
look at the passenger. But if we've got the registration number
I can track it down. There are ways.' He tapped his nose
suggestively. The vigil had got more interesting then as several
more cars turned up in close succession and drove inside, most
of them luxury cars, some with drivers and some without.

'Get him,' Price said sharply to Kate every time someone
who was obviously not a chauffeur got out to open the gates,
although he did not claim to recognize anyone by sight.
And she took her shots through the windscreen as unobtrusively
as she could.

'Something's going on there this morning,' Price muttered as
a fifth car entered Smith's driveway. 'They can't just be having
lunch. We may get better shots of the cars as they come out.'

But by noon most of the cars, including the cleaner's, had
driven out again one after another and Kate had done her best to
focus on whoever was driving or occupying the passenger seat.

'It's not going to be very clear through the glass,' she warned Price. 'And focusing on a moving car. I'll just shoot as many as I can and trust to luck on the quality.'

'Do your best,' he had said huffily. 'Just do your best.'

And when all the cars had departed, most of them swinging up the hill towards Blackheath and past where they were discreetly parked, he had reluctantly agreed that they needed a break and driven swiftly down towards Lewisham where they found a pub which served food.

'Do you think that's it?' she asked, tasting a sandwich which was curling at the edges. 'He's not likely to get more visitors this afternoon, is he?'

'Well, we haven't seen Smith himself yet,' Price said. 'If he chooses to go out it'll be interesting to see just where he goes.'

Kate shrugged. She found this assignment tedious but as Ken Fellows had sanctioned it she had no choice in the matter. She drank half a pint of shandy while Price downed a couple of pints and she ate the sandwich because she was hungry. But in the event Price's prediction was justified.

What happened next took Kate by complete surprise. Soon after they had driven back up the hill towards the heath and parked unobtrusively again, the gates opened to allow in a car which she recognized immediately.

'That's Harry Barnard from CID in Soho,' she said, her mouth suddenly unaccountably dry.

'Your boyfriend?' Price said, immediately on full alert.

'Not really,' Kate said.

'There's someone with him,' Price said. 'See if you can recognize him as well.'

Kate peered at the red Capri but could not make out who was in the passenger seat clearly.

'Take a couple of shots anyway,' Price said, and she followed his instructions.

'I don't suppose it's very odd that the cops should be paying Smith a visit but your man is well off his normal beat. I've got contacts of my own who may be able to tell me what's going on. If Smith is about to be nicked that's a big story. I'll follow up when I get back to the office. Let's wait a bit to see if Smith goes out. He won't be best pleased by that little visit I shouldn't think. He reckons he's far too influential to be bothered by detective sergeants. Unless, of course, he's got your mate in his pocket, like so many others down this way.'

'Don't be silly,' Kate said, though she feared her voice lacked conviction. But Price was right on one thing. Whatever was going on was getting more serious by the minute. They watched Harry Barnard's Capri leave after twenty minutes or so and she took another couple of shots.

'We'll see how Smith reacts to that,' Price said and settled back in his seat again, only to find his persistence quickly rewarded. After about five minutes, Smith himself drove to the gates, opened them and set off at speed towards Lewisham with Price close behind. It was difficult to keep the faster car in sight in the heavy traffic of the New Kent Road but as they approached central London Smith's car slowed at a junction and he signalled a turn towards Bermondsey and Rotherhithe.

'The Angel again?' Kate suggested.

'Could well be,' Price agreed and they followed at a safe distance towards the Thames. Smith parked in much the same place as he had chosen the last time they had seen him here, but instead of going straight into the pub he made his way to another car which was parked nearby, and opened the driver's door to allow someone out whose hand he shook enthusiastically.

'Well, well, well,' Price whispered. 'Get those two, petal. As many shots as you can.'

'Who is it?' she asked.

'He's called Mitch Graveney, and he's the father of the chapel for one of the print unions at the *Globe.*'

'Father of the what?' Kate asked, mystified.

'Chairman of the union branch,' Price said impatiently. 'Now what the hell is he doing down here meeting with Reg Smith?'

They sat watching the pub for half an hour but neither of the two men emerged and when Price sent Kate in to buy a packet of crisps at the bar she saw them sitting at a secluded table with pints of beer and plates of sandwiches in front of them.

'They look settled in for the duration,' she told Price as she opened her crisps.

'Well I don't suppose we can hang around here all day,' Price admitted. 'I'll make some inquiries about Mitch when I get back to the office.' He turned to look at her closely and his eyes were cold. 'There is one thing, sweetheart. I don't want you going back to your friend the copper and telling him what we've been up to. What we're doing is confidential and if you breathe a word out of turn I'll make sure you never work as a photographer in London again. You do understand that, don't you?'

Kate opened her mouth to protest but Price put a hand up.

'Your man may be as innocent as the day's long, dear,' he said. 'He might have been popping in to see Reg Smith with all the authority of the Metropolitan Police behind him. Or he might not. Until we know a bit more about what's going on you keep your mouth shut. Understood?'

'Understood,' Kate said, her mouth dry and her heart thumping. She was, she thought, not just out of her depth, she was in great danger of drowning.

SEVEN

D S Harry Barnard met up with Vic Copeland in the CID office half an hour before they were due to talk to Ray Robertson at the Delilah Club. Copeland had a tape recorder in a briefcase with a small microphone strategically placed just beneath the lock. It was, Barnard thought, a quite unnecessary stratagem to record a conversation which he knew would provide no admissions which could possibly be incriminating.

'I've managed to get us a meet with the Maltese later just in case our corpse is one of theirs,' Copeland said. 'But my money's on Robertson.'

'Well if you believe Reg Smith, you may be right,' Barnard said non-committally, not wanting to get into an argument. The morning's trip to see Smith, on Barnard's own insistence, had been frustrating and inconclusive. Smith had denied all knowledge of the tortured corpse found on the building site and been anxious to assure them that no one he was connected with had gone missing.

'You say he had lost his fingers and toes,' Smith had said, wide-eyed. 'What makes you imagine I treat people like that anyway? I look after my boys. Anyway, no one I work with is missing. You're on the wrong track completely, lads. You're on a wild goose chase. My activities these days are completely legit, whatever anyone else says. Believe me.' Barnard had not believed a word of it, but he was not prepared to go into details of his knowledge of Ray Robertson's affairs. The contacts between Robertson and Smith would inevitably reach official ears some time soon, perhaps even during the interview Copeland had arranged for this afternoon, but he saw no particular reason to highlight a liaison which he hoped Ray Robertson had decided to avoid. He shrugged himself into his trench coat and adjusted his tie in the glass panel of the door.

'Let's get on then, shall we?'

They walked the short distance from the nick to the Delilah Club where they found the doors open and Barnard led the way to the office at the back of the building. The door there was open too and they could see Ray Robertson lounging at his desk, smoking a cigar with a smile on his face which reminded Barnard of a hungry tiger eyeing up a sitting target.

'Good morning gents,' Robertson said. 'Come on in, come on in. Make yourselves at home. What exactly can I do for you?'

Barnard glanced at Copeland. 'My mate Vic has a few questions, Ray,' he said. 'We're pursuing inquiries about the murder victim who was found on the building site at Tottenham Court Road. We don't have an identity yet and we wondered if you had any idea who he might be.'

Robertson fixed a glare on Copeland and stubbed out his cigar viciously without adjusting his smile. He sat up in his swivel chair, elbows on the desk, every inch the predator in spite of his bulk. 'What makes you think that I might have anything to do with that poor beggar?' he asked, his voice silky. 'I heard what happened to him. That was pretty quickly on the grapevine. Nasty business, I heard. Very nasty.'

'Not one of your associates, then?' Copeland asked.

'Certainly not,' Robertson said. 'You could argue that not all my business dealings are lily-white – some people do – but Harry here will tell you that I don't go in for that sort of unpleasantness.' He gave Barnard a broad wink. 'I'm not a killer, or someone who tortures people, whatever my brother allegedly gets up to. I have a position to maintain doing my charity work. You should know all about that if you're going to be working in Soho for very long, Mr Copeland. You should have done your homework. I have friends in high places.'

'A bit different from your brother Georgie then? Or so you say,' Copeland sneered, his colour high, his temper also only just under control.

Barnard could feel the tension between the two men rising far faster than he liked or had anticipated.

'My brother Georgie is a bit of a psycho,' Robertson snapped back. 'I'm glad to see the back of him. He's been a bloody embarrassment to me for years, if you want the honest truth.

In fact since we were kids, as Harry here knows. He knew he was an evil little beggar when he was ten years old. Specialized in killing old ladies' cats.'

Copeland glanced at Barnard who shrugged. 'True enough,' he said, annoyed that Ray had dragged him into the conversation that way.

'So if he's not one of yours, this unidentified corpse, do you have any idea who our victim might have been working for?' Copeland went on relentlessly. 'Or who he might have annoyed? He must have been well into something to have been treated like that. Have you heard anything of that sort on your very efficient grapevine?'

'No I haven't,' Robertson said. 'This is a very big city and I don't have a finger in every pie.'

He didn't add more's the pity, though Barnard could see it was on the tip of his tongue. Ray, he thought, was too ambitious for his own good these days.

'Someone planned the disposal of that body very carefully,' Copeland persisted. 'It wasn't just a random street killing. And I'm told you've been having chats with Reg Smith recently so don't play the innocent with me. It won't wash.' Robertson glanced at Barnard angrily but did not respond to Copeland's charge.

Barnard shook his head almost imperceptibly, careful not to put too much on Copeland's recorder, but his reticence did not seem to improve Robertson's temper.

'It was pure chance that this poor beggar didn't disappear under concrete before anyone noticed he was there, Ray,' Barnard put in, trying to get the temperature down. 'Someone knew that was going to happen that morning and managed to get on to the site without security seeing anything amiss. Any ideas on that at all?'

Robertson focused again on Harry Barnard, but there was no warmth in his eyes now. 'You know as well as I do that there are players who wouldn't blink at murder if they were crossed,' Robertson said. 'You don't need me to spell it out. And I won't. Just leave me out of it. I don't know who your effing victim is and I don't know who might have killed him. I just want to make it very clear that it's nothing to do with me. I've got another boxing gala at the planning stage and I don't want my name dragged through the mud when I'm sending invitations out to my contacts in high places. I've a reputation to keep up.'

And that, Barnard thought with a faint smile, was what Ray Robertson truly believed.

'You don't think that the charges against your brother aren't going to do that anyway?' Copeland asked incredulously. 'You reckon you can cut yourself off from all that? Pull the other one.'

Robertson's face darkened again and he clenched his fists. 'Get this right,' he spat at Copeland. 'I won't be dragged into the mud by that bastard Georgie. Your job is to put him away for life. If I had my way I'd see him hang. It's a great shame they aren't going to do that any more. Now get out of here the pair of you before I really lose my temper.'

Barnard smiled again faintly as Copeland got reluctantly to his feet. 'I reckon we'll see you again, Mr Robertson,' he said.

'I bloody well hope not,' Robertson said, pulling out another cigar from his desk drawer and making great play of lighting it as they made their way to the door.

'Don't go away without telling us,' Copeland flung over his shoulder, as Robertson puffed a cloud of aromatic smoke in their direction. 'We don't want to have to track you down in Spain or anywhere like that. It's becoming a favourite hidey-hole these days but I don't think you'd like it. I don't think the climate would suit.'

Robertson just scowled at that and said nothing.

Barnard was sure he would be hearing from Ray later and he would vent his spleen then. But, he thought, there was absolutely nothing he was going to be able to do to even slow Copeland down, let alone stop him in his tracks. That way lay professional suicide.

The two detectives walked slowly back to the nick together but said little.

'He's a bloody con man,' Copeland offered as they walked past the desk sergeant and made their way back to CID. 'Thinks he's a bloody philanthropist of some sort with one hand while he rakes in protection money with the other. I'll put him away for something while I'm here, you see if I don't. If I get him in a cell he won't be so cocky, you'll see.'

And that, Barnard thought, sounded more like a promise than a threat.

DS Vic Copeland did not waste much time at his desk. Barnard watched with some anxiety as he marched out and headed in the direction of DCI Keith Jackson's office. Copeland banged on the DCI's door, putting his head around before being invited in.

'Thought I'd better report back, guv,' Copeland said, flinging himself into a chair, to the DCI's obvious irritation.

'On what exactly, sergeant?' Jackson snapped.

'I've just got back from a chat with Harry Barnard's old mate Ray Robertson. Softly softly's not in it with those two.'

'That's common knowledge,' Jackson said. 'Did you actually find out anything we didn't know already? What's Robertson got to say for himself?'

'He swears he knows nothing about the body at Tottenham Court Road,' Copeland said. 'And so, incidentally, does Reg Smith. We did a quick trip to see him this morning. Anyway, Robertson swears he doesn't know who it is or who might have dumped it there. Squeaky clean, he claims and Barnard did damn all to push him. I thought I might haul him in for a cosy chat here, without Flash Harry. What do you think, guv?'

'I think it's a bit early for that,' Jackson said. 'You said you were going to keep an eye on Barnard first anyway. Has that come to anything?'

'I followed him this morning as he was cruising around Soho. Nothing unusual. If he was on the take, which I guess he was, it was all very discreet. We'll have to set some sort of a trap if we're to catch him bang to rights. I'll work something out on that. The only odd thing he got up to was a trip to the queer pub. He's not that way inclined, is he?'

'I think you can rule that out,' Jackson said with distaste. 'There's not much doubt he's a lady's man.'

'Is he on the square, by the way? If he and Robertson are in the same lodge that could explain a lot of what's going on between those two. You know how it works.'

'Barnard's certainly not a mason,' Jackson said. 'I know exactly who is and who isn't in my nick. Like you, most are, but not Harry Barnard.'

'It was just another thought,' Copeland said. 'I like to know who I'm dealing with. I certainly saw him chatting up that old queen who flounces around like a pantomime dame. God knows what they were talking about. I only got a glimpse of them. I didn't go in. They'd have spotted me. In any case the only way I like to go into that place is with a squad of uniforms ready to give them a good seeing to.'

'I'll think about that,' Jackson said.

'I could pull the old queer in by himself? Give his bollocks a twist and find out what Barnard was chatting him up for? We might get something out of it.'

'Not yet, not yet,' Jackson said. 'You've only been here five minutes. Take it a step at a time and we've a much better chance of hanging Barnard out to dry. That's what AC Amis wants, as I understand it. We know he's been a mate of Robertson's for years. There's no way he hasn't been involved in something and this murder gives us an opportunity to pin them both down. There are other fish in the sea Mr Amis wants hauled out but Robertson and Barnard are target number one. So take your time. You can suss out the queer pub yourself if you like, see what you can turn up there. But keep a cool head and clean hands for the moment. This is too important to rush. And don't forget to have a look at the Maltese, just in case we can't prove the man without his fingers and toes is one of Robertson's.'

'Right, guv,' Copeland said, though he did not hide his disgruntlement. 'But in my experience you can prove pretty well anything you want if you really try.'

Kate met Harry Barnard after work in the Blue Lagoon for a coffee and she could see the anxiety in his face.

'You don't look as if you've had a very good day,' she said as he put a cappuccino in front of her.

He nodded bleakly. 'It started off badly and got steadily worse,' he said. 'Vic Copeland is on some sort of mission and I'm damn sure he has me in his sights as well as Ray Robertson.' He told her about the two sergeants' uncomfortable interview with the club owner and then the newcomer's threat to take Ray in for questioning. 'As far as I can see there's absolutely no evidence to link Ray with the murder victim but that doesn't seem to bother Copeland one bit.'

'Carter Price would be very interested in all this,' Kate said. 'Shall I tell him?'

Barnard shuddered slightly. 'I think that would do more harm than good,' he said. 'How are you getting on with Price, anyway? I had a nosy around with some contacts in Fleet Street and I didn't much like what I heard. He's got a lot of enemies, even on his own paper. And the press office at the Yard hate his guts.'

'If he's doing his job properly you'd expect that,' Kate said. 'Ray's not exactly an innocent is he? I know I've good reason to be grateful to him but he's still a gangster. If you did your job properly you'd probably want him in a cell too.' It was as critical as she had ever been about his link to Ray Robertson and she knew she was taking a risk.

Barnard flushed and stirred his coffee hard but refused to respond. 'Price has a reputation with the ladies,' he said.

Kate flushed in her turn. 'I've told you. I'm working with him. That's all.'

'OK, OK,' Barnard said. 'Just be careful, Kate, that's all I'm really saying. Trouble seems to follow you around and Carter Price is a maverick. Why won't the *Globe* provide him with a photographer if he's working on a legitimate story for them? I don't understand what's going on there at all.'

'He's not very explicit, but I think he has some sort of feud with the picture editor. The picture man certainly wasn't very friendly when Carter took me round the building. Not very friendly at all.'

'Well, be careful, Kate. That's all I'm saying.' Barnard put a hand over hers. 'I do care about you, you know.'

She smiled faintly. 'What you really mean is don't go to bed with Carter Price,' she said. 'I think I can guarantee you that I won't do that. I find him faintly repulsive in that way.' She got a faint smile in response to that unequivocal declaration but Barnard still looked strained. 'That's not all that's worrying you, is it?' she said.

He shook his head. 'I'm still not convinced the murder is gang related at all,' he said.

She took a deep breath. 'Carter Price took me down to Blackheath this morning to keep an eye on Reg Smith's place,' she said. 'Surveillance, he called it. He reckons Smith is planning something big . . . I shouldn't even be telling you this.' She hesitated and Barnard looked at her in astonishment.

'You saw me there, I take it?'

'You with someone else in your car.'

'Bloody hell, Kate. What did you think was going on? Or more to the point, what did Price think was going on? The worst I expect.'

'So what was going on?' Kate asked, her mouth dry.

'Sergeant Vic Copeland and I made a quick call on Reg Smith to ask him if he knew anything about the body that was found on the building site. Copeland is sure that it's a gangland killing, but of course Smith denied all knowledge of it. Nothing to do with him, he said. We weren't there more than fifteen minutes, I don't think. We had to get back for an interview with Ray Robertson to ask him the same question. You'd better put Price right on that.'

'I'll do that,' Kate said quietly. 'He thinks the worst every time, of course. I suppose it's his job. What did Ray say to Copeland.'

'Get lost, more or less. It's nothing to do with him either. Which leaves the Maltese to be tackled and they don't tell anyone anything if they can help it. So we're still left with no ID for the body. Nothing at all. I still think it could be the old tramp you met at the church that time.'

Kate shuddered slightly. 'In which case it could be more to do with Georgie Robertson than Ray?'

'And in which case the other witnesses could be at risk too. Especially Jimmy Earnshaw. He's only a kid and he must be worried about giving evidence, however well he's being looked after by the witness team. I had a quiet word with a mate of mine at the Yard who knows about protecting witnesses and he reckons he knows where Jimmy is. He gave me an address. Strictly out of order but he owed me a favour. I thought I might go down there and have a chat with him, see how he's bearing up. His evidence is absolutely crucial and I'd really like to know that he understands that and he's still up for the Old Bailey.'

'That he isn't getting cold feet, you mean,' Kate said.

'Will you come with me?' Barnard asked quietly. 'It might reassure him if he knew that there were people who were rooting for him.'

'When?'

'Now, if you're not doing anything this evening. It's not far to drive. We could be there in three quarters of an hour. I can drop you off at Shepherd's Bush on the way back. Or we could go out for a meal. What do you think?'

Kate hesitated for a moment but she could see that Barnard was wound up in a way that she had never experienced before. 'OK,' she said. 'Stop at a phone box and I'll tell Tess that I won't be in for supper.'

The drive down the A40 took slightly longer than Barnard had promised in spite of his expert weaving through the rush-hour traffic and Kate found herself becoming as anxious as Barnard evidently was about Jimmy Earnshaw's safety. Just beyond RAF Northolt, where fighters had taken off during the war, they took a right turn at traffic lights and made their way through a suburban landscape of tree-lined roads and semi-detached houses.

'Where are we?' Kate asked.

Barnard pulled into the kerb and consulted a map. 'This is Ruislip,' he said. 'Commuter-land. The tube comes right out here so people can use it to get to work in the centre of London. Now if we take a left here we're almost there.'

Within minutes he pulled up outside one of the many identical pebble-dashed semis, and switched off the engine. He looked at Kate, his face sombre.

'I think it would make sense if you knocked at the door,' he said. 'It won't do me any good at all if I'm recognized out here. The Yard will be furious. You can say you're a friend of Jimmy's and you've got permission to pay him a visit. Give them any name you like, so long as it's not your real name. And just see if you can be sure he's there and safe. That's enough for now. It's number twenty-two, just a few houses back.'

Kate sighed. 'Are you sure I won't get into trouble doing this?'

'No, but I'm sure I would if they found out. Come on, Kate. We need to know he's safe.'

'All right,' she said. 'I'd be devastated if anything happened to that boy.' She got out of the car and walked slowly back to the gate with twenty-two on it, and went up the short garden path to the door and rang the bell. There was silence inside and Kate was about to ring again when the door was opened quite suddenly by a man in jeans and shirtsleeves who looked half asleep and unshaven.

'Yes?' he said, his eyes unfriendly and the door held firmly only a quarter ajar.

'I think you have a friend of mine staying here,' Kate said. 'Jimmy Earnshaw. Can I see him?'

'Who told you that?' the man asked in even more unfriendly tones. 'Who the hell told you that?'

'I asked if I could see him and they said yes. Didn't they tell you?' Kate improvised. 'It's very important. I've got a message from his mother.'

'I don't care what you've got, miss. Nobody's told me to let anyone in.'

'He is here, then? Surely I can see him for just five minutes. That won't do any harm,' Kate insisted.

'Who are you?' the man asked, angry now and reaching out for Kate's arm.

She dodged back down the path slightly but still stood there, her arms folded. 'Jimmy,' she shouted, hoping her voice would carry through the half-open door. 'Jimmy, are you there?'

'Shut up, you little cow,' the man yelled back. 'Half the street will hear you.'

'Good,' Kate said and yelled again, taking care to back towards the gate where she knew Harry Barnard would be able to see her.

There was no response from the house and the man advanced threateningly down the path. 'He's not here, you stupid bitch.

He's gone. Now bugger off. I'm in enough bother already without you blowing my cover completely. Scarper!'

Back in the car, feeling hot and breathless, Kate told Barnard what had happened. 'He lost his rag,' she said. 'Told me more than he should have done, I guess. Jimmy's not there, though obviously he has been. He knew exactly who I was talking about and that I really shouldn't have tracked Jimmy down.'

Barnard nodded. 'We'd better go,' Barnard said. 'If he reports back to the Yard they'll send all the hounds of hell to track you down.' He started the car and drove back to the A40 without passing in front of the house Kate had visited. As they joined the main road a police car with lights flashing turned towards Ruislip at speed.

'Maybe nothing to do with us,' Barnard said as he accelerated towards Northolt. 'But it could be.'

'So what do you think has happened to Jimmy?' Kate asked, feeling slightly sick.

'What did the bloke say exactly?'

'He just said he's gone. But he certainly didn't seem pleased about it. He said he was in bother himself, whatever that means.'

'It probably means that Jimmy's either run off by himself or someone's taken him,' Barnard said.

Kate felt tears behind her eyes. 'That's not good, is it, either way?'

'No,' Barnard said. 'It's not good at all.'

EIGHT

Kate had spent an almost sleepless night in her own narrow bed after beginning to tell her flatmate Tess Farrell about her trip to Ruislip the previous day. She had rejected Harry Barnard's invitation to a meal and a night at his place out of hand, made tetchy by her anxiety for the boy. Yet she began to regret her decision as she saw her best friend becoming more and more anxious as she went on, until she stopped herself from spelling out her worst fears for Jimmy Earnshaw who had disappeared from supposedly safe police custody.

'You can't be sure he's run away, can you, la?' Tess asked, twisting her hands together in anxiety.

'It looked pretty certain to me,' Kate said quietly. 'And Harry's very worried.'

Tess hesitated and Kate decided she would not spell out for Tess all the details she knew about exactly why Harry was so worried.

'Is Harry dragging you into another adventure which could turn out badly?' she asked.

'Not really,' Kate had reassured her. 'He just needed someone with him to knock at the door. But it's very odd that if the boy really has gone the police themselves don't seem to be trying very hard to find him. Harry says there's been no word from Scotland Yard asking the local police to look in his old haunts in Soho. He's asked around himself but no one seems to have seen him or heard from him or even knows he's missing. He's only a kid, Tess, and he's fallen into a river full of crocodiles as far as I can see. Something very strange seems to be going on.'

'Could he have gone home?' Tess asked. 'Back to the north?'

'I don't think he has a home as such, la,' Kate said gloomily. 'As far as I can remember he said he'd been in a children's home in Doncaster or somewhere. That usually means trouble with the law or with his parents – if he has any. Anyway, he

said he ran away because he was being molested and then got
into even worse trouble when he arrived in London. People
pick kids up at the railway stations, apparently, and put them
on the streets. Or worse. He was lucky to get out of that mess
alive to give evidence and now it looks like a frying pan and
fire job. From bad to worse.'

'Holy Mother,' Tess said, looking appalled although Kate
did not know whether it was on Jimmy Earnshaw's behalf or
hers. Tess had always tended to mother her, both back in
Liverpool and when they had come to London as an adven-
turous threesome with their friend Marie.

'But there's nothing you can do about it, is there?' Tess asked.
'It's up to the police to find him and make a better job of keeping
him safe. Surely the trial must be coming up soon, isn't it?'

'At the Old Bailey but not for at least a month yet, Harry
says. If it comes up at all. If they're really losing witnesses it
may never get to court and Georgie Robertson will get away
with murder.'

Tess's eyes widened but she had no sensible advice to offer
her friend. The world Kate had fallen into was a foreign country
to her. 'Sleep on it,' she had advised, with a helpless look.

'I'll try,' Kate said, without any optimism at all.

And although she had gone to bed early sleep had not come
at all till the small hours and even then her dreams were
disturbing, full of anger and shouting which she could not
understand. She woke early and opened the curtains on to a
pale London morning, a grey dawn just breaking, in which
some people were already hurrying towards the underground
station at just after seven. She decided to have a bath after
she persuaded the huge grumbling gas geyser in the bathroom
to spurt out some hot water and she was sitting in the kitchen
in her dressing gown when Tess eventually emerged from her
room fully dressed for school.

'Are you seeing Harry today or going off again with your
reporter?' Tess asked, her face anxious as she made herself toast.

'More photographs for the *Globe*,' Kate said without enthusiasm. 'I can't really see what we're trying to prove with all
these pictures but Carter Price seems pleased with progress
so that's all that matters really. As far as I'm concerned it's

the most boring assignment I've had so far, sitting in a car all day waiting for something to happen.'

'Well, at least I suppose you're pretty safe sitting in a car,' Tess observed quietly. 'I do worry about you, you know.'

Kate smiled wanly. 'Thanks,' she said. 'But at least I can tell Carter Price today that Harry's visit to Blackheath was official, part of his murder investigation. And he was with the new sergeant he's working with who's certainly not his best friend. I don't want to be stuck in the middle if Carter decides to chase after him.'

When Tess had stuffed her bag with exercise books that she had marked the night before and set off to catch a bus to Holland Park, Kate made herself another cup of coffee and rang Harry Barnard's home number. He picked up quickly and sounded faintly disappointed by the sound of her voice.

'I'm just going to work,' Kate said huffily. 'I thought I'd check if you had any news of Jimmy.'

'Not yet,' Barnard said. 'I've asked my contact at the Yard to make discreet inquiries. I thought this call might be her.'

'I'd better get off the line then,' Kate said. 'I'll be out with Carter Price most of the day I think, but I should get back to the agency this afternoon to print up my pics. You can get me there if you want to talk.'

'Fine,' Barnard said and hung up.

'I think we'll just have a little mosey around this morning,' Carter Price said. 'See if Reg Smith is at home again and follow him if he goes out.'

Price was driving a white Mini this morning, the first time Kate had got anywhere close to this new model which had caused a sensation for the first few months of its life. He looked bulky and slightly ill at ease in the confined space.

'It's quite tiny, isn't it?' she said, feeling vulnerable as Price twisted his way through the heavy traffic on the New Kent Road, the lorries looming above them like whales beside a shrimp. 'They won't catch on, will they? It feels as if you're almost sitting on the road.'

'Not enough power,' Price said, tailing behind a double-decker bus impatiently. 'I'll be very surprised if they sell many of them.'

They parked again a discreet distance from Smith's gates and waited – and waited. Price occupied himself reading the *Globe* from cover to cover while Kate could do nothing except stare out of the windscreen, her camera on her lap and her frustration steadily mounting.

'Cheer up, darling,' Price said. 'I'll treat you to dinner tonight, if you like. I know this is as boring as watching paint dry but if we can pin this beggar down it'll be worth every minute. Here.' He passed her his paper and she began to read steadily through it without even bothering to react to his invitation.

It was not the first time he had made the proposal and so far she had persistently declined, but after this morning she thought she might take him up on it. There had to be some sort of reward for this dreadful assignment and it would annoy Harry Barnard, who deserved some sort of reaction to his brusqueness earlier this morning. An evening out with Carter Price might be an appropriate punishment. She guessed a good meal would go on his claim as a business expense somehow. She had watched her photographer colleagues filling in their expenses with an astonishing degree of imagination and knew that Fleet Street would – and did – trump them at every turn.

Kate's patience had begun to seriously fray when, just before twelve, Reg Smith's car emerged from his gates and he set off as before down the hill towards Lewisham, without apparently even glancing in their direction. A new Mini might be an object of interest to most people but not, evidently, to someone who drove a Bentley.

'The Angel again, do you think?' Price said as they followed. But this time Smith headed for central London, past the Elephant and Castle and over Waterloo Bridge before turning right into Fleet Street.

'Where the hell is he going?' Price asked as they passed Temple Bar into the City of London.

The answer was not long in coming. Smith swung his car to the kerb and parked immediately outside the *Globe* building, got out amid furious hoots from a black cab, and went inside. Price pulled up behind him.

'Can you see where he's going?' he asked Kate.

She peered out of the passenger window and through the glass doors of the newspaper office into the extensive marbled foyer. 'He's talking to someone in there,' she said. 'They're coming out I think.'

They both watched as the two men left the building and got into Smith's car.

'Mitch Graveney again,' Price said, evidently amazed. 'What the hell is going on?'

He swung the Mini into the traffic stream again but the road was busy and by the time they had reached Ludgate Circus there was no sign of the car they were following. Price waited at the traffic lights and peered left and right but Smith and Graveney had effectively disappeared.

'Damn and blast,' Price grumbled. 'He could have gone back south of the river over the bridge, or north towards Smithfield or straight on to St Paul's and God knows where after that. We've lost him, I'm afraid.'

'It's not turning out to be a very productive day, is it,' Kate muttered.

'Did you get a shot of the two of them coming out?' Price asked.

'Of course.'

'Well, I think I'll go back to the office, and see if I can get a clue as to why one of the *Globe*'s union officials is swanning round London with a major gangster. You, my dear, might as well go back to the agency. We'll call it a day on pictures for now.' He swung the small car in a tight U-turn and headed back towards the Strand. 'I'll drop you here,' he said, stopping outside Somerset House. 'You can pick up a bus back to the West End.'

'Thanks a lot, la,' Kate muttered as she opened the car door, but Price seemed oblivious to her sarcasm.

'I'll call you later to talk about tomorrow,' he said. 'Or maybe a meal tonight?'

Kate slammed the car door without answering. Harry Barnard could be annoying, she thought, but he was not in the same league as this bloody fat man.

It turned out that by the end of the afternoon Harry Barnard did want to talk to Kate again. He tracked her down at the agency just after four and took her out for coffee.

'I've got a meeting tonight with one of the lawyers putting together the prosecution case against Georgie Robertson,' he said. 'Strictly off the record. You know I'm out on a limb here. I'm meeting her for a drink in Highgate later. Can you come with me?'

'Why?' Kate asked, puzzled.

'Protection, really,' Barnard said quietly. 'If anyone sees us together I can claim it was just a chance social meeting if you're with me. We popped into the Flask for a drink before going out for a meal. We can do that too if you like. But I need to know what's going on with the case against Georgie. If it's really falling apart why aren't we looking for missing witnesses? In other words, what the hell's happening?'

Kate hesitated for only a moment. 'Will she know if Jimmy Earnshaw's really missing?' she asked.

'She should do,' Barnard said. 'That's what the prosecution lawyers are there for. And she sounded a bit worried when I spoke to her on the phone. She was happy enough to have a meeting.'

'All right,' Kate agreed. 'Will you pick me up at the office?'

'Five thirty,' Barnard said. 'You're a doll.' He gave her a quick peck on the cheek.

'No,' Kate said sharply. 'I'm not.'

The Flask stood on a corner site in the centre of Highgate village, an old pub with empty tables on its forecourt on a dark and chilly evening but already crowded indoors when Barnard and Kate arrived. There was comfortable fug inside as they peered through the hazy cigarette smoke swirling under the low nicotine stained ceiling looking for Barnard's contact.

'There she is,' he said eventually indicating a pale, anxious-looking young woman in a dark coat, her hair pulled back severely from a face with little make-up, blue eyes shaded by a pair of tortoiseshell glasses. The table in front of her was bare.

He made his way through the crowd of drinkers with Kate close behind.

'Ruth,' he said. 'It was good of you to come. This is my friend Kate O'Donnell who was involved in the Georgie Robertson case. You'll have seen her witness statement, no doubt. Kate, Ruth Michelmore.'

The two women eyed each other somewhat warily for a moment.

'Can I get you both a drink?' Barnard asked and when they had made their choices he went to the bar to order.

Kate sat down opposite the lawyer.

'You were the one who caught up with Jimmy Earnshaw, weren't you?' Ruth asked.

Kate nodded. That was a night which still caused her to wake up from her dreams occasionally soaked in sweat and paralysed with fear.

Barnard came back and put two G and T's in front of the women and took a sip of the foam on his pint before sitting down.

'Kate is indirectly responsible for us having a case against Georgie Robertson at all,' he said.

'Ah yes,' Ruth Michelmore said. 'Of course. I knew I recognized the name.'

'But my worry is that we're not keeping Jimmy, and the other witnesses, as safe as we should be,' Barnard insisted. 'Have you seen him recently?'

'I haven't seen any of them recently,' Ruth Michelmore said. 'But then I'm only a junior cog in the machine. But my bosses should have been talking to them and all I've picked up from them over the last couple of weeks is a general worry and a few angry phone calls to the Yard. I don't know what's going on but I get the impression that it's something bad.'

'Would it surprise you to know that we think Jimmy Earnshaw is missing from his safe house? Jimmy and maybe the old tramp Hamish Macdonald?'

'It wouldn't surprise me at all,' Ruth said soberly. 'It would fit with the worries I've been having. Hamish might have gone looking for a drink, of course. He could be out on a bender. But the boy? What is he? Fourteen? Fifteen? Why would he run off? And where would he go if he did?'

'He came from somewhere up north,' Kate said.

'I wonder if they managed to make contact again and they've gone off together,' said Ruth. 'Jimmy regarded Hamish as his only friend in London. He didn't trust anyone else, including the police and the lawyers.'

'If they've both gone you'll have a hard time making the case against Georgie stick, won't you?' Barnard asked.

'Too true,' the lawyer agreed. 'So who wants the case to collapse do you think? Georgie's brother? Is it a family loyalty thing?'

'Not likely,' Barnard said sharply. 'Ray Robertson wants Georgie put away even more than we do, believe me. I've known the two of them since I was a kid in the East End and there's never been much love lost there.'

'Ah, that explains why an alleged mate of his, the trainer at his gym, has been put on to the list of potential witnesses too. I thought it was odd, but maybe I've got the brothers' relationship wrong.'

'Who is it? Rod Miller? There's a couple of blokes help out at the gym,' Barnard said.

'I think that was the name.'

'Rod will say whatever Ray tells him to say, but a good defence lawyer might make mincemeat of him in the witness box,' Barnard said thoughtfully. 'He's no substitute for the two who seem to be missing.'

'Well, if we've lost some of the major witnesses we may have to move on the secondary ones. Maybe you too, Miss O'Donnell,' the lawyer said.

Kate shuddered slightly, knowing that to face Georgie Robertson at the Old Bailey was the last thing she wanted to do.

'Is Georgie Robertson a queer?' Ruth asked.

'I've no evidence for that, though he did have some contacts who frequent the queer pub in Soho,' Barnard said. 'I always thought it was because there might have been a few blokes there who enjoyed the services he was providing. He's got no form.'

'I heard some talk of a man called Vincent Beaufort possibly being useful to the prosecution case. But he's not on the official list of prosecution witnesses that I've seen.'

'I'm pretty sure Vincent isn't into boys, but he may have heard something relevant I suppose. That pub's a hive of gossip. Do you want me to talk to him?'

'Could be helpful, maybe,' the lawyer said. She glanced at Barnard warily for a moment. 'The other thing I wondered is whether Georgie Robertson is a Freemason?' she asked carefully.

'Or are you, for that matter? In which case you probably won't tell me.'

'I'm not,' Barnard said, looking angry. 'And I don't think Georgie is, as far as I know. But as you must realize, they're a secretive bunch. Why do you ask?'

'Just that if you're a woman in legal circles you soon become aware that an awful lot of lawyers are. And coppers too, I'm told. I've come to the conclusion that it's best to know just who is and who isn't. They talk about being on the square but as far as I can see it's more like wheels within wheels going round in some very dubious circles. If you're to survive, you need to know what connections the men have. If Georgie Robertson is a mason, he'll have a few friends in high places, I guess.'

Barnard nodded. 'A lot of coppers are involved. People have tried to persuade me to join, told me I'll never get promotion if I don't, but I can't be bothered with secret societies.'

'Well, if you're not eligible, like me, maybe you never do get promotion,' Ruth said bitterly. She laughed. 'I get that feeling. But you'd not find many women wanting to wear a pinny for fun when they wear them most of the time at home. And a lot of legal men think that's what we should all be doing, that's all we're good for.'

'I know the feeling,' Kate said.

'It's a lot more than a bit of fun in a pinny and a nice meal after,' Barnard said, looking gloomy. 'From what I'm told quite a few dodgy characters join thinking it's some sort of insurance because there are so many coppers involved. But not the Robertson brothers, as far as I know.'

'So if his brother doesn't want him to get off, who else might like to see Georgie Robertson on the loose again?' Ruth asked. 'Who else might be trying to interfere with the witnesses?'

'Apart from his mother, I can't think of anyone,' Barnard said.

'His mother?' Ruth sounded surprised. 'Could his mother try to derail the trial, do you think? Surely she must be too old.'

'Ma Robertson is a little white-haired old lady who looks as if butter wouldn't melt in her mouth,' Barnard said. 'But she always doted on Georgie, her baby, and when push comes to shove she's as tough as old boots. So it's not impossible, I suppose. When her husband was alive she was in there with the best of them but I don't know how fresh her contacts are in criminal circles now. I think Ray's got most of the East End gangsters sewn up and he won't lift a finger to help Georgie. I don't think his mother could do anything without his say-so. And springing witnesses from police protection takes some serious organization.'

'You sound as if you've already been looking for Jimmy Earnshaw and Hamish,' Ruth said.

Barnard hesitated for only a moment. 'I think Hamish might be dead,' he said quietly.

Ruth Michelmore froze. 'What makes you think that?' she asked.

'We've an unidentified body,' he said. 'Found on a building site. No one reported anyone missing, but then if it was Hamish, no one would. No one would know he'd gone except his minders at the Yard and they're not saying a dicky bird, for reasons I don't understand.'

'I don't like this one bit,' Ruth said. 'I'll ask my boss if I can talk to both the witnesses again. I'll have to go through him. I can't ask the Yard direct. But if I get a dusty answer I'll let you know. Let's keep in touch, Sergeant Barnard. I'm getting a very bad feeling about all this.' She pulled on her thick coat, wound a wool scarf round her neck and got up. 'You'll keep an eye open for the boy as well?' she asked.

'You bet,' Barnard said. 'Call me at home if you need to, not at the nick. I'm not sure who I can trust there.' He gave her his number and when she had gone he and Kate finished their drinks in silence.

'Come back to my place,' Barnard said. 'I need to change, then we'll go out for a meal.'

Kate sighed and nodded. She felt unsettled and uneasy now about her own situation as well as Jimmy Earnshaw's. She had not dreamed she might have to give evidence and hated the idea with a passion. 'Do you think anyone would try to stop me giving evidence?' she asked as they got back into Harry's car for the short drive down Highgate Hill.

'I don't think so, do you? What you know isn't exactly crucial, just circumstantial. Without Jimmy and Hamish the case will fall apart.'

When they got back to the flat Barnard made no amorous advances. He shut himself in his bedroom to change while Kate flipped through his record collection and spun round aimlessly in his revolving chair.

When he came back he put his arm round her. 'Stop worrying,' he said. 'I don't think you're in any danger.' Before she could reply, the phone rang and she watched him tense as he listened to whoever was at the other end. 'Thanks,' he said briefly. 'I'll see if we can find him.'

'Who was that?' Kate asked.

'It was the vicar at St Peter's. You remember him? David Hamilton who runs the refuge for kids on the street? He says one of the boys he's looking after at the moment saw Jimmy Earnshaw, actually saw him and spoke to him. He said Jimmy was very frightened and told him he was getting out of London as soon as he had the train fare. I don't like that, Kate, I really don't. The first place anyone looking for him would go would be to the stations. They know he came from the north. They might guess he'd go back there. Though what he imagines he's going back to I can't imagine. From what he told us about his previous background he'd be jumping from the frying pan back into the fire, I should think.'

'Doncaster, wasn't it?' Kate asked.

'I'll call social services there in the morning,' Barnard said. 'See if they've seen him. And take a swing round King's Cross. There are places in the back streets round that old dump you could hide an army.'

'Why isn't there an army of coppers out looking for him anyway?' Kate asked angrily. 'What the devil's going on, Harry?'

'I wish I knew,' Barnard said. 'But believe me, I intend to find out. Come on. Let's put all this out of our heads and enjoy ourselves for this evening at least.'

But Kate thought that in the circumstance that might prove quite hard.

NINE

When Sergeant Harry Barnard got to the nick the next morning he found Vic Copeland sitting at his desk with a self-satisfied look on his face.

'I thought you should know,' Copeland said.

'Know what?' Barnard snapped back.

'I've just got the OK from Jackson to bring Ray Robertson in for a formal chat,' Copeland said, leaning back in his chair with a grin. 'That beggar is running rings round this manor as far as I can see.'

'Are you going to do the same with Reg Smith? Or the Maltese?' Barnard asked.

'Nah, waste of time. It's a Robertson on trial and I reckon a Robertson trying to get him off. No question.'

'I take it I won't be invited to join the party,' Barnard said.

'Dead right, mate.' Copeland got up and pulled on his coat. 'See you later though,' he said. 'Promise you that.'

Barnard swallowed hard and followed Vic Copeland out but while Copeland headed for the front office, no doubt to assemble some uniformed troops to go with him to bring Robertson in, Barnard headed to the DCI's office and knocked on the door. Summoned inside he met a distinctly unfriendly stare from the opposite side of Keith Jackson's immaculate desk.

'Yes?' Jackson snapped.

Barnard affected to look as innocent as possible. 'I thought you might want to fill me in on what Copeland's planning to question Ray Robertson about, guv,' he said. 'I do know him quite well. I thought I might be able to help.'

'You know him far too well,' Jackson said. 'You are part of the problem that AC Amis has identified. Not that he really needed to. I've been aware of it ever since I walked through the door of this nick. You're not the only one, or even the worst, perhaps. We'll see in the fullness of time. But the AC wants to see some action and Ray Robertson is as good a place for Copeland to start as any.'

Barnard thought he might as well be hung for a sheep as a lamb. 'The trouble is, guv, that if you destabilize the present situation you could end up with something significantly worse,' he said. 'Robertson and the Maltese have reached an accord which has kept violence off the streets in Soho for a year or more. If you take either one of them out you can be sure that someone else – Reg Smith perhaps – will try to break in and there'll be a gang war. And that could be much, much worse. That's the way innocent punters don't just get ripped off, they get hurt.'

'That's the pessimistic view, sergeant, and it's one which the AC and I believe is totally defeatist. What you're saying is that we go along with the status quo for a quiet life for fear of something worse. That is not the policy of the Metropolitan Police and the sooner officers like you get to grips with that the better for all of us, especially the law-abiding citizens of the West End of London. Pandering to these gangsters leads to corruption all round and Mr Amis will not stand for it.'

'No chance of sitting in on the interview with Ray Robertson, I suppose, guv?' Barnard asked.

'No chance,' DCI Jackson said. 'Carry on, sergeant.'

The phrase threw Barnard back to his days of national service and he shuddered slightly at the memory. 'Sir,' he said, almost saluting and spinning on his heel to leave the room with distinctly military precision. He wondered what exact part Keith Jackson had played in the forces. The imprint was certainly indelible.

Back in the CID office he put his coat on and walked out into Regent Street and found a phone box. Fred Bettany's secretary answered promptly and put him through quickly.

'Fred,' Barnard said without identifying himself. He was sure the accountant would know his voice. 'Ray's in trouble. Vic Copeland's planning to haul him into the nick for a going over. Can you make sure his brief is there? And could you pass on a message from me? Tell him I'll call in at the gym about six. I need to talk to him. OK? That's assuming they don't arrest him.'

There was a silence at the other end.

'Tell me about it,' Bettany said eventually.

'Not now, mate,' Barnard said and hung up.

For the rest of the morning he followed his usual routine, keeping his finger on the pulse of Soho, meeting useful contacts, chatting up the street girls as they emerged towards lunchtime from their flats, bleary-eyed and un-made-up, saving what charms they still possessed for the arrival of clients much later in the day. But he kept his fingers out of anyone's till and ended up at lunchtime with a visit to the queer pub which had already attracted a substantial clientele. One or two looked up warily as Barnard walked in but relaxed when they recognized him.

The knot of anxiety which had tightened his stomach since he had absorbed the implications of Vic Copeland's plans was still there, but he knew if he tried to intervene in any way at the nick his career would be immediately on the line. If it wasn't already, he thought as he approached the bar and ordered a half pint, leaning back against the mahogany, glass in hand, assessing with sharp eyes who was there while trying to look his normal relaxed self. He turned back to the barman eventually.

'Has Vincent Beaufort been in yet?' he asked. 'I need a word.'

'I haven't seen him for a couple of days, Harry,' the barman said. 'Do you want me to give him a message?'

A sharp shiver of alarm ran up Barnard's spine. Beaufort lived to flaunt himself and for him to be absent from Soho's streets and bars was distinctly unusual. 'Do you know where he's living now?' he asked.

The barman shrugged. 'I heard he had a new boyfriend but I've no idea where they hang out.'

'If you see either of them can you ask them to get in touch?' Barnard said, telling himself that his sense that something was not right was in no way justified by the facts. But he did not convince himself. He finished his drink and walked slowly back to the nick to be met in the front office by the alarming sight of Ray Robertson himself, being helped towards the door by a tall man in a dark suit he half recognized as one of the lawyers who found it lucrative to work for Robertson's varied enterprises. Robertson's face was bruised and there was a cut above his right eye as if, in a reprise of his early career, he had just left the boxing ring defeated.

Robertson caught sight of Barnard in the doorway and directed a snarl in his direction. 'What the hell's going on, Flash?' he hissed. 'That's what I'd like to know. What the bloody hell is going on?'

Barnard nodded in the direction of the two men but said nothing as he passed them and paused at the main desk where a chubby sergeant was watching the scene with avid interest. 'What the hell happened to him?' Barnard asked quietly as the two men vanished down the steps outside.

The sergeant shrugged. 'The official story from Vic Copeland is that Robertson lost his rag and threw a punch when they invited him down to the nick, so Vic threw a few back. He's been in an interview room with Copeland and the DCI most of the morning and been bailed with a charge of resisting arrest.'

'And the unofficial story?' Barnard asked.

'Well you know Copeland's rep,' the sergeant said. 'I'm damn sure he wasn't as battered when he came in as he is now going out, so I leave it to your imagination. His solicitor didn't arrive till about half an hour ago so they had him on their own for a fair length of time. The solicitor's playing merry hell.'

Barnard nodded. Nothing the sergeant told him surprised him but he knew that he was on a hiding to nothing if he tried to interfere. He made his way into the interior of the building and headed for the custody sergeant's office. The officer on duty did not seem too pleased to see him, perhaps suspecting that he wanted to talk about Ray Robertson's treatment, but Barnard had something else entirely in mind.

'Has a queer called Vince Beaufort been brought in over the last couple of days?' he asked. 'Small bloke, flamboyant dresser, could have been done for cottaging, soliciting, any of that.'

The sergeant visibly relaxed. 'Don't think so,' he said, flicking through pages of records quickly. 'Has he got a record?'

'I think he's done time once or twice, for the usual,' Barnard said. 'I wanted a little chat but the word is he hasn't been seen on his usual haunts for a few days. It seemed a bit odd. He's not exactly the retiring type.'

'Some of them flaunt it,' the sergeant said. 'I'd have their balls off if it were me.'

'Sounds a bit drastic,' Barnard said lightly, though there was no humour in his eyes. He spun on his heel, made his way out of the nick and into the nearest pub, where he ordered a double scotch.

The Red Lion was a small dark pub down one of the narrow alleys off Fleet Street which led downhill to the river Thames.

Carter Price led the way from the *Globe* building where he and Kate had met that morning and pushed open the door for her. 'This is the *Globe*'s pub,' he said. 'You find out all the gossip in here.'

The lounge was already busy and Price had to wait to get served at the bar and they only found an empty table after a hunt in the darker regions at the back of the room.

'The printers tend to come in early,' he said. 'Then at lunchtime this might as well be the newsroom, except for those who prefer El Vino down the road. A bit more exclusive down there. The theatre critics from the posh papers hold court but you'll not get served if you're a woman. You have to sit still and wait for the men to bring you something.'

'You're joking, la,' Kate said.

'I'm certainly not,' Price insisted. 'I'll take you there one day, but today I'm keen to talk to Mitch Graveney's mates, see if we can find out how the hell he knows Reg Smith so well.'

Kate raised an eyebrow and sipped her tomato juice. It felt too early in the day to join Price on the hard stuff. They sat in silence for a while watching a succession of blue-overalled printers come in and out for a quick drink.

'First edition of the evening paper's just gone,' Price said glancing at his watch. It was nine thirty. 'Some of them get a break after that.'

Most of the printers glanced in Price's direction, flashed

appraising glance at Kate, raised an eyebrow and then ignored the pair of them. But eventually one of the men coming in waved a hand in their direction. 'Can I get you another, Carter?' he asked. 'And your lady friend?'

'Double scotch, and a tomato juice,' Price said quickly.

After a few minutes, the man came back with their drinks and a pint for himself and pulled up a stool to their table.

'Aren't you going to introduce me?' he asked, giving Kate a flashing smile.

'Pete Archer, Kate O'Donnell. Kate's helping me with a story I'm working on,' Price said airily.

'Very nice too,' Archer said before taking a long drink from his foaming glass. 'I wish I could summon up a dishy assistant out of thin air like you do.'

'She's not an assistant, she's a photographer.'

Archer gave a low whistle and looked surprised. 'Not looking for a staff job, is she?' he asked. 'Bill Kenyon must be going soft in his old age.'

'I've met Bill Kenyon,' Kate said sharply. 'He's living in the dark ages as far as women are concerned.'

Archer and Price laughed loudly.

'Well I'll bet Carter here a fiver that we don't see a female photographer here in the next ten years.'

'You're on,' Price said complacently. 'I've told her to be satisfied with the job she's got. And it'll be twenty years before you printers let a woman near a machine. Mitch Graveney would do his nut at the very thought.'

'It's very like typing,' Kate said, thinking of the Linotype operators she had seen at their keyboards. 'What's the difference?'

'You'll get us drummed out of here if anyone hears you committing heresy like that,' Price said and it was clear he was only half joking. 'Which reminds me, I saw Mitch in a pub south of the river the other day. You live in Lewisham, don't you? I don't think he noticed me but I was a bit surprised at the company he was keeping. Do you know a bloke called Reg Smith? Some sort of big shot in that area, not necessarily legit, you know what I mean?'

Archer looked uneasy for a moment but then his face

cleared. 'Ah yes, I know what it would be,' he said. 'I'm
not on the square myself. Brought up a Catholic, I was, and
they don't like that sort of thing. But I know Mitch is a
mason and someone told me Smith was something big in
one of the local lodges. Worshipful something or other, don't
they call it. They're probably in the same lodge. Mitch
Graveney lives in Lee Green which isn't far away. You can
bet your life they'll be wearing pinnies together and
scratching each other's backs the rest of the time. You know
how it is?'

'That explains it,' Price said easily. 'So who's going to win
the Chelsea game on Saturday? It's going to be a tight one,
isn't it?'

Archer shrugged. 'Don't have much time for football
myself,' he said. 'I've got an allotment. That keeps me out of
the wife's way at weekends. Anyway, I've got to get back.
We're short-handed today. Mickey Mouse and Donald Duck
didn't turn up.' He finished his drink in one, grinned and left
them, leaving Kate looking bemused.

'Was he serious?' she asked.

'Oh yes,' Price said. 'You don't get a printer's job in Fleet
Street unless your dad and your grandad had one before you.
The unions see to that. And it's not unknown for them to add
a few fictional characters to the payroll. It's one of those
custom and practice issues. If the management query it the
presses stop rolling and a day or night's paper goes down the
tubes. No paper, no income, QED.'

'Isn't that illegal?'

'It's industrial relations, dear,' Price said. 'Not pretty but
it's been going on for years. And I can't see anyone sorting
it any time soon. Come on, let's go back to Smith's place and
see what we can see. Later I'll see if I can find out which
lodge those bastards are frequenting. And if you're very good
I'll treat you to dinner later.'

'I've got a date tonight,' Kate said, not for the first time,
thinking of Harry Barnard and finding that option preferable
to Carter Price's hospitality, which she was quite sure came
with strings.

*   *   *

The evening did not turn out quite as Kate expected. She had returned to the agency soon after lunch when Carter Price had got tired of sitting outside Reg Smith's house, which this morning appeared deserted.

'You might as well go back to the office and print up every-thing we've got so far,' Price had said grumpily. 'I need to have a quiet chat with some of my Masonic contacts and see if I can find out exactly what connections there are between Smith and Graveney. It may be just coincidence. I can't see what Mitch is going to get out of palling up with a gangster like Smith but maybe he's got something Smith wants, infor-mation most likely. Maybe he's got wind that I've got him in my sights.'

'That could be very dodgy, couldn't it?' Kate had asked.

'Oh, I've been on a few dodgy characters' hit lists over the years,' Price had said airily. 'They make threats and huff and puff but so far I've survived and they've ended up in jail. That's what the *Globe* pays me for, after all. It's my job.'

But not mine, Kate thought uneasily, wondering how long this surveillance could safely continue.

Later in the afternoon Harry Barnard called her and they arranged to meet for an early meal at an Italian restaurant they both liked in Charlotte Street; early because he was hoping to see Ray Robertson later, but before she left the office he had rung her again with an urgency in his voice which frightened her.

'I've just had a call from David Hamilton at St Peter's refuge for homeless youngsters. Can you meet me there as soon as you can?'

Kate did not argue. She tidied her desk, put on her coat and hurried through the crowded after-work streets of Soho to the looming Victorian church which held so many unwelcome memories for her. She found Barnard standing in the porch with the vicar, both men looking grim.

'What's happened?' she asked, feeling slightly sick with apprehension.

'Nothing – yet,' Barnard said. 'One of the lads here told Mr Hamilton that he had seen Jimmy Earnshaw hiding in the churchyard, freezing cold and starving hungry. He had taken him something to eat after he was given his own tea but when they both went back to look for him soon afterwards Jimmy had gone.'

'So we were right to be worried about him,' Kate said.

'Where else might he try to hide?' Hamilton asked. 'There's nowhere here where he could shelter for any length of time. The outbuildings have all been securely locked up since . . . since what happened last time. And we've cut the shrubberies back. Liam, the lad who saw him, thought he was trying to get into the boiler room where he would at least have been warm. Jimmy asked him if he had any money. Said he wanted to catch a train.' The vicar shrugged helplessly. 'I'm sure he doesn't know how much train tickets cost,' he said.

'He may have gone back to the embankment by Faringdon underground, where he camped with Hamish Macdonald,' Barnard said. 'Or if he really wants to get on a train he may have gone to King's Cross. That's the station he must have arrived at from Doncaster when he first came to London. But there are hundreds of places to hide round there in those back streets and goods yards behind the station. Kate and I will have a look around for him, Mr Hamilton.' He pulled a slip of paper out of his pocket, scribbled something on it and handed it to the vicar. 'That's my home number,' he said. 'Call me there later if by any chance he turns up here again. I can be here in fifteen minutes from Highgate if you need me.'

Hamilton looked at him angrily. 'I thought this boy was being kept safe by the police,' he said, obviously controlling his temper with difficulty. 'They don't seem to have been making a very good job of it, do they, sergeant?'

'Tomorrow I'll try to find out how he managed to give his minders the slip,' he said. 'But for now we need to find him if we can. He's not safe out there on his own.'

Barnard drove Kate quickly away from Soho and into the quieter streets of Holborn and then Faringdon. He pulled up eventually alongside the fence surrounding the still derelict bomb sites above the tube line which here ran along the steep-sided, long-covered course of the River Fleet. Barnard hoisted himself on to the top of the fence and realized that there was no longer any sign of the vagrants' encampment which had existed here eighteen months ago. The banking above the train tracks was in total darkness until fitfully lit up by a train rattling past in the direction of King's Cross.

Barnard jumped down on to the pavement beside Kate again. 'There's no one there as far as I can see,' he said. 'They've obviously fenced off the whole area more securely to keep the vagrants out. And if he gets in there all the trees and bushes have been cleared. Anyone with a powerful torch would be able to see him without any trouble. Even more so when the trains run past.'

Kate leaned against the fence feeling defeated.

Barnard looked at his watch and sighed. 'I have to see Ray tonight if I possibly can,' he said. 'He may have some idea why the witnesses have panicked and run, if that's what's really happened.'

'Don't worry about me,' she said. 'I can go home to eat.' She glanced up and down a deserted Faringdon Road and stiffened, putting a hand on Barnard's arm. 'Look,' she whispered. 'Isn't that him?'

A slight figure was heading towards them and they realized that they must be pretty well invisible standing still beside the dark fencing.

'I'll do it,' Kate said softly. 'He'll trust me more than you. He'll remember me.'

'Be careful,' Barnard whispered. 'He might panic.'

With infinite care she detached herself from the fence without the boy apparently noticing and let him draw level.

'Jimmy?' she said quietly and she was close enough to put a hand on his arm. He made a panicky attempt to free himself but Barnard closed quickly on the other side and hemmed him in. The boy's shoulders slumped and he seemed to gasp for air.

'We're not going to hurt you, Jimmy,' Barnard said. 'We want to make sure you're safe.'

There was another gulp from the boy, who was trembling in their grip. 'I'm not bloody safe am I?' Jimmy said, the Yorkshire accent still strong. 'I was looking for Hamish. He'll see me right.'

'Hamish isn't here,' Barnard said. 'No one's here any more.

They've cleared the embankment completely.' He could not tell Jimmy what he feared had become of Hamish now, he thought. That would panic him completely. 'Come on, there's a caff on the corner. We'll get you some tea and something to eat. Then we can decide where you can be really safe. All right?'

'Aye, all right,' the boy mumbled and began to cry.

'We can't keep him here,' Tess said in a desperate whisper as she shut the door of her bedroom on Jimmy Earnshaw who was sitting on their sofa in the small living room demolishing the second cheese sandwich she had made him and gazing at the small black and white television in the corner.

'I know, I know,' Kate said.

'What's he going to do when we're both out at work? He'll either run off with anything he can carry or lie on the sofa all day taking drugs.'

'I know, I know,' Kate said again. 'It's just temporary, I promise. Harry said it was too dangerous to take him to his place. Someone might work out where he was hiding if it leaked out from the kids at the church he'd been there. It's Saturday tomorrow so we'll sort something out for him properly tomorrow, preferably out of London. Harry says he'll come round in the morning. Don't worry. It's only for tonight.'

Tess still looked mutinous but she went to the cupboard in the corner of her room where they kept spare sheets and blankets and pulled some of the bedding out.

'I'll lock the front door and put the key under my pillow so he can't get out,' Kate said. 'That's the best we can do, I think. Then we'll see what Harry comes up with in the morning.'

TEN

Once he had dropped Kate and a reluctant Jimmy Earnshaw off at the Shepherd's Bush flat where he reckoned the boy would be safe for one night at least, Harry Barnard headed east and parked outside Ray Robertson's gym just off the Mile End Road. He could hear the sound of some fairly vigorous training going on inside even before he pushed open the door but he was surprised to see Ray himself, in singlet and shorts beating merry hell out of a punchbag. Robertson had been a contender himself in his late teens but Barnard could see now how far he had let himself go. His arms were flabby and his paunch hung over his shorts and the exercise had left him breathless and sweating.

'Flash,' he gasped. 'Come in, come in, and tell me how to get this beggar Copeland off my back, will you. The man's a menace.' As Robertson turned in his direction Barnard could see that his left eye was bruised and half-closed and there were other bruises on his jaw and the side of his neck. Barnard winced but Robertson gave him a faint grin.

'I didn't duck fast enough,' he said. 'I'm out of condition. All this went on before my lawyer got there. He's raising the roof with your DCI. I didn't get that sort of treatment when I was a nipper in Bethnal Green.'

'Copeland was in the City force,' Barnard said. 'They're well known for it.'

'That's not all they're well known for,' Robertson muttered. 'Some of them make you lot in Soho look like amateurs. I know one ex-super who's living the life of Riley in a ten-bed mansion in Essex.' He led the way to his office, and towelled himself down before pulling on slacks and a polo-neck sweater.

'Well, Copeland got away with murder in my book, so watch out,' Barnard said. 'And I do mean murder. He's a violent bastard. And as far as I can see he's gunning for me too. So I'm walking on eggshells.'

'I thought you must be keeping your distance,' Robertson said. He reached into the bottom drawer of his desk and pulled out a bottle and two glasses. 'Here, don't let the kids out there see you but I reckon it's time for a drink.' He handed Barnard a generous measure and knocked his own back quickly. 'This is all getting out of hand,' he said. 'I've got plans just now that I don't want disrupted. Copeland's got nothing on me. He's just playing games.'

'Are you still talking to Reg Smith?' Barnard asked. 'If Copeland gets a whisper of that he'll not let go.'

'Nah, he blows hot and cold does Reggie,' Robertson said dismissively. 'I don't reckon it's going to come to anything even if I volunteer to help, which I'm very doubtful I will. He's got other irons in the fire. Anyway if you're up the swanny yourself the less you know the better. I'll keep out of his way for a bit, though I still think he's a good man to work with.'

'Maybe,' Barnard said, not hiding his scepticism.

'Anyway the thing I'm worried about is nothing to do with all that. It's my plans for a gala, if you must know. That's not going well.'

'I'm sure it'll work out,' Barnard said. 'The sort of toffs you invite are always ready for a good night out.'

Robertson grinned and poured another measure. 'Anyway, is this just a social call or what?' he asked.

'Not quite,' Barnard said. 'I wondered if you'd had any feedback on Georgie's case recently. I'm getting suggestions that he might get off.'

Robertson's face darkened.

'I only ask because I know for a fact that at least one of the prosecution witnesses is running round London on his own scared witless, and another of them might be dead.'

'How the hell did that happen?' Robertson asked, knocking back his Scotch and almost choking. 'I thought the Yard was looking after all that.'

'The Yard's gone amazingly quiet about the whole business. But it's only a matter of time before they wonder if you might be trying to get Georgie off by nobbling the prosecution's witnesses,' Barnard said. 'I'm happy to tell them that's garbage but they're not likely to believe me. Or you, if they come asking.'

'Jesus wept,' Robertson said. 'Could they really think I want that psycho on my back again? Blood might be thicker than water in some people's books but not if it's as curdled as my little brother's. He's a complete liability, Flash. You know that.'

'I might know that but I get the impression that there's a few people at the Yard who might not believe you if it suited their book. And Copeland's their stooge, make no mistake about that. He'll prove what he wants to prove if he's got backing from on high. You know how these things work.'

'He doesn't want to believe me, you mean,' Robertson said, his face flushed. 'He fancies nailing two Robertsons instead of just one? That's one of the things Copeland was going on about till my brief told him to back off. I gave the bastards all the help I could when all that was going on in spite of having my ma on my back going bananas. You know what she's like.'

'Are you sure she couldn't still be trying to help Georgie out somehow? I reckon someone is.'

'Nah,' Robertson said. 'I told you, she's well past it, over the hill.'

'It's a line of inquiry Copeland might follow up however old she is,' Barnard said. 'I'd warn her to look out for him, if I were you. He'd thump his own grandmother if he thought it would get him somewhere. In the meantime I've got a legal contact who's trying to find out what's happening to the witnesses. I'll let you know if she comes up with anything. In the meantime I'll keep well out of your way. Nothing personal, mate, but I need to cover my own back.'

'Yeah, you do that Flash. You're a damn sight more use to me in the force than out of it. Contact me through Fred if you must, but keep me in touch with what's going on.'

The narrow network of streets behind King's Cross and St Pancras railway stations, with their sharp bends and tunnels and semi-derelict archways beneath the tracks were avoided by all law-abiding Londoners by night. Only the street girls lingered on foot on ill-lit corners waiting for clients, who generally cruised by in cars flicking their headlights over the talent before pulling into the kerb and opening an inviting door, or for the police to descend mob handed and bundle them all into vans, lining them up next morning for the ritual fines which did nothing to stop them working again the very next day. That night the rain had set in by nine and the young women and girls were shivering in their skimpy clothes. A group of them huddled under a railway arch for protection, keeping close to generate some warmth with little sense that the punters would bother to come out tonight. Only the desperate would brave the elements and they were the ones to be feared.

'There's a bit of a pong back there,' one girl said, peering into the Stygian darkness behind them.

'Never mind, at least you can see the street from here,' someone countered. 'If I don't turn any tricks tonight my bloke is not going to be best pleased. I need to see if any cars turn down here.'

'It's getting worse,' another woman said watching the puddles outside overflowing the broken down kerb and turning into a small river which threatened to invade their space. 'I'm off.' And she unfurled a battered umbrella and plunged into the dim rain-drenched street and quickly disappeared. The four more persistent women stayed under the shelter of the archway and inched further back to avoid the flurries of icy water which were being flung towards them by biting gusts of wind.

'What is that disgusting smell?' one asked. 'It's getting worse.'

'Dead dog?' another suggested. Another lit a cigarette and while the match briefly flared raised it to offer a flicker of flame which penetrated towards the back of the arch revealing a clutter of rubbish.

'Dead man more like,' she said matter-of-factly lighting a second match. 'There's a foot sticking out back there under that box.

'Christ,' the youngest girl whispered. 'I'm off too. I don't want anything to do with dead men.'

The woman with the cigarette grabbed her arm. 'We're all off, darling,' she said. 'But who's got some change? I'm not saying we hang about but someone needs to call the rozzers, don't they? Whoever he is we can't just leave him there to rot, poor old bastard. We've got to call the Old Bill.'

'I think you can dial nine nine nine for free,' another offered before spinning on her stiletto heel and plunging into the downpour outside.

When the Old Bill eventually turned up in the shape of two patrolling constables with powerful flashlights all the women had long gone, but the bad smell they had noticed was quickly identified by the older bobby.

'That's not just a tramp,' he said, his face lugubrious by nature and not about to change at all whatever the job threw at him. 'That's a dead tramp.' He directed his light over what was visible of the dead man beneath the boxes and other rubbish piled up at the back of the arch, illuminating to his surprise all the signs of a well-dressed middle-aged man beneath the debris with one hand limp in a welter of congealed blood and a knife slash across his throat which had obviously killed him.

'Well, well,' the constable said. 'Not a tramp at all then, by the looks. A job for CID for sure. I wonder where the little tart who called it in has got to? For all we know it could be one of her johns and she might have some explaining to do.'

'Nah,' the older officer said after looking more closely. 'Not a tart's crime, that. There's more to this than meets the eye.'

By the time detective sergeant Harry Barnard arrived at work the next morning a second murder inquiry was already cranking into gear. Although the body had been found well off the West End patch they soon found themselves involved, with the vice squad in the front line as the case clearly involved prostitution.

'Nigel Wayland,' DCI Keith Jackson told Barnard and his colleagues when he called vice squad officers together for a briefing. 'Lived in a flat in Berwick Street, well-known nancy boy who liked to pick up partners in the queer pub. Though he seems to have eased off recently. Someone said he had a live-in lover.'

'I know him,' Barnard said quietly. 'He's been around for years. A couple of convictions for cottaging. God knows what he was doing so far from his usual haunts. I've never heard of queers hanging around King's Cross before. They're more likely to get a kicking than strike lucky. Someone must have taken him up there, in a car maybe. There are lots of quiet corners for a bit of how's your father, as the street girls know only too well.'

'We've been asked to make inquiries on our own patch,' Jackson said. 'So you and Copeland can concentrate on the queer pub, get in there as soon as the doors open and find out when Wayland was last seen and who with, who his regular partners were. We need to be seen to be going through the motions, I suppose, even for one of those perverts.'

Copeland laughed loudly, and most of his colleagues allowed themselves a titter, though Barnard remained stony-faced. As far as he knew he was the only person in the nick who was the least bit sympathetic to Soho's queers and he found it politic most of the time to keep his views to himself.

'I know that someone else who's in that bar a lot of the time has gone missing,' he said. 'The barman mentioned it last time I dropped in there.'

'Not being seduced are you, Flash?' Copeland asked to general merriment.

Barnard waited until the room fell quiet again. 'Bloke called Vincent Beaufort – or at least that's what he calls himself. I shouldn't think it's the name he was born with. Flamboyant dresser. Some of you must know him by sight. Purple suit, as often as not, yellow cravat, green fedora, the full works. Tourists stop in the street to stare and he loves every minute of it. He seems to have dropped out of sight for some reason.'

'Didn't we interview him in the George Robertson case?' DCI Jackson snapped.

'We did,' Barnard said. 'But he wasn't much help. He simply confirmed that he's seen Georgie Robertson in the pub once or twice. But he couldn't identify who he was talking to – or said he couldn't – so he was no real help.'

'Is George Robertson a bloody poofter too?' Copeland asked.

'Not as far as we know, but he was certainly making use of boys in his various enterprises. He might have been in there making contacts. But we never followed it up. We had enough evidence from other sources. Vincent Beaufort was surplus to requirements.'

'Well, don't waste any time on him, unless you think he might be involved in this killing,' Jackson said. 'People go missing for their own reasons, as you very well know. Concentrate on Wayland and report back to me. I'll liaise with the murder team at King's Cross myself. But it's not our case and we've no reason to bust a gut over it. Not that AC Amis will mind us stirring up the queers. He doesn't like them any more than I do. But in terms of results it's more important to identify the body we found at Tottenham Court Road. Any progress on that?'

'Not so far, guv,' Barnard said. 'A couple of dozen labourers on the site over the last month or so have simply disappeared. Some have gone back to Ireland.'

When Jackson had marched back to his own office, Copeland slapped Barnard on the back. 'Come on, Flash,' he said. 'Let's go and stir up a few shirt-lifters. Beats chasing petty thieves any day.'

Seething quietly Barnard followed Copeland out of the nick into the rain which was still beating down. 'Are you on the square, Vic?' Barnard asked as they crossed Regent Street and moved into the narrow lanes of Soho.

Copeland gave him a sharp look. 'I am, as it goes. You're not, I'm told.'

'Never saw the point,' Barnard said.

'Why do you ask?' Copeland said. 'I was wondering the same thing about Ray Robertson, especially since he took up with Reg Smith. Is Robertson on the square? Smith certainly is.'

'Not as far as I know,' Barnard said cautiously. 'He's never mentioned it to me.'

'It just crossed my mind that he must have good contacts with the Yard to have kept himself out of the frame for so long. It can't just be because he's an old mate of yours, can it? And I know for a fact that Smith has pulled in some favours in that quarter.'

'Masonic favours?'

'Sure. That's what it's all about, isn't it? It's certainly done me some good over the years, when things got a bit rough. You should give it a go, Harry. In your situation I'd make it a top priority. I'll give you the names of some top brethren in the police lodges, if you like. Could do you a lot of good.'

DS Barnard did not reply and as they were approaching their destination Copeland did not appear to expect any response to his gratuitous advice. They swung into the queer pub which was crowded on a Saturday lunchtime and made for the bar where the barman acknowledged Barnard with a nod and went on serving two men in motorbike leathers who were surveying the scene via the mirror behind the optics. They obviously liked what they were seeing and pushed away into the crowds with a determined expression.

'Pete, my boy, have you seen anything of Vincent Beaufort since we last spoke?' Barnard asked.

The barman shook his head. 'He's not been around,' he said. 'He's usually in here most days but not today, nor for a few days, as it goes.'

Copeland slapped a blurred photograph on to the counter and stabbed a finger on to what was clearly an image taken after death rather than before. 'This one of your customers too?' he asked.

'Nige?'

'Nigel Wayland,' Copeland agreed.

'Yeah, he's a regular. Lives local, I think. Have you lost him too?'

Copeland did not respond to the question. 'Can you point out any of his mates?' he asked.

The barman looked doubtful. 'Not really,' he said. 'He used to chat to Vince regularly but on the whole he'd just pop in and out – come in on his own and then leave with someone, you know how it is?'

'Not really,' Copeland snapped. 'See anyone here now who he's ever left with?'

The barman looked uncomfortable and flashed an appeal in Barnard's direction which he ignored. 'Not really,' the barman said. 'No one I can remember for definite.'

Barnard knew that there was no way that the barman was going to start identifying people whose liaisons were certain to be illegal. 'Nigel Wayland has been killed, murdered,' he said quietly. 'I think maybe you should give some thought to who might have had contact with him recently? Give it a serious go and we'll come back to see you after the weekend when your memory might be a bit better. And if you do happen to see Vincent Beaufort can you tell him I want a word?'

The barman swallowed hard and nodded and watched the two sergeants intently as they spun and made their way through the deeply suspicious crowd to the door.

'You let him off the hook,' Copeland complained as they headed west again. 'Half an hour in an interview room would soon bring his memory back.'

'He'll give us what we want,' Barnard said. 'Just give him a bit of time. You don't need to beat information out of people. It's more reliable if it's volunteered.'

'Huh,' Copeland grunted with evident disbelief.

'Come on, let's go and take a look at Wayland's flat while we're here,' Barnard suggested. 'I dare say the King's Cross mob have already given it a going over but they might have missed something.'

'Knowing their DCI, you can almost guarantee that,' Copeland said.

'On the square as well is he?' Barnard asked.

'He wouldn't be where he is today if he wasn't,' Copeland said and gave Barnard a knowing smile.

It was mid-afternoon before Kate heard anything at all from Harry Barnard and she and Tess were running out of ideas to keep the boy they had reluctantly given house room to occupied. He had slept for most of the morning under blankets on the sofa and then paced the living room like a nervous animal expecting the arrival of a predator at any minute. When the doorbell rang he stiffened and grabbed Kate's arm.

She disentangled herself from his fierce grip and looked out at the window. 'It's all right, la,' she said. 'It's Harry. Let's hope he's found you somewhere better to stay.'

Tess let the sergeant in and he arrived at the flat looking cheerful.

'OK, Jimmy. The Rev Dave has done the necessary again. Not the same place you went to last time, obviously, but someone else up in Hertfordshire. They've agreed to keep you there until the trial so you shouldn't have any more problems. If the prosecution lawyers want to talk to you I'll get Dave Hamilton to take them out there, no one else. So not even I will know where you are. OK?'

Jimmy nodded, twisting his hands together nervously. 'OK,' he said. 'I suppose.'

'You're a witness,' Barnard said flatly. 'You know too much. Scotland Yard hasn't kept you safe. You've got no money and no prospects. This is the best I can do. The trial will be on at the Old Bailey in a month or so and then you'll be in the clear. Come on, let's go. Mr Hamilton's expecting us. I could lose my job over this so don't mess me about.'

As he hustled the boy towards the door, Harry turned back briefly. 'What about a meal tonight,' he asked.

Kate shook her head. 'Carter Price has been pestering me for days so I said I'd have dinner with him tonight,' she said. 'He's picking me up at eight.' When she saw Barnard's flash of anger she smiled. 'Sorry,' she said sweetly. 'Another time?'

As it turned out, Carter Price arrived late, contenting himself with blowing his horn outside the flat until she appeared, and opening the door for her without getting out of the car. She slid into the passenger seat and glanced at him without much enthusiasm.

'Sorry,' he muttered. 'I got held up at the office.' He revved the engine and drove back to central London without any further comment. He was looking, Kate thought, unusually haggard but by the time they had arrived back into the West End his mood seemed to have lightened and he ushered her out of the car and into a restaurant in Charlotte Street with impeccable courtesy.

'You'll like this,' he said. 'Genuine French food, the real deal, be a change from all that Italian stuff you say you like.'

'I draw the line at snails,' she whispered as they were shown to their table by a supercilious waiter in black tie. 'And frogs' legs. Don't fancy them, la.'

'You really are a provincial little lady, aren't you? You need taking in hand, you know.' He gave her a self-satisfied smirk which almost persuaded her to turn tail and leave.

'Am I worth the trouble?' she asked tartly.

'Oh, I think you might be,' Price said. 'Time will tell.'

The waiter handed them menus which Kate found bewildering as most of it was written in French with only the most sparse English translations underneath.

'Let me choose for you,' Price offered as she hesitated and the waiter hovered. 'Is it fish, chips and mushy peas where you come from, or – what's it called – Scouse?'

'Scouse,' Kate snapped. 'And I like fish. What's wrong with that?'

'Nothing at all,' Price said. 'Fish you shall have then, my dear. What about *sole bonne femme.* That's cooked in butter. And to start with let's go for the soup, that's a safe choice. I'll have the same.' He relayed the order to the waiter and consulted the wine waiter over a suitable accompaniment and then settled back in his chair with a heavy sigh.

'I'm sorry, petal, I had a fairly difficult meeting with my boss this afternoon. It seems that the picture editor you met, Bill Kenyon, has somehow found out that I'm doing some research with you instead of one of the staff photographers and is not best pleased. I'm infringing his monopoly apparently. The news editor knows what I'm doing and had no objections initially but now it seems there are a few. I guess it's because I claimed the cost on my expenses. Normally they go through more or less on the nod but this time apparently not.'

'Do you think Mitch Graveney could have found out that you've been following him and Reg Smith? He might have complained,' Kate suggested.

'He could, I suppose, though if he had a grievance he's more likely to raise it through his blasted union than through my bosses. I've been very, very careful with the printers I've talked to about him. I don't want to risk bringing the paper to a standstill, for God's sake. The only other thing I've done about him is ask someone I know in the Masonic hierarchy who owes me a favour to see if they can get a list of the members of the lodge Graveney and Smith belong to. I've not heard back from him yet. But in the meantime I seem to have been dropped in the mire somehow.'

'So are we going to be able to carry on?' Kate asked,

knowing that Ken Fellows had almost certainly drawn up a watertight contract which would not let Price wriggle out of paying what had been agreed.

'For the moment,' Price said. 'But they're breathing down my neck for some reason. But I won't let that stop me. I didn't expect this to end up on my home turf but if it has it's all the more reason to follow it up, don't you think?'

The soup arrived and Price filled up Kate's glass, which was already half empty.

'You'll get me tipsy,' she said.

'Mmm,' Price said. 'Don't worry. I'll get you home safe and sound.'

But where, Kate wondered, her head already muzzy, will we be going in the meantime?

ELEVEN

Kate arrived late at the agency next morning, pale and faintly nauseous, and was not totally surprised to see Harry Barnard watching the office door from the opposite side of the street.

'I rang you earlier,' he said as he crossed the road. 'I was worried about you. Tess said you didn't come in last night.'

'I don't see what business that is of yours,' Kate snapped. 'As a matter of fact I did come in. It was just very late. Tess was fast asleep. She'd gone to school when I got up.'

'He invited you back for coffee, did he? As the saying goes.'

'He did as a matter of fact, la. And that's what I had. Coffee, a brandy and a coffee. As I say, it's none of your business.'

'Did you know Price is notorious for picking up pretty girls?' Barnard persisted.

'Is this the pot calling the kettle,' Kate said. 'I'm working with Carter Price, Harry. I work with men all the time because there aren't any women to speak of in the sort of thing I do. So you'll have to live with it.' She glanced at her watch. 'I'm late,' she said. 'I have to get on.'

She turned away with half a smile. His jealousy amused her and, if she was honest with herself, secretly pleased her, but she was not going to let him see that.

'I'm supposed to be meeting Carter in ten minutes,' she flung over her shoulder before opening the door and pounding up the stairs to Ken Fellows' agency to do little more than pick up fresh film for her camera.

When Price appeared, on time and looking keen, driving a Ford Anglia this time, she was ready and Harry Barnard was nowhere to be seen. 'So where are we going this morning?' she asked.

'Well, I'd dearly like to know where Mitch Graveney and Smith went yesterday, but I think we'll have to follow them a bit more closely next time to work that out. I know Graveney's

at work this morning, working on the evening paper, so he's
not going to be able to get away from the *Globe* before lunchtime, so I thought we'd have a look round his local neighbourhood, visit a few pubs, see what we can discover. He's a well
known boozer so he must have a local. He lives in Lee Green,
a couple of miles from Lewisham and Blackheath, so we'll
have to brave the traffic again.' Kate sighed.

'It sounds a bit like looking for a needle in a haystack,' she
said.

'Never fear,' Price said as he headed to Piccadilly Circus
and then swung along the Strand to Waterloo Bridge. 'I've
done my homework. I've chatted to some of Graveney's
mates. A lot of them live down there because the trains
come in to Charing Cross or Holborn and then it's a short
walk to Fleet Street. Graveney apparently has a wife and a
couple of kids. So we'll go and have a look at his home
territory.'

The Ford stopped and started its way through the heavy
traffic heading out of London towards Kent. Eventually Price
turned off the main road and threaded his way through increasingly leafy streets on the incline back towards Blackheath and
pulled up at the end of a row of well-kept modern houses with
garages and flourishing front gardens.

'Very nice,' Price said. 'Just confirms what I told you. The
printers do very well for themselves. He quite likely gets two
pay packets, one in his own name and one for Bing Crosby
or Frank Sinatra.'

'So if he's doing so well for himself why would he want
to get involved with Reg Smith?' Kate asked.

'In my experience people who are doing well for themselves
never turn down an opportunity to do even better,' Price said.
'You can do a little recce for me. Go to number sixteen and
knock at the door. If someone answers, say we're lost and
want to get to the centre of Blackheath. And while you're
there just have a little scan at what you can see inside and
out. Don't appear too nosy. Use your common sense.'

Kate shrugged and got out of the car before strolling down
the street to number sixteen, opening the gate and ringing on the
doorbell. The garden was neat, with the first signs of spring

bulbs appearing in the flower beds, and a small car parked outside the closed garage doors. At first she thought there must be nobody at home and she peered round the side of the house to catch a quick glimpse of an extensive garden beyond, with apple trees and a greenhouse behind the long stretch of lawn before she heard someone call out behind her. She turned to find a middle-aged woman in coat and hat looking at her with a suspicious expression on her face.

'What do you want?' she asked, her voice sharp with suspicion.

'I'm sorry, I thought I'd try the back door,' Kate said quickly. 'I'm sorry to bother you but we're a bit lost. We're trying to get to Blackheath and I think we've taken the wrong turning. I've tried a few doors but no one seems to be at home.'

'You can't cut through this way,' the woman said shortly. 'It's a dead end. You'll have to turn round and go back to the main road. I'm sorry, I'm in a hurry.' She hesitated for a moment. 'You can follow me if you like. I'm going in that direction. I'm going to my daughters' school. They're both at Blackheath High, you know.'

'That's very kind,' Kate said. 'We'll turn around and follow you if you don't mind.' She spun round and hurried back to Price's car. 'Follow her,' she said as the woman she assumed was Mrs Graveney reversed out of her drive and drove past them with an impatient wave of the hand. 'She's going to Blackheath High School. Sounds a bit posh.'

'Not just posh, bloody expensive,' Price said. 'Even if he's claiming for two jobs, I'm gobsmacked Mitch Graveney can afford the fees. On top of what that house must have cost. Houses round here aren't cheap.'

'So you reckon he's into something beyond the job at the *Globe*?' Kate asked.

'Up to his neck, I should think, though what it is I can't begin to guess. But if he's thick with Reg Smith whatever it is is unlikely to be legal.'

When he left Kate at the agency, Harry Barnard made a call from a phone box and immediately went back to his car. Shirley Bettany had picked up the phone quickly but she did not seem quite as enthusiastic to hear from him as she usually was when he proposed a meeting.

'Fred's at home this morning,' she said quickly. 'He was with Ray late last night and decided to sleep in.'

Barnard smiled faintly at the thought of the bed he had occupied himself so often being taken over by its rightful owner for once. No wonder Shirley didn't sound warmer. 'Sorry, sweetie, it's actually Fred I want to talk to,' he said. 'Ask him if I could come round to your place in . . .' He glanced at his watch. 'In an hour?'

The line went quiet and Barnard amused himself by wondering if Shirley was wearing the blue satin negligee she favoured after sex with him. Thick and silky, she pulled it tight round waist and hips and left it loose at the top, more often than not provoking Barnard to pull her back into bed when she had planned to get up.

She came back on the line quickly. 'That will be fine, Harry,' she said, her voice chilly. 'See you shortly.'

Barnard hung up regretfully and walked slowly back towards his car, stopping for a coffee in Camden High Street before heading up the hill towards Hampstead. He did not need to park anywhere today except immediately outside the Bettanys' gates, and he was not surprised when Fred himself opened the door. Fred looked haggard and grey and was wearing casual slacks and short-sleeved shirt. He nodded him into the sitting room without a word.

'Shirley's gone out to get her hair done,' he said as he waved Barnard into one of the comfortable armchairs. Fred flung himself into another chair and gazed at Harry for some time without speaking, steepling his hands beneath his chin. 'How long's Ray got, Harry?' he asked at length. 'Everything tells me he's on the edge and likely to topple off at any moment. Shirley's nagging me to bail out before the balloon goes up.'

'He still seems to be dithering about Reg Smith,' Barnard said. 'That's what I came up here to ask you. Why the hell doesn't he just tell him to bugger off south of the river where he belongs?'

'He keeps saying he will and then changes his mind. He's still feeling annoyed that he didn't get into Notting Hill,'

Bettany said. 'You know he doesn't like to be thwarted. But if he lets Smith into Soho he'll be mincemeat. Smith's as ruthless as they come.'

'Was the poor beggar we found on the building site one of Smith's men?' Barnard asked. 'That's what the Yard seem to think but we've found no evidence for it. I even went down to Blackheath with one of my colleagues to ask him but he just laughed at us. Personally I think the body is one of the witnesses against Georgie but that idea doesn't seem to hold water with the brass.'

Bettany leaned towards a shelf under the coffee table and handed Barnard a couple of colourful travel brochures. 'I fancy Spain myself, but Shirley has a yen for Bermuda.'

Barnard's heart thudded and he struggled to keep his expression neutral.

'She's on at me to make a decision.'

'You're serious?' he asked.

'Oh, yes,' Bettany said. 'I've had a good run with Ray, salted plenty of money away but I can't see a future in it any more. I want out before the balloon goes up. If he hooks up with Smith I don't want to be a part of it. I suppose you could say it's time to retire before your mates at the Yard come looking for me. There's no way I want to spend the rest of my life in Pentonville when all I did was look after Ray's books.'

'No, that's not a good thought,' Barnard said. 'Personally I'm trying to keep well clear of Ray myself. There's another purge going on at the nick and I need to keep myself squeaky clean.'

Fred Bettany smiled, an unusual reaction from him. 'The best of luck with that, Harry,' he said.

Harry Barnard drove back to town, his thoughts in turmoil. He hesitated for a moment at Oxford Circus, wondering whether he dare call in on Ray at the Delilah, and then swung the car back towards the nick as the safer option. DS Vic Copeland was at his desk, looked ostentatiously at his watch and grinned wolfishly.

'Late night, Flash?' he asked. 'Was she worth it?'

Barnard shrugged non-committally, hung up his jacket and slumped down at his desk, still obsessed with what he had

learned from Fred Bettany. It was maybe time, he thought,
for him to break decisively with Ray Robertson too. Their
relationship had always been ambivalent ever since he had
decided as a teenager to join the police, by which time Ray
and Georgie had decisively headed off into the East End
underworld. And yet he could not rid himself of the knowledge
that Ray, when the three boys were flung together as wartime
evacuees on an unwelcoming farm in Hertfordshire, had been
the one who had protected him from the unfriendly village
lads and, more importantly, from the rampagings of his already
unstable brother Georgie. He could still remember exactly
what it was like to be on the floor with Georgie pressing his
face into the mud until he was sure he would suffocate. And
the relief when Ray took Georgie by the scruff of the neck
and pulled his brother off, giving him a vicious cuff around
the ear for good measure. He sighed and jumped slightly when
Vic Copeland, who had come up quietly behind him, put a
heavy hand on his shoulder.

'Come on, Flash, it's time for a wander round our patch
isn't it?'

Barnard got up.

'Aren't we supposed to be looking at this dead shirtlifter's
lifestyle? We'd better go through the motions at least. There
was nothing at his flat that helped so we'd better trawl the
queer pub again, press a bit harder, maybe.'

'I suppose,' he said, without enthusiasm.

'By the way, are you doing anything tonight?'

'I don't think so,' Barnard said warily.

'There's a knees-up at my old nick in the city I thought you
might like to come to. Six o'clock till you have to be lifted
into a cab. Do you fancy it?'

'Yeah, why not,' Barnard said, wondering whether cultivating
Copeland might get him off his back. 'Let's do that, mate.'

By the end of a fruitless day, Harry Barnard had hoped that
Vic Copeland might have forgotten his promise to take him
to his old nick's party, but he underestimated the former City
officer's memory or his determination, or maybe both. At five
thirty Copeland wandered back into the CID main office with
his coat on and waved a hand in Barnard's direction.

'Ready, mate?' he asked. Barnard nodded and slipped into his trench coat and pulled his trilby on carefully at what he considered to be the most fetching angle.

Copeland laughed. 'There'll be no tarts there,' he said. 'Except possibly a couple of old boots from uniform you wouldn't want to pass the time of day with. This'll be strictly a lads' night out – or in, in this case, the entire nick. The super down there's one of the lads himself most of the time. Doesn't stand on ceremony out of hours. In fact most of the time he's the life and soul of the party. Not like your miserable old sod of a DCI here. Have you got your car?'

Barnard nodded.

'You can leave it down by Smithfield and take a cab home if you need one. Pick it up tomorrow.'

'Fine,' Barnard said. 'Let's go.'

The noise when they finally arrived at Copeland's former nick hit the two men like a blow. The party had evidently started well before the advertised time and raucous groups of shirt-sleeved officers, some still partially uniformed, met them with a generalized welcome for Copeland which seemed to be seamlessly extended to his companion from the West End and instantly plied them with tumblers of Scotch. Copeland was obviously still a popular visitor to the nick where he had come within an ace of being charged with murder, which said all Barnard needed to know about the notorious solidarity of the City force. He hoped, though without much confidence, that when AC Amis had completed his revamp of the Met things might change in the City as well. Taking the odd backhander was one thing, he thought. Beating someone to death in a cell was quite another.

Losing Copeland in the crowd Barnard accepted a top-up from a tall, red-faced plain clothes officer with a cheerful smile.

'Welcome to the City of London,' he said, his words slurred. 'Vic tells me you're trying to do something about Ray Robertson at last. About bloody time, too.'

'Well, we did succeed in pinning down his brother Georgie,' Barnard countered. 'He's a much more dangerous proposition than Ray.'

'So they say,' his new-found friend agreed. 'But I reckon Vic's right when he says the mother's not to be sneezed at either. And she's got two sons. Vic reckons there's damn all to choose between them.'

'She's an old woman,' Barnard said.

'There could still be a big bad wolf under grandma's pinny. Vic seems to think so anyway. Says he's going to stake her out.' Barnard spluttered into his whiskey and tried to turn it into a cough. That was not something Copeland had chosen to confide in him and he was sure that was deliberate. If DCI Jackson and Vic Copeland between them did succeed on pressing major charges against Ray Robertson, he thought, or even his mother, they wouldn't stop there. He would be in their sights too. He drained his glass and made for the door, but before he got there he felt the weight of a heavy arm across his shoulders.

'Not going, are you, Flash,' Copeland said. 'Come on, you've hardly met anyone yet. Come and talk to my old guv'nor. He wants to persuade you to join his lodge.'

Barnard sighed. There was no way he wanted to join the superintendent's lodge, one of those which he knew recruited mainly police officers, or anyone else's lodge for that matter, but he knew that this was not a good place to annoy Vic Copeland. It would be noted and speculated on and filtered back to the Met and Copeland would take whatever advantage of it he could. He followed the sergeant back into the increasingly noisy throng with a distinct sense of his vulnerability. Maybe Fred Bettany had the right idea, he thought. Get out now while the going's good.

He allowed himself to be steered towards the bar area where a paunchy man in plain clothes, sweating heavily, his face flushed and the hand holding the whiskey glass not entirely steady, was holding forth to an admiring group of younger officers who appeared to be hanging on his every word. He spotted Copeland and waved an expansive arm.

'Vic, my old mucker,' he said. 'How's it going in the big bad Met?'

'Not too bad, guv,' Copeland replied. 'Interesting times in Vice.' He waved in Barnard's direction. 'This is one of my new mates. Harry Barnard. The one who pinned Georgie Robertson down, remember? He's interested in joining the brethren and I thought maybe you would give him a helping hand.'

The superintendent's bleary gaze fastened on Barnard and he nodded cheerfully. 'We've a full complement here now,' he said. 'Apart from the girls, of course, but I don't rush about recruiting them in the first place. Let's face it, it's a man's job. Any copper who tells you anything different is a bloody fool.' There were nods of agreement all round. 'Anyway Harry,' the superintendent said putting a brotherly arm around Barnard's shoulder and giving Copeland a conspiratorial wink. 'Anyway, let me buy you a drink and we'll have a little chat about the craft.'

TWELVE

Harry Barnard woke late after his trip to the City, bleary-eyed and with a thumping headache. He could not remember exactly how he had got home in the small hours although when he glanced out of his bedroom window he could see his car was parked askew in the car park below so he assumed he had driven. Not, he thought, the most sound decision he had ever made. The phone began to ring before he had finished making the coffee which he hoped would help restore him to some sort of normality. It was DS Vic Copeland, who did not sound in the best of moods either.

'Where the hell are you?' Copeland demanded. 'I thought we were supposed to be talking to Ray Robertson's accountant this morning. He's due here in ten minutes.'

'Were we?' Barnard asked. 'I won't be in for a while. I've the mother and father of all hangovers.'

'I'll go ahead on my own then,' Copeland snapped and Barnard heard the phone slammed down at the other end.

He groaned. He knew that being interviewed by Copeland would be the last straw as far as Fred Bettany was concerned. Shirley was probably booking their flights at that very moment. He wondered bitterly who had won the argument over Spain or the Caribbean. He could not imagine buttoned-up Fred enjoying life in a Hawaiian shirt in either destination. He made his coffee and sniffed the aroma gratefully. Perhaps the morning had not turned out so badly after all if Vic Copeland was closeted with Fred Bettany for an hour or so. He could, he thought, take advantage of that.

He showered and dressed quickly and by nine thirty was exceeding the speed limit down the Holloway Road in the direction of the East End. He pulled up outside Robertson's gym, not very optimistic that he would find him there, so was not surprised when the sole occupant turned out to be one of Ray's long-time trainers Rod Miller, in grubby singlet and shorts.

'Long time no see, Rod,' Barnard said enthusiastically. 'Do you know where the boss is?'

Miller shrugged. 'Not expecting to see him today Harry,' he said. 'He said something about going to see his ma.'

'Really?' Barnard asked, surprised. Since Georgie Robertson's arrest he did not think relations between Mrs Robertson and her other son had been anything more than frigid. As he heard it, the old lady did not think Ray was doing nearly enough to help Georgie escape the several serious charges he was facing, not realizing – or choosing not to realize – that Ray was more than content to see Georgie go down for life.

'That's what 'e said,' Miller said. He seemed to have shrunk since Barnard had last seen him, he thought, and he looked distinctly anxious. 'Did you know he wants me to give evidence at the trial?'

Barnard shook his head. 'What does he want you to say?' Barnard asked, knowing that whatever the trainer was supposed to testify to would probably bear little relation to reality. Miller flushed slightly and glanced at the floor.

'That he made a pass at me,' he muttered at last.

'And did he?'

'Nah,' Miller said. 'I'm not a bloody nancy boy, and I don't think Georgie is either. It's just something Ray dreamed up to make sure Georgie goes down, innit? Juries don't like queers.'

'They don't,' Barnard agreed. 'But I'd duck out of that if I were you, Rod. It's a dirty trick too far. And Georgie's brief will make mincemeat of you if you can't make it sound kosher. You know what they're like.'

'He told me to tell Mr Copeland that I'd do it, not you,' Miller said, his eyes shifty.

'And did you?'

'Last Monday.'

'Well, next time I see Vic Copeland I'll tell him you've changed your mind. Will that do?' Barnard demanded. 'In the meantime I'll catch up with Ray at his mother's place and tell him not to be so effing stupid. That's a favour too far, that is.' Barnard felt genuinely angry at the hapless trainer but even more annoyed with Ray Robertson for thinking that he might get away with such a blatant interference in the case. Barnard could not count the number of times he had warned Ray not to interfere in the judicial process, obviously to no avail, and he wondered now just what else he had got up to in the interests of putting Georgie away.

He went back to his car and headed east towards Bethnal Green and the densely packed streets he and the Robertson brothers had known so well as boys. Barnard had met them both at primary school before they were thrown together irrevocably by being sent to the same farm in Hertfordshire as evacuees to escape the German bombing, the scars of which were still visible in parts of the East End. Georgie was already running wild and revealing a seriously vicious streak before they arrived in the country and Ray had continued to protect Barnard from the younger boy's attacks and the hostility of their local schoolmates, who had resented the arrival of these outsiders when they arrived in their rural village. Ray had always regarded Harry Barnard's decision to join the police as inexplicable and deeply regrettable and Barnard was sure that if he had not followed that path after grammar school he would have become as inextricably involved in crime as the Robertson brothers. They had not been thrown together much during Barnard's early years in the force but once Barnard graduated to the vice squad in Soho they inevitably came face-to-face again and Barnard seriously began to wonder if his career could survive their closely entwined history.

It never ceased to surprise Barnard that Ma Robertson still lived in the small terraced house where she had brought the two boys up, a couple of streets from where the Barnards had lived. Unlike Barnard's father, her husband had not survived the Normandy landings and by the time Ray and Georgie were fully grown it was their mother who played a crucial role in East End crime, taking over and building on what her husband had started, and expecting her sons to succeed her.

Barnard parked in an anonymous car park near Bethnal Green station and walked slowly down to one of the few pre-war terraced streets which had survived the bombing and post-war redevelopment. He glanced up and down the street before he knocked on the neatly painted front door but could see no one on foot and only a few parked cars at the far end of the road near the local shops. The door was opened quickly by Mrs Robertson herself and Barnard had no difficulty in recognizing the Robertson brothers' formidable mother, a little shrunken, a little greyer and slightly stooped but still with the sharp, steely eyes he had always known and a face which had only hardened over the years into an expression of complete implacability. She stared at her visitor for a moment as if scanning it for changes too and allowed a hint of a smile to dominate her features for no more than a second.

'It's you,' she said, holding the door open. 'I'm very popular this morning. But if it's Ray you want, duck, you've missed him. He left about ten minutes ago.'

'How are you Ma?' Barnard asked, stepping straight from the front door into the living room where a coal fire crackled in a grate which had never been modernized.

'How do you think?' she snapped back quickly. 'With Georgie still banged up, like he is.'

'He may be banged up for much longer if the trial goes against him,' Barnard ventured.

The expression which crossed the old woman's face and was gone again almost instantly was fierce in its intensity. 'We'll have to see about that,' she hissed. 'But I know I'll get no help from you in spite of all Ray's done for you.'

'Ray, maybe,' Barnard said equably. 'But not Georgie. You know as well as I do there's never been any love lost there.'

'Is that all you came for?' she asked. 'To tell me that? As if I didn't know.'

'I came to catch up with Ray, but I can tell you what I wanted to say as easily as Ray now I've taken the trouble to come so far. I was out last night with some coppers at a party in the City and I picked up a hint that their interest in Ray extends to you too. I think you're being watched, Ma, so be careful, that's all. If you're doing anything you shouldn't be, I'd pack it in if I were you.'

'Pah,' Ma Robertson said contemptuously. 'They'll have to get up early in the morning to catch me out.'

Barnard shrugged helplessly, knowing he was wasting his time here. 'Do you know where Ray's headed? I really need to talk to him.'

'I don't know, duck. I've no bloody idea. He doesn't tell me much these days. He spends too much time on his poncey boxing galas to give me or his brother any help.'

Barnard sighed and turned back to the front door. He could, he thought, make much the same complaint but in his case Ray Robertson's increasing isolation was a definite plus. This was a time when his relationship with any of the Robertson clan was a liability he could do without.

Back at the nick, after a leisurely stroll round Soho, Barnard reluctantly sought out Vic Copeland who was sitting at his desk looking like a particularly smug cat who had just located a copious source of cream.

'How's the hangover?' he asked Barnard. 'I told you you'd have a good time.'

Barnard shrugged. 'It's improving,' he said. 'I've had worse. How did you get on with Fred Bettany?'

'Ah now, there's an interesting thing,' Copeland said. 'He didn't turn up, did he?'

'Did he let you know why?' Barnard asked, a tiny worm of worry intruding into his stomach.

'Nope,' Copeland said. 'And didn't answer his phone, either. When I asked the plods in North London to take a look they said the house was deserted.'

'Ray Robertson will know where he is,' Barnard said, trying to project some confidence into his voice. 'Bettany's worked for him for years.'

'Which is precisely why we need to talk to him,' Copeland said. 'If anyone knows where the bodies are buried it will be Fred Bettany. And maybe where people get their toes and fingers lopped off. I'd like to get a warrant to search Robertson's gym down in Whitechapel. I reckon that's a thieves' kitchen at the very least. Maybe worse.'

Barnard shrugged. Copeland, he reckoned, was clutching at straws now. There was no evidence that he could see that the body on the building site had any connection with Ray Robertson at all. 'So did you make any progress on anything at all this morning?' he asked irritably. 'What about the other murder, Nigel Wayland? Anything new there?'

'I'd other fish to fry this morning, once I realized Fred Bettany had stood me up,' Copeland said evasively. 'But I thought we could pop into the queer pub at lunchtime, see if his mate Vincent has turned up there yet. If he doesn't put in an appearance soon I reckon we should put out a call for him. If one of the shirtlifters is dead and another's disappeared, chances are the second one is either another corpse or a killer, don't you reckon? Find Wayland's mate and we've cracked the case for those layabouts in King's Cross. Simple.'

Barnard shrugged. He had no doubt that for someone with Copeland's history fitting up Beaufort for Wayland's murder was all in a day's work. But he wanted no part of it. 'Let's have another look at the gay pub then,' he said. 'It can't do any harm.'

'And we can have a bevvy while we're about it,' Copeland said, getting to his feet. 'If your hangover will take it, mate. I didn't have you down as a quitter.'

Kate got back to the Fellows' agency in mid-afternoon. She took the film out of her camera and shut herself in a dark room to develop her pictures but within minutes she had to stop work because her hands were shaking so much. She sat down on the high stool next to the workbench and put her head in her hands.

She had met Carter Price at nine that morning. 'Where are we off to today?' she had asked.

'I thought we'd take a spin around some of the pubs and caffs in the East End and see if we could get a hint where Smith and Mitch Graveney were headed the other day. Neither of them lives out east and I should think if any of Ray Robertson's associates saw Smith on their turf there would be trouble. He'd be noticed. They stick to their territories on the whole, these crime gangs. They don't waste time treading on each other's toes unless they're seriously provoked.'

Kate sat thoughtfully for a moment before coming to a decision. 'I do happen to know that the police are worried about Ray Robertson's contacts with someone from south of the river.'

'With Smith, you mean?' Price's eyes had lit up when she nodded uncertainly.

'I shouldn't be telling you things I've picked up from Harry Barnard,' she had said.

'Don't worry about that, petal,' Price said as he slid the Jag he had turned up in this morning into gear. 'If anyone ever wants to know, we've found that out all by ourselves. As we've been following Smith around for days no one could ever prove anything different. And I know Ray Robertson still owns a gym in Whitechapel. We'll mosey on down there and see what we can pin down.'

It was easy enough to find Robertson's gym but when they pushed open the door it appeared deserted apart from one rather skinny lad beating a punchbag in one corner to within an inch of its life. He slowed down as Price approached and Kate wrinkled her nose and drew back at the smell of sweat.

'I'm looking for Ray Robertson,' Price said with the warmth of an old friend. 'You haven't seen him this morning, have you?'

To Kate's surprise the boy nodded.

'He was in the office with Rod Miller a while back. They went out together.'

'Any idea where they were headed?' Price asked.

'Nah,' the boy said. 'All I heard was Rod telling Ray to give his regards to his Ma. Sounded a funny thing to say.'

Price had pondered for a moment. 'Is there a phone book in here? I reckon Ma Robertson must be on the phone.'

'In the office, I reckon,' the boy said, giving his punchbag another tentative bash and waving in the direction of the glassed off cubbyhole where the paperwork was done.

Price peered through the window before pushing open the door and appropriating one of the hefty volumes of the London phone directory. 'There,' he said triumphantly, jabbing at a page. 'Mrs Dorothy Robertson, in Bethnal Green. I know for a fact she's known as Dolly. If her son's gone down there it's certainly worth a look. But we need to be quick.'

They had hurried back to the car and Price had thrust a London A to Z into Kate's hands. 'Find me Alma Street,' he said, as he swung the Jag recklessly back into the Mile End Road and headed east again and embarked on a nerve-jangling ride, inexpertly navigated by Kate, and culminating at the end of Alma Street where he pulled into the kerb close to the corner and gazed down one of the original terraced streets and obviously one which had survived the worst the Blitz and the developers could do.

'Number thirty-three,' he had said. 'The one with the green door. The lad at the gym was right. There's a Jag parked right outside. That must be Robertson's. Isn't that touching. The gangster's come to see his dear old mum. But I'll put money on it being something more significant than that. Just who else has he come to see?'

Slowly Kate pulled herself together, although her eyes still prickled with tears, and began to develop her film. As she printed each one and hung them up to dry she knew she had a detailed record of Ma Robertson's succession of visitors that morning. She devoutly wished she hadn't.

The first print, which Price had carefully timed at nine forty-five, showed Ray Robertson himself coming out of his mother's house and getting into his car. He had driven away at speed down the narrow street. By ten another car had nosed into Alma Street and Kate had gasped, looking horror-struck.

'What is it?' Price had asked sharply.

Her mouth dry Kate had taken a moment to answer. 'That's Harry Barnard's car,' she said.

'Well, well, well, of course it is,' Price breathed. 'And he's by himself this time. No one to cover his back. Make bloody sure you get a clear shot of him.'

The red Capri had pulled up outside number thirty-three and reluctantly Kate had taken several shots of it as Barnard got out and knocked on Dolly Robertson's door.

'He's known the whole family since he was a kid,' she said faintly as the door opened and the sergeant went inside without a backward glance.

'Not a great qualification for a copper,' Price had said. 'Let's see if anyone else turns up. Maybe he's meeting someone here, though obviously not Ray.' Kate had sighed and settled back in her seat again and was immensely relieved when they saw Barnard leave the house, get into his conspicuous red car and pull slowly away as she reluctantly took more shots of his departure.

'So what does that prove?' she asked Price defiantly.

'Nothing at all,' Price said. 'Unless we can find out what he came to talk to Dolly Robertson about. And I guess she won't invite us in to tell us. You may have to prise it out of him yourself.'

Kate had shaken her head at that but now, as she stood gazing down at the picture of Harry getting back into his Capri without, it seemed, a care in the world, she knew she would have to do exactly that for her own peace of mind, regardless of Carter Price.

But their vigil in Alma Street had not ended there. Less than half an hour after Harry Barnard had driven away another car came slowly into the street and pulled up outside number thirty-three.

'She's a very busy lady this morning,' Price said triumphantly. 'Look who we've got here. Not just Reg Smith but Mitch Graveney as well. Now tell me there isn't something big going down. I reckon someone's persuaded them to get Georgie Robertson out somehow. A rescue on the way to court, maybe, or just using the law somehow, nobbling the witnesses perhaps.'

He had glanced at her sideways with a questioning look but Kate had looked away. After all that she had seen this morning she had not been prepared to speculate.

The photograph of Smith and Graveney arriving and leaving went up on the line to dry off alongside the rest and Kate cleared away. They had followed the two men when they had driven off about half an hour after arriving and Price seemed convinced no other significant visitors were likely to turn up. Smith had dropped Graveney outside the *Globe* offices in Fleet Street and this time Price had taken Kate back to the agency to develop her pictures.

'I'll call around at five to pick up copies,' he said and Kate had nodded unenthusiastically. When she had been persuaded to take on the assignment for the *Globe* she had no idea where it would lead. This, she thought, was the worst possible outcome if Barnard was involved with not one serious criminal but two.

*   *   *

Kate waited impatiently in the Blue Lagoon after work, staring gloomily into her cappuccino. The place had not felt the same since her friend Marie, an aspiring actress filling in time working in the coffee bar, had decided to go back to Liverpool and seek her fortune there. She had often met Harry Barnard here, a regular punctuation in their erratic relationship and maybe today the terminal point.

Harry had never disguised the fact that he cut corners and lined his pockets in Soho, she thought. It was, he said, the way policing worked there and had always worked. The line Kate thought should exist between the criminals and the coppers on the street had, Harry said, always been blurred, the priority to concentrate on the mortal sins rather then the venal, to infiltrate the ever-changing world of pubs and clubs and strip-joints, porn shops and brothels, and learn to distinguish between the myriad of jackals and the dangerous kings of the jungle. Running with the jackals, he said, occasionally brought down the lions. She had believed him because she wanted to, she thought. But she wondered if she could believe him any more.

He came into the coffee bar soon after five, his trench coat slung around his shoulders, his hat pulled over his eyes, as if to try to hide the fact that he looked pale and tense and there were dark circles beneath his eyes. He nodded to Kate and went to the counter to order coffee before taking off his coat and hanging it on a hook by the door and slumping heavily into the seat opposite Kate.

'How are you doing babe?' he asked.

'I'm fine,' she said. 'You look shot at.'

He nodded and flashed her the faintest of smiles. 'Heavy night last night,' he said. 'And a lot of hassle today. Everything's going pear-shaped.'

Kate gazed down at the foam on her coffee and stirred circles in it, transfixed for a moment by the idea that this might be the last time she and Harry Barnard sat here together.

'Carter Price took me to the East End today,' she said slowly.

Barnard stiffened but said nothing. 'We were looking for Ray Robertson. We saw Reg Smith and a printer from the *Globe,* a bloke called Mitch Graveney who's something big in the union, heading in that direction the other day but we lost him in the traffic so we don't know where he was going. But Carter is sure Smith is trying to stitch up a deal with Ray so he decided to have a look at what Ray was doing. A lad at the gym told us he'd gone to see his mother.'

Barnard nodded grimly. 'So you went to Bethnal Green?' he asked.

Kate nodded and glanced down at her coffee again.

'And what did you see?'

'Ray Robertson's car was parked outside when we got there but he left just as we arrived. Carter decided to stay there and see if Mrs Robertson had any more visitors.'

'And of course she did,' Barnard agreed, his voice flat and his expression unreadable.

'What were you doing there, Harry?' Kate asked. 'Carter's got you down as part of some conspiracy with Ray Robertson and Reg Smith to do something massive – rob the Bank of England, steal the Crown Jewels, get Georgie out of jail . . . I don't know. You tell me.'

'Why Reg Smith? What's he got to do with what happened this morning?' Barnard asked.

'I told you,' Kate said. 'We've been following him, taking pictures, and he turned up at Mrs Robertson's after you left, with Mitch Graveney, a union official from the *Globe*. Carter reckons he's on to a cracking story, although he's not sure what they're planning yet.'

'Jesus wept,' Barnard whispered. 'And you've got photographs of all these comings and goings?'

'I gave Carter a set of prints when he called round before I left the office. I've got the negatives in a safe place.'

'You realize this could finish me off too?'

'Why were you there, Harry? What on earth is going on?' Kate demanded.

'I wanted to talk to Ray, that's all. I just missed him at the gym. He's been telling me for weeks that he wasn't going to get involved with Smith but he has this crackpot idea that together they could pull off something like another train robbery only without anyone getting caught this time. I've told him he's crazy but I've never been sure that he's taken any notice. Yesterday I discovered that his money man is bailing out and that panicked me. I really wanted to talk to Ray to find out what he's up to.' Barnard chose not to mention that, if he failed to find Ray, he wanted to warn Ma Robertson himself about Copeland's interest in her.

'Have you tracked Ray down?' Kate asked.

'No I haven't. I don't know where he's gone. His mother didn't know.' He looked at Kate with desperation in his eyes. 'Can you persuade Carter Price to leave me out of whatever he's planning to write?' he asked quietly.

'I doubt it,' Kate said. 'He doesn't listen to me. I'm just necessary baggage.'

'I only stayed five minutes with Ma Robertson, for God's sake. I've known her since I was a kid.'

'I'm sorry,' Kate said. 'I don't know what I can do.'

Barnard walked slowly across Soho to where he had parked his car. It was beginning to rain and he turned his coat collar up as he brooded on what he began to see as the unravelling of his life. It was ironic, he thought, that the threat was coming from the first woman he had harboured strong feelings about for a very long time. Kate O'Donnell had charmed him from the first time he met her and he had barely realized how far he had let down his guard. He should have seen the threat her camera posed, especially as her photographs had proved useful in previous cases, catching suspects unawares. This time he had been caught unawares himself, and if her pictures were published, which was no doubt what Carter Price intended, he was unlikely to be able to explain them away.

He turned into Regent Street and waited to cross the road when his attention was caught by a small man on the opposite side of the road amongst the crowd waiting to cross towards him. He was muffled in a black raincoat and had a trilby pulled down over his eyes, but Barnard was sure that his eyes were not deceiving him. He waited until the traffic lights changed and then hung back as the oncoming crowd approached. In the resulting melee he made his move and grabbed Vincent Beaufort's arm in a steely grip.

'Vince, you old queen, where have you been hiding.'

Beaufort did not resist. He seemed to physically deflate in Barnard's grip and his eyes bulged with fear. 'What do you want?' he asked.

'We want you for a little chat about your mate Nigel Wayland,' Barnard said. 'You know he's dead, I take it?'

Beaufort gulped and nodded.

'OK,' Barnard said steering him across the road and towards the nick. 'Think we'll book you a cell for the night and in the morning you can fill us in on what you know about Wayland and how he came to get his throat cut underneath the arches at King's Cross.'

THIRTEEN

Harry Barnard sat drumming his fingers intermittently on his desk the next morning. He had arrived at the nick early in the hope of talking to Vincent Beaufort only to find that his plans had been scotched by Vic Copeland who, he was told, was already shut in an interview room with the prisoner and a detective constable, Trevor Jones, who had overtly become one of the DS's most enthusiastic disciples. Barnard ground his teeth impotently and settled to riffling through the paperwork which had piled up on his desk, and typing some reports with two fingers, furious with himself for allowing Beaufort to fall into the clutches of Copeland.

The hands of the squad room clock seemed to advance almost imperceptibly as he waited for Copeland to emerge, but in the end it was DCI Keith Jackson, red-faced and clearly furious, who pushed open the door and, without a word, beckoned to Barnard to follow him. In the corridor outside Barnard could hear a commotion downstairs in the reception area and, as he followed Jackson in that direction, the sound of an emergency bell not far away.

'What's going on, guv,' he asked as Jackson marched down the stairs.

Jackson did not reply but when Barnard reached the ground floor the outline of the crisis was clear enough. Vincent Beaufort was huddled face-down on the floor with his hands handcuffed behind his back, his jacket covered in blood, groaning loudly, while Copeland, his DC and a couple of uniformed officers stood round him in a threatening position and two ambulance men, whose vehicle could be seen in the street outside, blue lights flashing, manoeuvred a stretcher through the swing doors.

'What the hell happened,' Jackson demanded of Copeland, who turned towards him and shrugged.

'Bastard had a knife,' Copeland said, his DC, Trevor Jones, nodding energetically behind him. 'We should have known but I thought he would have been searched last night.' He glared in his turn at Barnard.

'Custody sergeant should have done that,' Barnard said. 'He's got no history of violence as far as I know.'

'Well he has now,' Copeland said. 'He went completely dool-ally in there. We're lucky not to need an ambulance ourselves.'

Jackson glared at both the officers. 'My office. Now,' he said.

The ambulance men were crouching by their patient who seemed to have relapsed into unconsciousness. 'Can we get these handcuffs off,' one said. 'We can't get him on the stretcher like this. And he's bleeding from this hand anyway. He'll bleed to death if we're not careful.'

One of the uniformed officers released Beaufort's wrists, getting his hands covered in blood but allowing the ambulance men to turn their patient over, revealing the extent of the battering he had obviously taken.

Barnard winced but Beaufort's eyes remained closed and one of the ambulance men checked his pulse and was appar-ently satisfied that at least he was alive. They put a tourniquet above the hand which was bleeding heavily and placed him on the stretcher.

'Shall I go with him?' Barnard asked the DCI, but Jackson shook his head angrily.

'My office,' he said. 'I want chapter and verse on how this happened. Uniform can send someone to the hospital to keep an eye on him and let us know if and when he comes round. I hope for all your sakes we've not got a carbon copy of what happened in the City, Sergeant Copeland. I really do.'

Barnard followed the other three men back up the stairs and into the DCI's office where Jackson closed the door firmly and placed himself behind his desk, his expression grim. Copeland maintained a defiant sneer but DC Jones, who had followed him in, was beginning to look distinctly uneasy. Barnard for his part felt immensely relieved that whatever else he had to hide he had taken no part in what had happened in the interview room downstairs.

'Right,' Jackson said 'I want it straight, nothing left out, nothing invented. Barnard, tell me how you happened to bring him in last night.'

Barnard went carefully over his accidental encounter with Beaufort the night before. 'He was obviously trying to avoid being noticed,' he said. 'He wasn't in his usual flamboyant gear. But I've been around Soho long enough to recognize him even when he was trying not to be recognized. I told the custody sergeant he was wanted for questioning about the Nigel Wayland murder and we would talk to him in the morning. And that's where I left it. He wasn't very happy but I didn't give him any options. It was too risky to let him loose to disappear again. I came in early this morning but Vic here was in even earlier and had begun to question him when I arrived. And that's all I know about it.'

'Did you ask him any questions last night?' Jackson asked.

'No. I thought it was better to let him stew,' Barnard said.

'Right, now you, Copeland. What state was he in when you fetched him out of his cell this morning?' Jackson asked.

Copeland shrugged. 'Well, I wouldn't say he was very happy. And he was even less happy when he realized he was going to talk to us and not Flash Harry here.' Copeland flashed Barnard a glance of sheer malevolence.

'Any idea why that might be, Sergeant Barnard?'

'No sir,' Barnard said flatly.

'Carry on, Copeland,' Jackson snapped. 'What happened next?'

'Well, nothing unusual happened next. Beaufort was evasive, said he hardly knew Nigel Wayland, denied he'd ever had sex with him or lived with him. I didn't believe him but I let it go at first. I asked him why he'd disappeared, why he'd left his usual haunts, why he was creeping around more or less in disguise, and again he was evasive, said he'd gone out of London with a friend but wouldn't give the friend's name, said we'd only pull his mate in for gross indecency if he did that. So I went on to ask him about the night Wayland's body was found, and the previous day. Did he have an alibi, in other words? And that's when he lost it. He suddenly stood up and vaulted over the table with a knife in his hand. We were lucky not to get slashed. Took us completely by surprise. But I managed to grab his right arm and DS Jones here got hold of the knife. But Beaufort didn't give up. He went at us hammer and tongs until I caught him on the chin and he went down poleaxed. He doesn't look as if he could scare a cat but he's a bloody nutter. I've never seen anything like it.'

Barnard looked hard not at Copeland but at DC Jones, who was looking increasingly uncomfortable, and he knew Copeland was lying. Jones, he thought, was the weak link and he wondered how to get the DCI to appreciate that.

'What happened to the knife?' Jackson asked.

'It's in an evidence bag,' Copeland said. 'My guess is it's the one he used to kill Wayland. They might even be able to tell. You never know.'

'Make sure it goes to forensics,' Jackson said. 'Barnard, you check on that please.'

Barnard nodded.

'I want written reports from all three of you by lunchtime,' Jackson went on. 'The Yard will want to hear about this and I don't think any of you will come out smelling of roses. So get out of my sight.'

The three men left the DCI's office in silence and while Harry Barnard headed back to the CID office to type out his simple report the other two hurried downstairs and, he thought, no doubt out of the building to coordinate their stories.

Behind them DCI Jackson put in a call to Scotland Yard and asked to speak to Assistant Commissioner John Amis. He was put through quickly and the AC listened to his description of the morning's events in silence.

Jackson hesitated and then ploughed on. 'Can you recall Copeland, sir?' he asked. 'He's causing more trouble than he's worth.'

'Certainly not,' Amis said. 'You know why he's with you. There have to be some changes in Soho. It's seeping out to the Press, I'm told. You risk becoming a national disgrace, front page of the *News of the World*. I want the manor cleaned up and cleaned up fast. Top priority is your man Barnard. Is there no way you can involve him in this latest debacle? He brought your victim in, after all.'

Jackson drew a sharp breath. 'I don't think that's feasible, sir,' he said. 'The whole nick knew what was going on with Beaufort. He's a well-known character in Soho, something of a celebrity queer, you might say, and we've had him on our wanted list for days, since the body was found in King's Cross. He seems to have disappeared as soon as Wayland was found which is suspicious, to say the least. And now he's pulled a knife. I've had all the beat officers keeping an eye out for him for days. But his friends very soon found out where he was last night and there was a lawyer banging on the counter downstairs almost as soon as Copeland started his interview.'

'Doesn't say much for your security,' Amis snapped.

'Someone outside must have sent him, but Copeland wouldn't let him into the interview room,' Jackson came back defensively. 'More or less told him to sod off. But there's going to be outside interest as soon as it gets out that Beaufort is in hospital. So there will be complaints from that direction as well as from every nancy boy in the neighbourhood as soon as they realize Beaufort has been seriously hurt. Barnard wasn't even in the nick when most of this was going on. But he might have alerted a brief.'

'Pity,' Amis said. 'Leave it with me, chief inspector. I'll have a word with the press office and see what we can do to keep the evening papers at bay. In the meantime search Beaufort's flat. And get forensics on to that knife.'

'Sir,' Jackson said, and hung up with an expression of deep dissatisfaction on his face. He could see nothing but trouble ahead.

Barnard occupied himself for the rest of the morning but Copeland and Jones did not reappear. They must have a lot to talk about, he thought. Then, just as he was beginning to think about lunch a colleague called across the room with a smirk.

'A call for you from a bird.'

Barnard picked up the receiver half expecting to hear Kate's voice but it turned out to be the prosecution lawyer Ruth Michelmore.

'Can we meet for a chat?' she asked. 'I'm at Oxford Circus.'

'Outside Peter Robinson's main entrance in ten,' Barnard said, glancing around the half-empty squad room to make sure no one was listening.

He hung up and flung on his trench coat and hat and made his way to the north end of Regent Street at a brisk pace. He saw Ruth across the busy junction gazing into the store's display as if window-shopping for miniskirts, which seemed unlikely as she was wrapped in a long bulky coat which Barnard guessed his mother might have worn. He crossed the junction quickly.

'Follow me into the first cafe on the left in Great Portland Street,' he said as he passed her.

When she arrived looking flustered, and sat down opposite him, he allowed himself a faint smile. 'Sorry about the tactics, a bit what's-his-name, James Bond?' he said. 'But we really ought not to be seen together.'

'You're right,' she agreed. 'But I found out for sure this morning that what we suspected is true. The old Scot and the boy, Jimmy Earnshaw, are both missing. The case against Georgie Robertson is collapsing. That has to be really bad news doesn't it? There'll be no witnesses left soon and those there are seem to be pretty peripheral, like your friend Kate O'Donnell. But that may be all we've got. Or maybe one or two people from the queer pub who may have heard or seen something that we didn't think we needed up to now.'

'Damn and blast,' Barnard said. 'That's all I need. You realize the Yard are still saying officially there's no problem with the witnesses?'

'Yes, I know. That's why I'm keeping all this a bit cloak and dagger. My boss doesn't accept that they could be lying, but one of my colleagues has failed to get interviews with either of them for a couple of weeks now. Something is seriously wrong. The director of public prosecutions is beginning to take an interest in the evidence and he can pull the plug on the whole prosecution if it won't stand up in court.'

'I'm sure you're right,' Barnard agreed. He thought for a moment. 'Can you leave Kate out of it for now?' he asked. 'And I can reassure you about Jimmy Earnshaw at least. He turned up at the shelter St Peter's church runs and the vicar has made sure he's being looked after in a safe place. Even I don't know where that is, but when he's needed he'll be there, I promise.'

'That's a relief, at least,' Ruth said.

'As for the Scot, I just don't know. I have to say I fear the worst.'

'That's not good news,' Ruth said. 'I don't understand how this could have happened.'

'No,' Barnard said, his face grim. 'Something very dubious is going on and I've had no luck pinning it down. In the meantime, I'll follow up the queer angle. Any suggestion that Georgie has inclinations that way will give the jury conniptions. It won't do his case any good at all.'

'That's true, even though it's not true and the defence won't like it. But mud will stick, and mud may help.'

'Leave it with me,' Barnard said. 'I promise you we'll nail this bastard if it's the last thing I do.' A vivid memory of taking a beating from Georgie Robertson as a boy when Ray was not around flashed into his mind. Even then Georgie had enjoyed inflicting pain, he thought, as he recalled writhing in the corner of a field as his tormentor ran away laughing, and Georgie had gone downhill ever since.

Ruth Michelmore finished her coffee and gathered her things together, still looking anxious. 'Keep in touch,' she said before hurrying out of the cafe and moving quickly out of sight in the swirling shopping crowds.

Barnard stayed where he was for a moment gazing into his own coffee cup. His own time might well be running out, he thought, and he needed to act fast if he was to keep Kate's name out of sight as a possible witness. He took a deep breath, paid for the coffees and set off at a brisk pace for the Middlesex Hospital.

He found Vincent Beaufort sitting up in bed, pale and heavily bruised, one eye half closed and his hand and forearm bandaged. A uniformed constable was sitting by his bed. 'Give me ten minutes, Gerry,' he said to the PC. 'Go and get a cup of tea, why don't you?'

Happy enough with that offer, the officer ambled out of the ward and Barnard took his seat beside Beaufort's bed.

'Sorry about all that, Vincent,' he said.

'You're all bastards when it comes down to it,' Beaufort said, his voice faint. 'But your Sergeant Copeland is something else.'

'What happened to your hand?' Barnard asked.

Beaufort glanced at the bandage. 'It got slashed by the knife I'm supposed to have pulled.'

'So where did the knife come from? It was obviously there, in the interview room.'

'One of them pulled it out from somewhere. They dragged me across the desk and for a minute I thought Copeland was going to cut my throat. He'd already beaten me to a pulp. I must have grabbed the blade to push it away. I bloody nearly lost a finger.' He waved his bandaged hand in the air as if to illustrate the point.

'What did he want?' Barnard asked. 'What the hell was it all for?'

'He only wanted to fit me up with Nigel Wayland's murder,' Beaufort said. 'He practically had my confession written for me. We were lovers, we fell out and I knifed him. No doubt he chose to plant a knife on me, just to make the whole fantasy that I'm a dangerous maniac more believable. Jesus wept.' Beaufort sagged back on to his pillows, wincing with pain, his eyes terrified.

'He's insisting you pulled the knife on him.'

'You know that's ridiculous,' Beaufort whispered. 'I've never carried a knife in my life. It's crazy. *You* know it's crazy, Mr Barnard.'

'Tell me about Nigel Wayland,' Barnard said. 'Are you sure you never had any relations with him?'

'Never,' Beaufort said. 'He had other interests, dear.'

'Which were?'

'If you want the unvarnished truth, he liked young boys, at least until recently. He wasn't very popular in the circles I moved in.'

Barnard stiffened as pieces of the jigsaw began to make a sort of sense. 'And recently?'

'Rumour was that he'd suddenly got a steady partner but I've no idea who.'

'Did you ever see Wayland with Georgie Robertson?'

Beaufort nodded imperceptibly. 'More than once,' he said.

'Is that why you disappeared?' Barnard persisted.

'When Nigel was killed I wondered if I might be next,' Beaufort said. 'I thought I'd make myself scarce for a bit. You know I'm a bit conspicuous around the place. And Georgie Robertson must have known I'd seen him once or twice back then, chatting about boys with Nigel. I just thought maybe they would want me as a prosecution witness after all. He may be banged up but don't tell me he hasn't got friends on the outside who'll be doing their damnedest to make sure he gets away with it. Goes without saying, doesn't it?'

'You say you've got an alibi for the night Wayland was killed?' Beaufort nodded again.

'You're going to have to use it now,' Barnard said. 'Get a brief organized and tell him who you were with. There's no choice. They'll charge you for what Copeland said happened in the interview room anyway, however much you deny it. You need to get your defence well organized.'

'You think that'll stop Copeland?' Beaufort said. 'You know what he said to me in there when he was slapping me around? He said there was no way out for me. I'd go down for murder. He had friends in high places who would see to that.'

'Did he now,' Barnard said quietly. 'We'll have to see about that.'

In the meantime, he thought, with Georgie Robertson's friends apparently out to get rid of not just the major witnesses due to give evidence at his trial but peripheral ones as well, he needed to make sure Kate was safe. And that, he knew, might be difficult.

Kate O'Donnell sat in Carter Price's car which was parked close to Scotland Yard waiting impatiently for him to emerge from police headquarters. He needed to pop into the Press Office briefly before they started another day's investigations he had said when he picked her up from the agency and headed down towards the Embankment. He had been gone about half an hour before Kate spotted him heading back, looking red-faced and annoyed. He got into the driving seat and headed quickly back into the mainstream traffic.

'Problems?' Kate asked.

'A bloody stone wall,' Price said. 'I wanted a chat with Peter Manning, who's the press officer I mainly deal with. Good bloke normally. He's given me some cracking exclusives in his time. Mind you I must have paid for them in malt whiskey if not in cash. But not today.'

'What were you looking for?' Kate asked. 'Something to do with the Robertsons?'

'Not really, no,' Price said. 'I got a whisper this morning from a contact that someone took a serious beating at the West End nick this morning. An ambulance was called. But Manning wasn't having any of it. False alarm, he said. Ambulance attended but wasn't needed for someone who'd just fainted. Nothing to worry about at all. As if! I didn't believe a bloody word of it.'

'I can probably find out for you from Harry Barnard,' Kate said. 'Do you want me to call him?'

'Maybe,' Price said. 'But leave it until after I've talked to my contact again. Either he's got it all wrong or the cops are covering up for someone again. And as Vic Copeland's based there now I wouldn't bet against him being at the bottom of it. And if he's done someone serious damage again I promise you I'll nail him this time. Mind you he'll have more difficulty getting away with things now he's in the Met and not the City force. Everyone knows the City police are out of control. The Met's top brass are at least trying to clean up. John Amis seems to be a good bloke.'

'Who's he?'

'Assistant Commissioner. The Press Office says he's putting pressure on the West End, especially Soho. May not do your boyfriend any good though.'

'Huh,' Kate said defensively. 'The way you talk about Fleet Street it sounds as though they could do with a good clean up as well.'

'Yes, well, you're probably right, babe, but as long as we're all living on our expenses and banking the salary cheques for a rainy day I suppose there's no one who'll do anything about that. But the cops? That's another kettle of stinking fish altogether, isn't it?'

'If you say so,' Kate said. 'So what are you planning now?'

Price glanced at his watch and sighed. 'I was hoping we could catch sight of Reg Smith again,' he said. 'But what with one thing and another I think we'd better postpone that until tomorrow. I haven't had chance yet to look at your pictures from yesterday. And I need to talk to my contact again about this alleged violence at your lover-boy's nick. And I'm waiting for another contact to call me back with some details of Smith's Masonic Lodge. I reckon I'd best stick to my desk for today. Do you want me to drop you at your agency, or would you rather go home? Ken Fellows need never know. He'll charge me for today anyway, so it's no skin off his nose.'

'Drop me at Piccadilly Circus and I'll see if I can tempt Harry Barnard out for a quick lunch,' she said. 'I'll find out what was going on at the nick this morning if you like and tell you tomorrow. OK?'

'Yes, why not,' Price said. 'Let's do that. It may be something or it may be nothing, but if Vic Copeland's been up to his old tricks again I'd like to know. It's a cracking story and it's high time someone exposed that bastard.'

'Well I don't think Harry would have any objections to seeing him exposed on the front page of the *Globe*,' Kate said. 'He hates him with a passion, believe me.'

Price turned the car and swung round Trafalgar Square and then Piccadilly, dropping Kate at the end of Shaftesbury Avenue.

'Tomorrow at nine,' he said as she slammed the car door and he headed east again towards Fleet Street.

She waved in acknowledgement and then looked around for a phone box. Barnard came to the phone quickly and accepted her suggestion that they meet for lunch with an enthusiasm which surprised her.

'Half twelve at the usual place,' he said, and she agreed and was not surprised when he hung up quickly. She knew that he would not want to have any sort of a private conversation with her in the CID office where he could easily be overheard.

She spent some time window-shopping in Regent Street and Oxford Street before making her way into the narrow streets of Soho, to find Barnard already at a corner table in the Blue Lagoon stirring the froth on a cappuccino. He gave her a faint smile as she arrived and slid into the seat opposite him.

'You look glum,' she said, her own face anxious. She was increasingly convinced that she was in far deeper waters on Carter Price's coat-tails than she could possibly have anticipated when she took on the assignment and she guessed that if she had problems Barnard's would be far worse.

'What's happened?' she asked and quietly Barnard told her what had happened to Vincent Beaufort that morning.

Kate glanced around the empty tables around them before she responded. 'So what will happen to him?'

'They'll charge him with assault as soon as he's fit enough to be taken back to the nick,' Barnard said. 'That's serious enough for him to be remanded to prison where he'll have a very rough time. Meanwhile no doubt they'll try to work out how to fit him up with Nigel Wayland's murder. They'll put it across as a convenient falling out amongst queers, I guess, and we know how that will go down with a jury. And nothing at all will come out about Wayland's connections to Georgie and young boys.'

'Carter Price seems to think that John Amis is a good man. Couldn't you go to him with your suspicions about Copeland?'

'John Amis is the man who put Vic Copeland in place to clean up Soho,' Barnard said angrily. 'The only mystery about Amis is why he's not broadcast the fact that the prosecution witnesses for Georgie Robertson's trial are missing – or dead. I suppose the Yard's seriously embarrassed if it thinks the prosecution's going to collapse because of their carelessness with witnesses. So no, I don't think Assistant Commissioner Amis is going to be much help to me.' He hesitated for a second before going on. 'I met Ruth Michelmore yesterday, the prosecution brief. You remember?'

Kate nodded.

'She hinted that they may have to turn to some of the more circumstantial witnesses if they can't put the main ones into the box, and that could mean you,' Barnard said. 'I just wanted to warn you to be very, very careful where you go and who you talk to for a bit, that's all. Watch your back.'

Kate nodded warily. 'I'm with Carter Price most of the time,' she said. 'I know you don't like that much but at least it means I'm not on my own. He may be a bit of a self-satisfied pig but I expect he'd defend me if he had to. So don't worry. I'll take care.'

FOURTEEN

'So how's it going?' Kate asked Carter Price when he picked her up at the office next morning looking gloomy.

Price put the car into gear and to Kate's surprise headed north to Regents' Park where he parked under trees close to the zoo. He sat in silence for a moment and Kate was surprised to hear the roar of a lion between the noise of passing traffic.

'You don't look too pleased with life,' she ventured as the silence grew.

'No,' he said eventually. 'I'm not. I reckon this inquiry has just run into the sand.'

Kate looked at him, not able to hide her astonishment. 'Why?' she asked. 'I thought with the pictures we got the other day we were just beginning to make progress.'

'We may have bitten off more than we can chew.' Price said. 'As Mitch Graveney put it to me last night, even I can't win them all.'

'Mitch Graveney?' Kate asked. 'You talked to Mitch Graveney?'

'I did and it was a serious mistake,' Price said. 'My Masonic contact came back to me and said that Graveney and Reg Smith were in the same lodge, somewhere in Lewisham. And I thought I'd cracked it. That was the connection we were looking for. So I went for it. I tackled him in the pub after the first edition went. Turned the conversation to 'the craft' as they call it, pretending I was interested in joining, asked him where his lodge was and was it a good one to get into. Eventually I raised Reg Smith's name casually. Said I'd seen him with Smith as I drove through Bethnal Green. More or less asked him in the end what he and Smith were up to and why they were chatting up old Ma Robertson. Said I'd happened to see them there as I passed, him and Smith together. He went doolally.'

'You were taking a chance, weren't you?'

'I told you. I must have been mad to wade in like that. Mitch more or less hustled me out of the pub and backed me up against a wall. I thought he was going to hit me. He told me to lay off. There was no story there. It was union business. And worse, he said if I didn't lay off he'd see to it that there was a wild cat walkout and stop the paper. Leave it dead in the water and I'd be blamed for interfering in union affairs and provoking it.'

'Could he do that?' Kate asked.

'Oh, yes, he could do that,' Price said. 'He could do that very easily. And if he let slip that I'd provoked the union I'd be toast. Bill Kenyon is already moaning to the editor that I'm avoiding his photographers and using you instead. At the moment they don't really know what I'm digging into. On the whole they leave me alone to research my own stories and they don't care too much about my methods so long as I come up with a good front page lead at regular intervals. But if the boss asks me point blank what I'm up to I'll have to tell him and if I let on I'm trying to find out what Graveney's up to in his spare time I'll be for the high jump. Provoking the printers' unions is about as bad as it gets in Fleet Street.'

'And that'll be the end of the investigation?'

''Fraid so,' Price said.

Kate gazed out at the park where the still-bare trees marched into the distance making it difficult to believe they were in central London. 'What do you really think is going on?' she asked.

'I don't know,' Price said. 'But I know that if you see Ray Robertson and Reg Smith visiting that particular old lady it can't be for any reason that isn't seriously criminal. Mitch Graveney is the wild card. I can't imagine what he was there for. But you can be sure that it wasn't just to wish her happy birthday.'

'And Harry Barnard,' Kate said quietly. 'He says he was looking for Ray and just missed him.'

Price looked at her hard. 'You'll have to decide whether you believe that or not, babe.'

Kate thought about that for a moment and then sighed. She wanted to believe Harry but she had always sensed his ambivalence about Ray Robertson and when push came to shove she did not really know where his loyalties lay. 'So what do we do now?' she asked.

'I'll drop you back at your agency,' Price said. 'We'll keep a low profile today and see what happens. Tell your boss I'm not sure how much longer I'll need you. I'll be in touch.'

Back at the office Kate sat disconsolately at her desk filing some of her recent work. Ken Fellows had not looked particularly pleased when she explained that her collaboration with Carter Price might be coming to a premature end. She might have been bored for much of the time she had spent with Carter Price but she knew that he must be on the edge of uncovering something seriously criminal. And Ken Fellows was very happy to pocket what he was paying for Kate's services.

'He'll have to cough up the full fee,' Ken had said sourly. 'We had a deal. What's the problem anyway?'

'He's hit an unexpected snag,' Kate said. 'He may be able to find a way round it but I doubt it.'

'Right, see if he wants you tomorrow. If not, I'll put you back on our rotas,' Ken said. 'But there's nothing outstanding for you to do today.' He turned back to the contact prints he had been studying, dismissing Kate without another word.

Sorting her prints, Kate came across the negatives of all the photographs she had taken for Carter Price. Strictly speaking they probably belonged to him, but she reckoned it was up to her to keep them safe and she was not totally sure now that the agency office was the best place for them to be, and she certainly did not want to take them home with her. She could do nothing now about the set of prints Carter already had, which included the shots of Harry Barnard arriving at Mrs Robertson's house. She looked at that negative for a while, pondering again just what it meant and whether she should simply destroy it. But that would not prevent Carter Price revealing everything that had happened in Bethnal Green if that's what he felt made a story he could eventually publish, using his own prints as proof. She wished that Barnard would finally cut his ties with Ray Robertson but suspected he was too closely linked to him to ever do that. But whatever Ray Robertson was involved in now was even more opaque than usual and almost certainly as much a danger to Harry as it was to him. She thought for a moment longer and then put all the negatives into an envelope with a note to her mother, and addressed the package to her Liverpool home. She would post them at lunchtime and know they were safe until they were needed – if they ever were.

That task accomplished at the post box on the corner of Soho Square she headed back towards the Blue Lagoon. She had not contacted Harry Barnard today. It might be better, she thought, if she resolved some of her own uncertainties before she saw him again. She bought an *Evening Standard* and sat in the corner of the coffee bar eating a sandwich with her usual cappuccino and reading the paper. Just as she had decided that it was time to go back to the office she was surprised by a burly man in a leather jacket, dark-haired and with an aggressive expression apparently etched in place. He had come into the coffee bar and made a beeline to her table before she could even stand up, taking the stool opposite her, blocking her way out.

'Excuse me,' she said irritably. 'I was just going, if you could let me by.'

'No Flash Harry today, then,' the stranger said. 'Sorry, we haven't met yet but I've heard a lot about you, young lady.' He pulled a warrant card out of his pocket and flashed it in her direction. 'DS Copeland,' he said. 'We need a word.'

'I'm not sure I need a word with you,' Kate said faintly.

'You don't have a choice, darling,' Copeland said, his face darkening. 'It's either here over a nice cup of coffee or down at the nick in an interview room, and I can guarantee you won't like that.'

'I suppose it had better be here then,' Kate said angrily. 'I hear people don't come out of interview rooms in one piece when you're around.'

'You'd better believe it,' Copeland said. 'Your boyfriend's not in a position to help you any more. He's got more than enough problems of his own.'

'So what do you want to talk about?' Kate asked.

'This reporter from the *Globe* you're swanning around with. What the hell is he up to?'

'I think you'd better ask him that,' Kate said. 'I'm just the hired help. I take the pictures he wants taken.'

'I don't bloody believe that for a minute,' Copeland said. 'You're a smart cookie. I don't believe you don't know exactly what's going on. Who's he talking to? I saw you both watching Ma Robertson's house yesterday. Why was he there, for God's sake? She's eighty years old if she's a day. Going ga-ga if what I'm told is true. He must have had a reason for turning up out there in the darkest depths of Bethnal Green.'

'I told you. I just go along for the ride and take pictures when we get there.'

'So you took pictures down at Ma Robertson's house?' Copeland snapped back.

Kate hesitated but could not see any way out of answering. She nodded and sipped the last of her coffee. 'And where are these pictures now?'

'Carter Price has got them,' Kate said. 'He's paying for them so I print them out at the agency and then hand them over to him.'

'You haven't got copies?'

'No,' Kate said. 'There's no reason to keep copies.'

'Not even the negatives?'

'No,' Kate said, thinking of her packet winging its way to Liverpool. She had taken that decision just in time, she thought thankfully.

'But you know what you've taken, where and when, and that's what I want to know,' Copeland said. 'You must keep records of some sort.'

'You'll have to ask Carter Price,' Kate said. 'They're his pictures, his records. He makes the plans, takes the decisions. I told you. I just do as I'm told.'

'So how long has this been going on? Where else have you been taking pictures?' Copeland was looking more and more disgruntled, leaning across the table with his face turning red and uncomfortably close to Kate's, his fists opening and closing in frustration.

'I told you. You'll have to ask Carter Price. If I start handing out confidential client's information I could lose my job.'

'If I find out you've been lying to me I'll throw the book at you,' he said, his face contorted with anger. 'These pictures of yours look like being material evidence in a criminal case. I'll follow up on your friend Carter Price and if I don't get what I want out of him I'll get a search warrant for your office and your flat. So don't try any funny business like trying to hide your pictures.' Kate thought again of the packet of negatives now safely in the hands of the Royal Mail and allowed herself a faint smile.

'You'll have to talk to Carter,' she said. 'He's the boss, I'm sure he'll be very helpful. He's a crime reporter, for goodness sake. He's on the same side as you are.' Although that, she thought, might not be strictly true.

'I'll do that,' he said. 'Why aren't you working with him today, anyway?'

'He wanted to do some work in his office today,' she said, feeling guilty that she was pointing the sergeant so forcefully in Price's direction but sure she needed to disentangle herself from Copeland before he started probing even more sensitive areas of her life. She was surprised and relieved he hadn't gone in that direction. Harry Barnard, she thought, could certainly do without that.

Kate strap-hung most of the way home on the Central Line and arrived at Shepherd's Bush feeling tired and wrung out. There was a slight drizzle drifting over Shepherd's Bush Green as she strolled under the wintry trees in the direction of Goldhawk Road and home. She crossed the main road at the lights and headed towards the turning where she lived and glanced over her shoulder ready to cross again but just as she stepped off the pavement she was aware of a car she could have sworn was safely parked heading towards her at speed. In a split second she leapt out of its way, falling heavily back on to the pavement where a concerned passer-by hurried to help her.

Shaking as she tried to assess the damage, hoping that nothing was broken, she allowed herself to be helped to her feet. 'He came out of nowhere,' she said. 'I barely saw him.'

'The maniac was accelerating towards you,' her Good Samaritan offered, helping her pick up her bag and collect the bits and pieces, including her precious camera, which had been scattered across the pavement. 'Are you sure you're OK? Did he actually hit you?'

'No,' Kate said, realizing she was trembling uncontrollably and feeling unaccountably cold. 'He came close but didn't actually touch me. I don't think I'm badly hurt. I'll have a few bruises I expect.'

'Where are you going? Do you need a hand?'

'I live just over there,' Kate said, waving at the tall Victorian house where she could see lights on in her flat. 'My friend's in, by the look of it. I'll be fine, thanks.'

The two women crossed the road together and her new friend waited at the gate until she saw that Kate had opened the front door safely and made her way inside. But by the time Kate got up the stairs and through her own front door she could not hold back the tears.

Tess was in the kitchen and looked up in alarm as Kate walked in. 'Whatever's the matter?' she asked. 'You look a bit of a wreck.'

'I think,' Kate said through her tears. 'I think someone just tried to kill me.'

Tess gasped and put her arm round Kate, helping her to sit down on the sofa. 'Stay there,' she said. 'I'll make you some tea. Hot sweet tea, isn't that what you're supposed to have for shock? We don't have any brandy.'

She busied herself in the kitchen while Kate tried to control the shaking which had increased in intensity as soon as she sat down. Her sobs eased as she sipped the tea Tess brought in but it did nothing for the hollow feeling of fear in the pit of her stomach. In a whisper, she told Tess exactly what had happened.

'I swear the car wasn't in sight when I stepped off the pavement,' she said. 'It appeared suddenly from nowhere, accelerating at me. I only had a split second to get out of the way.'

'What makes you think he was aiming at you? It could just have been a bad driver who didn't see you. The lights out there are not very good.'

Kate thought carefully again about what had happened. 'I don't think the car had any lights on,' she said. 'I think he was waiting for me to come home. Which means he knows where I live.' She felt suddenly sick and hesitantly she began to tell Tess why Carter Price seemed about to pull the plug on his investigation. 'He's not someone who can easily be frightened off,' she said. 'He's done stories about villains for years, and he's got lots of contacts in the police who should be able to help him. But he's scared. Really scared. So I think I should be as well, don't you?'

Tess looked tense. 'Hadn't you better ring Harry?' she said.

'I've been trying to contact him all day,' Kate said dully. 'I had a run in with another detective sergeant at lunchtime, asking about Carter Price's pictures, and I'd like to get him off my back. But this is much worse.'

'Let's call him now,' Tess said. 'If what you say is true, maybe we shouldn't stay here tonight.' She shuddered. 'You remember what happened last time someone found out where you lived in Notting Hill. We were lucky to get out of that flat alive.'

Kate took Tess's hand and gripped it hard. She had always blamed herself for the fire which had stranded her and her two flatmates on the top floor of the house they had been living in. The thought of a repeat of that almost panicked her. 'Will you make the call? I'll write his number down.' She scribbled the Fitzroy number and Tess dialled but as they waited, even Kate able to hear the ring tone from across the room, it became clear that Harry Barnard was not at home.

'Do you want to call the local police?' Tess asked, but Kate found that an impossible question to answer. Her faith in police officers was at a very low ebb. She shook her head helplessly and Tess nodded.

'Right,' Tess said, recognizing that if decisions were going to be made, she was going to have to make them. Kate, she reckoned, was in shock. 'This is all too much, after what happened before. Let's spend the night somewhere else. I'll ring my friend Eileen. She teaches art so at least you'll have something to talk about and I know she has a spare room. I stayed there after a party once.'

Kate nodded dully. 'I'll pack a bag,' she said, as Tess picked up the phone again. 'You're right. We can't stay here. It's too dangerous. And if I can't get hold of Harry I don't know where else to turn.'

FIFTEEN

Kate did not sleep well on a lumpy mattress on the floor of Tess's colleague's spare room. She got up early and the two of them accepted a sketchy break-fast in the kitchen and then walked the short distance back from Hammersmith to their own flat to wash and change for work.

'Do you think that was a needless panic,' Tess asked as they unlocked their front door and took a look round their undisturbed home.

Kate shrugged tiredly. 'I just don't know,' she said. 'I'll talk to Harry later and see what he thinks.'

Tess looked at her sceptically, taking in her pale face with dark smudges under her eyes. 'I'm not sure Harry is any good to you,' she said with unaccustomed bluntness. 'And if this job with the man from the *Globe* is coming to an end that might be a very good thing too. It's a very odd sort of assignment.'

'Well it looks as if that's run into the sand, anyway,' Kate said. 'It wasn't the most exciting job I've ever had, though watching Carter run around like a bloodhound is quite fun. But I did think he was beginning to get somewhere and then suddenly he decided to stop. Said he had upset the trade unions at the paper and that could lead to a strike, which sounded very odd. But he said that was the one thing even a paper like the *Globe* couldn't afford.'

'So what happens now?' Tess asked.

'I'll see if he turns up this morning. If not, I think that's the end of it. Ken Fellows won't be best pleased. He'll have to chase Carter Price for what he owes him, I'm sure. But for me it just means I'll be back on the rotas, doing whatever comes up. It's no skin off my nose, really.'

'Well, I think after last night, that might be a jolly good thing,' Tess said, tumbling a pile of exercise books into her bag. 'That camera of yours tends to lead to too much excitement, if you ask me, not to say dire trouble. You'd be better off with a quiet life for a bit.'

Kate gave a shrug and did not look entirely convinced. 'Maybe,' she said as she pulled on her coat, wound a scarf round her neck and followed Tess out of the flat. 'I'll meet you back here at teatime,' she said. 'See you later, alligator.'

'In a while,' Tess responded automatically before turning back. 'Your turn to cook, remember. Or shall we go to the chippie? I could fancy a fish supper.'

Kate laughed. 'Friday night,' she said mockingly, with instant recall of fish for tea with confession to follow. 'We don't have to do any of that any more, la. Remember?'

At the office after her half hour strap-hanging, Kate waited for Carter Price to contact her but when she had heard nothing at ten o'clock she pushed open Ken Fellows' door and stuck her head round.

'Hasn't he been in touch at all?' Fellows asked irritably.

'Not yet,' Kate said.

'Give him a call at his office. He can't expect you to hang around all day on the off chance that he needs you. He either does or he doesn't. He should know by this time in the morning.'

Kate nodded and turned back into the now almost deserted photographers' office and picked up a phone. *The Globe*'s switchboard answered quickly and put her through to an extension, but the phone was not picked up by Price's familiar voice but by someone she did not recognize at all. 'I'm trying to contact Carter Price,' she said.

'Are you indeed,' the voice said and she detected an undercurrent which was not friendly. 'So am I, as it happens. He's not in yet and he damn well should be. We were supposed to be having a meeting at ten.'

'Could you please ask him to call Kate when he comes in,' she asked.

'Kate? Are you the photographer girl he's been swanning around with? This is the news desk you're talking to,' the voice snapped. 'Didn't you know he wouldn't be needing you any more?'

'He wasn't exactly definite,' Kate stammered.

'Well, he should have been,' the voice which now sounded very definite indeed came back before the phone went dead.

Kate sat for a moment staring at the receiver before hanging up. That, she supposed, was that, and she was unsure whether she felt slightly sorry or not that her relationship with the portly reporter was over. In spite of her reservations, and her recent scare, she had become curious about Reg Smith and Mitch Graveney and wondered where Carter's inquiries might ultimately have led. She reported the result of her phone call back to Ken Fellows, who scowled.

'Bastard,' he said. 'He told me he'd need you for at least a month. I'll bill him for that anyway. He signed on the dotted line.'

'I think his boss's got cold feet,' Kate said. 'His investigation was getting a bit close to home.'

'Well, never mind about that now. I'll find you something else to do tomorrow. Today you can concentrate on filing what you've accumulated while you've been swanning around with Price.'

'Fine,' Kate said, not at all reluctant to spend a day in the office, though she knew that if Ken became aware that she had no longer got the negatives of Carter's pictures there might be trouble. But for the moment, as far as Carter Price's inquiries were concerned, she would talk to Harry Barnard about her scare the previous night and see whether he thought it might have been deliberate. In the clear light of day the idea that someone might have aimed a car at her on purpose had begun to seem more unlikely.

But Kate's hopes for a humdrum morning in the office in the end came to nothing. Just before lunchtime, when she was planning to call Barnard and arrange a meet at the Blue Lagoon, the door to the office was flung open and DS Vic Copeland walked in looking even more belligerent than usual. He made for Kate's desk and loomed over her for a moment before he spoke.

'You again?' she said faintly.

'Me again, young lady,' Copeland said. 'And this time I do want you down at the station, no messing. Carter Price was found in a back alley near Fleet Street this morning, beaten to within an inch of his life. He's not going to be talking for a while, if ever, so it's down to you, isn't it? I want chapter and verse about what you've been doing together all this time. And there'll be no nonsense about client confidentiality. This is a case of attempted murder already, according to the City force, and according to the hospital it could turn into a murder investigation any time soon. So get your coat on while I tell your boss where you're going. You may be some time.'

Kate had lost track of time, sitting across a table in a windowless, bleak interview room which smelt of stale cigarette smoke and sweat. Copeland occasionally sat opposite her, leaning menacingly in her face and slapping his hand down flat when he apparently did not get the answers he wanted, but most of the time he strode around, breathing heavily as he waited for her replies, which were often slow in coming.

'What did Price think Reg Smith was up to?' he asked repeatedly, and when she insisted that she did not know he became even more aggressive. 'He must have given you some idea,' he snarled. 'There must have been some motive to justify all the time he spent following Smith around. That was costing the *Globe* money, after all.'

'Nothing that he ever revealed to me,' Kate said. 'I told you before. I was just the hired help. We went where he wanted to go. He did the driving. I took pictures of what he decided to take. Or who he wanted to take. I don't think his bosses at the *Globe* had a clue what he was after. He told me they left him to his own devices. So long as he came up with good stories. And he's famous for doing that.'

'And this was going to be a good story, was it?'

'So he said. A bloody good story, were his exact words.'

'Did he tell you who Smith was meeting, who he was talking to? Come on, girl. If someone's tried to kill Mr Price, there has to be a motive and the chances are it's someone he's annoyed in a big way. So who exactly did you take pictures of?'

'Smith used to go to a pub in Bermondsey,' Kate said slowly, feeling sick. 'We followed him a couple of times and saw him meet people there. There was someone called Graveney who Carter knew. He worked at the *Globe* and he seemed very surprised to see him there with a major crook.'

'Anywhere else you saw him. Come on, come on. You have to tell me everything.'

Kate watched Copeland's fists clench and unclench and suspected that if she had been a man he would have been using them by now. She shuddered slightly. 'Withholding information in a major inquiry is a criminal offence. You know that, I'm sure. Anyway, you must want Carter Price's attacker caught.'

Kate nodded bleakly at that and Copeland started his march around the room again, making a claustrophobic space even more panic-inducing than it already was. Kate felt sick again.

'Did you see Smith with Ray Robertson? I expect you know him, don't you, given the company you keep.' His voice was raised to a near shout now.

'I know Ray Robertson,' Kate said, summoning up her last reserves of defiance. 'I took pictures at one of his galas at the Delilah Club.'

'So did you take any pictures of Robertson on this assignment? Did you see him with Reg Smith?'

Kate shook her head but guessed she had hesitated too long.

'I bloody well know you took pictures outside his mother's house,' Copeland said. 'You must have seen him there.'

She nodded, guessing where this was leading. 'Yes,' she said. 'He was there. And Reg Smith and Mitch Graveney.'

'And your bent friend Harry Barnard,' Copeland said triumphantly. 'He was there too, wasn't he? I know he was.'

Kate nodded again, feeling breathless and aware of her own heart racing. 'Yes,' she whispered. 'We saw him there too.'

'Of course you did,' Copeland said with an expression of pure satisfaction. 'Of course you bloody did.'

A tear crept down Kate's face and she brushed it away angrily.

Copeland watched her in silence for a moment and then grinned wolfishly. 'Did your mate Harry tell you why he was there?' he asked.

Kate shook her head. 'He just said he was trying to catch up with Ray Robertson. He wasn't there at the same time as Ray Robertson or the other two. He came on his own and went away quite quickly. Harry said he was looking for Ray.'

'And you took pictures of all these comings and goings?'

Copeland said. It was hardly a question and Kate nodded again. 'You didn't by any chance cull the more inconvenient ones?'

'Of course not,' Kate said. 'Carter knew exactly what I'd taken. I couldn't have done that even if I'd wanted to.'

'So Carter Price should have all these pictures? At his office? At home? Do you know where they are? Do you know where he kept them? There was nothing on him when he was found.'

'No,' Kate said. 'I've no idea. His office would be the most likely place, wouldn't it? Haven't you looked there?'

Copeland glanced at his watch. 'They should have searched the place by now but if they'd found anything they'd have let me know. So why aren't there any copies? Where are the negatives? That's not normal is it? Surely your boss keeps some record of what's been taken, what he can charge for?'

'It wasn't like that, it was an unusual contract arrangement,' Kate said. 'Carter was buying my time not specific pictures. Sometimes we spent hours without taking anything at all. Surveillance, he called it. And he regarded anything I did take as his property. In fact he took everything. I think he was very frightened of anything leaking out. And it looks as if he was right to be scared, doesn't it?' Kate wondered if Price would ever be able to contradict her version of the story. It seemed unlikely.

Copeland scowled at her. 'You'd better get out,' he said curtly. 'I'm not sure I believe you. And if Mr Price doesn't survive I'll be wanting to talk again, you can be sure of that. But for now you can go. You can report back to your boyfriend, if you like. I'm not bothered. He's going to have plenty of other things to worry about very soon.'

Kate walked slowly back to her office through the pale sunshine thinking it odd that the world had not changed at all during the time she had spent in DS Copeland's pressure cooker of an interview room. She had not ventured to ask whether Harry Barnard was in the building, knowing how much the question would annoy Copeland, who escorted her to the main door, but when she passed a phone box she pulled open the heavy door and rang the CID number. But the voice which answered told her that the sergeant was not at his desk and did not seem inclined to speculate as to where he might be. She tried his flat but the phone there went unanswered.

At the end of the afternoon she had come to a reluctant decision. The incident with the car the previous evening had unsettled her, but the news of the attack on Carter Price, and her interview with the menacing DS Copeland had panicked her completely. If she had succeeded in contacting Harry Barnard he might have persuaded her to come to a different decision, but on her own she found that she could not even summon up the confidence to go home. She asked Ken Fellows if she could leave early, which he grudgingly accepted, then put on her coat and trudged the half mile to St Peter's church where she found the Rev Dave Hamilton supervising a meal for a dozen or so noisy teenagers, who regarded her arrival as an excuse to become even more riotous as if this were a way to impress her.

Quickly taking in her pale face and anxious eyes, Hamilton took her arm and led her into the vestry where he had a makeshift office. 'What can I do for you?' he asked, waving her into a sagging chair with concern in his eyes. 'You don't look very happy.'

'I'm not,' Kate said quietly. 'My life seems to be running out of control.' She told him about her brush with death the previous evening, her uncomfortable session at the police station and the attack on Carter Price the previous night. 'I know you're good at finding safe places for people to stay. I wondered if you could find one for me, just for a couple of days really, until I can sort out with Harry Barnard and the rest of them whether I'm really at risk or whether it's all my imagination.'

Hamilton nodded. 'I'm sure I can do that,' he said. 'Give me an hour to make a few phone calls and hand the kids over to the night staff who put them to bed. If I can sort you something out we can go to your place together in my car and pick up your gear and then I'll take you to a safe place. You have a genius for getting into tricky situations, Kate. Maybe you should try to lead a quieter life.'

'I think what's going on now has something to do with Georgie Robertson's trial,' Kate said, her voice hoarse with tension. 'I haven't been told I'm wanted as a witness but if some of the other people have gone missing I might be called. Harry Barnard thinks the old tramp is dead and the lawyers were worried about Jimmy Earnshaw, so I don't think I'm wrong to feel worried.'

'It all seems like a good enough reason to get away from London for a bit,' Hamilton said. 'Let me make a few calls and see what I can do.'

DS Harry Barnard had spent a frustrating morning interviewing workers from the building site where the mutilated body of the still unidentified man had been found. The few who knew anything about the timetable for pouring concrete on the morning the corpse had been excavated from its shallow grave turned out to be a motley collection of labourers, most from other parts of England and Ireland, who even at a cursory glance were unlikely to be members of any of London's criminal gangs. The information they had had, if it had been passed on, could only have been bought and if a serious price had been paid the worker would very likely have already left the city, Barnard thought as he sifted through the records junior officers had obtained. He knew that tracking down casual labourers in the construction industry defeated even the Inland Revenue as employers connived in the avoidance of tax and national insurance. This was like looking for a single cracked brick in a brickyard and Barnard wondered why DCI Jackson had insisted on wasting time on the task.

He strolled back to the nick at lunchtime, called Kate's office and, when he was told she was not there, thought he might stroll up to the Blue Lagoon to see if she was grabbing a sandwich on her own. But before he could put that plan into action he was waylaid in the corridor by DCI Jackson.

'Did you know the crime correspondent at the *Globe*?' he asked peremptorily. 'Carter Price? I heard your girlfriend was working with him.'

Barnard could not disguise his surprise. 'She has been, guv,' he said. 'Why do you ask?'

'I've just had a call from the City police. He was found in a back alley last night beaten half to death. He's in Bart's hospital and it's touch and go whether he'll survive. I've sent Vic Copeland to have words with Miss O'Donnell, as she's on our patch. City want to know exactly what the two of them have been up to. She hasn't been confiding in you, by any chance, has she?'

Barnard shook his head, bewildered. 'She doesn't tell me what she's doing,' he said. 'I've hardly seen her for days.'

'Well, it could be a random attack, I suppose,' Jackson said. 'Or it could be that someone Price has annoyed wants him out of the way. Anyway, you keep out of it. If he survives it'll all be clear enough. If he doesn't it'll be another murder investigation and we'll assist the City police in any way we can. And your lady friend will be a witness – again. She seems to be making a habit of it, doesn't she?'

DCI Jackson strode off towards his office, leaving Barnard leaning against the corridor wall feeling breathless. He wondered where Kate was if she was already talking to sergeant Vic Copeland and he was filled with foreboding at the thought, although he knew that if he ignored Jackson's instruction not to interfere he would be in deep trouble. He thumped the wall in frustration and decided that he could not hang about waiting. He would leave Kate to the tender mercies of Vic Copeland, because he had no choice, but in the meantime he would make some inquiries of his own.

He drove as fast as he dared up Regent Street and along New Oxford Street and High Holborn before turning down a short steep street which delivered him to the lower level road which undercut Holborn Viaduct. He was in the City now, not far from the nick where Vic Copeland had taken him to the drunken party a few nights before. He knew that technically he had no jurisdiction here, but when he presented his Metropolitan Police warrant card at the reception desk at Bart's the young woman made no objection. She consulted lists and then said Ward Seven. 'He came in last night from Casualty for Professor Nixon to have a look at. He specializes in head injuries.'

'Thanks, love,' Barnard said and took the long corridor indicated to Price's ward. The swing doors opened almost noiselessly and a nurse engaged in paperwork at a desk looked up in surprise but also nodded obligingly when he showed her his warrant.

'Third bed on the left,' she said, pointing to one of the high beds where most patients appeared to be hitched up to drips

and oxygen and machinery which Barnard did not even
recognize. 'Not that you'll get anything out of him. He's still
unconscious.'

In fact Barnard could see that very few of the ward's patients
seemed to be conscious, most were swathed in bandages and
staff were obviously busy with someone who was concealed
behind drawn curtains. The bed the nurse at the door had indicated contained a motionless body, head heavily bandaged, eyes
closed and with an oxygen mask covering most of his face.

Barnard glanced round for the nearest nurse who looked
surprised to see him. 'Has he come round at all?' he asked.

'No,' the nurse said. 'He's fractured his skull in two places.
Hairline fractures but not good. Are you a relative?'

'Police,' Barnard said.

'It's touch and go,' the nurse said, with the faintest of shrugs.
'He may never come round at all. On the other hand he might
be chatting me up tomorrow, like most of them do.'

'Were you on duty when he was brought in?'

'Yes, he wasn't transferred until about ten o'clock this
morning. Professor Nixon operated earlier to stop the internal
bleeding.' She shrugged slightly, glancing at another patient
who was sitting up in bed and waving feebly at her. 'I'll be
with you in a second, Mr French,' she said.

'Just one more thing,' Barnard said before she could turn
away. 'When he was brought in did he have anything with him?
A bag, a briefcase? We want to know whether he was robbed.'

'There's a hospital bag in the locker which I think has just
got his clothes in,' she said. 'Have a look if you like.' And she
turned on her heel to attend to the vocal patient behind her.

Barnard opened the locker and found a large brown paper
bag containing what was obviously Price's clothes, dirty and
torn and in some cases carrying traces of blood. But as far as
Barnard could see there was nothing else there, certainly nothing
which could contain what he imagined would be a bulky collection of Kate's photographs. Just to be sure he went through all
Price's pockets but found nothing more significant than a packet
of cigarettes and a lighter, a crumpled handkerchief, his wallet
and some change – so this wasn't a robbery, he thought – and
in the inside pocket of his jacket a piece of thick paper folded

over tightly into a wad. But it was photographic paper, he quickly realized with some excitement as he flattened it out carefully on the blankets of Price's bed. He looked in astonishment at a page of contact prints with a cross or a tick against each picture and a message in what he guessed was Kate's handwriting asking Price to confirm which ones he wanted enlarged and printed. Barnard let out his breath in a low whistle.

If Carter Price had been carrying pictures or negatives they had obviously disappeared but this crumpled record of at least some of the photographs Kate had taken had survived against the odds. He refolded the document, put it in his pocket and glanced at Price's motionless form and left the ward quickly. Back in his car he could not resist pulling it out of his pocket again and spreading it out on the steering wheel. It was not, he quickly realized to his relief, a record of pictures taken outside Ma Robertson's house in Bethnal Green but of some previous day's work south of the river. To his relief he knew that he would not appear in any of these pictures, most of which seemed to have been taken outside a pub near the Thames. But Reg Smith was in there and so was Ray Robertson and another man Barnard did not recognize. And if it told Barnard anything at all it was that Ray was still seeing Smith long after he had told him that he wasn't. It told him that Fred Bettany had made a wise move, choosing to bail out before the going got too rough. It was just a pity he'd taken Shirley with him, Barnard thought with a wry smile. But he didn't need that distraction anyway he told himself more soberly. What he needed to do now was find Kate O'Donnell very quickly and make sure she was safe. She may have known too much about the crimes Georgie Robertson was charged with for months but a day was too long for her to know too much about Reg Smith's affairs. With Carter Price out of action, and quite possibly dying, she must by now be top of the gangster's list of people to see.

SIXTEEN

Barnard drove as fast as he dared down Oxford Street where the sales shoppers were spilling off the pavements into the paths of buses and cars and sat fuming in the usual jam at Marble Arch. Finally he cleared the congestion and put his foot down as far as Shepherd's Bush. He glanced at his watch as he turned down Goldhawk Road. He knew Tess was a teacher and hoped that at four forty-five she would already be home. But he leaned on the doorbell for some time before anyone responded and when they did it was only to reveal a face in the narrow crack allowed by a security chain.

'Oh, it's you,' Tess Farrell said, releasing the chain and opening the door. She was in a dressing gown, with a towel wrapped turban style around her head. 'I hoped it was Kate, but I didn't like to wash my hair without the chain on the door. I don't think there's anyone else in the house, and after what happened last night . . .' She shrugged and Barnard took in how pale and anxious she looked.

'Kate isn't back yet?' Barnard asked, his heart thumping.

'I hoped she was with you,' Tess said. 'You'd better come in if you haven't seen her yet.' She led the way up the stairs to the first floor flat she shared with Kate and flung herself on to the sofa looking exhausted.

'Sorry,' she said. 'We didn't get a very good night's sleep. We stayed with a friend. Kate didn't want to sleep here. I think we were both thinking about what happened in Notting Hill.'

'So what happened?' Barnard asked. 'I haven't seen Kate today so tell me. What the hell is going on?'

Tess told him what had happened to Kate on the way home from work the previous evening and his face darkened as he listened. He glanced at his watch.

'What time does she usually get home?' he asked.

'About six,' Tess said.

'Can I use your phone to ring the agency? If she's not left yet I'll go and pick her up.'

'That would be good,' Tess said.

But when Barnard spoke to Ken Fellows it was only to discover that Kate had already left. 'Her contract with Carter Price has fallen apart so I told her to go early. She looked a bit shattered actually, but she just said she thought she was getting a cold.' Fellows sounded as if he regretted this unusual act of kindness now it had been revealed.

'Carter Price is in hospital at death's door,' Barnard said angrily. 'He was attacked in the street last night.'

'Jesus,' Fellows said. 'Does Kate know about this? She didn't seem to when she came in this morning.'

'She knows now,' Barnard said. 'One of my colleagues was talking to her earlier. Did she say she was going home when she left or what?'

'She didn't say anything,' Fellows said. 'Just thanks.'

'Right, I'm with her flatmate now so we'll wait for her to turn up.'

'She shouldn't be too long,' Fellows said. 'She left about four thirty. She said she wasn't feeling good and she certainly looked as though she should be in bed.'

Barnard hung up and glanced at his watch. It was half past five. 'She's on her way,' he said. 'She should be here soon.' He flung himself back against the sofa cushions and their eyes met for a moment in shared anxiety.

'I'll go and dry my hair,' Tess said getting to her feet. 'Make yourself a cup of coffee if you want to.'

Barnard shook his head and lit a cigarette instead. But he found he had smoked several more before seven as his mood had darkened from anxiety to serious concern. Kate, he thought, was almost certainly not coming home. 'I don't like this,' he said to Tess. 'I'll go back to the nick and put out a call for her.'

'You think she's really at risk?' Tess whispered.

'If someone wanted to get rid of Carter Price I think someone might be looking for Kate too,' he said bluntly. 'Let me know if she turns up back here, and I'll keep in touch at my end. And don't let anyone into the flat.' He gave her the CID number and his own.

Tess gazed at him with tears in her eyes. 'She can't keep out of trouble, can she? What are we to do with her?'

Barnard shrugged, his eyes bleak, standing by the door. 'I'll find her,' he said with far more confidence in his voice than he really felt. 'I promise you I'll find her.' He let himself out quietly and went back to his car where he thumped the steering wheel in frustration. 'I'll tear this city apart if they've hurt a hair of her head,' he muttered as he accelerated away from the kerb. 'I'll bloody swing for them.'

Barnard slept badly and went into the nick late after checking with Ken Fellows that Kate had not turned up at the picture agency that morning. Seriously worried now, he hardly noticed as he went into the CID office and hung up his coat that he was attracting one or two curious looks as he made his way to his desk. But terrified for Kate he thought no more about them as he checked out the night's reports terrified that more bodies – and in particular one body – might have been found dumped somewhere in the city overnight. What made him most afraid was the fact that Kate did not seem to have tried to contact him after her interview with Copeland, who was nowhere to be seen this morning. But he was not to be left with his anxieties for long. Before he had chance to set in place the procedures for an official effort to trace her, DS Vic Copeland came into the CID office looking grim and beckoned Barnard peremptorily.

'The DCI wants to see you, mate,' he said. Barnard took a deep breath and then decided to say nothing. He followed Copeland in silence to Jackson's office where the DCI was as usual sitting behind a pristine desk, with a single file in front of him. He did not ask Barnard to sit down although Copeland took a chair to one side of him, placed strategically to give the impression that in whatever discussion was about to take place he was not on Barnard's side.

'Guv?' Barnard asked uneasily.

'I have been asked by Assistant Commissioner Amis to launch an inquiry into your relationship with Ray Robertson and associated criminal elements.' Jackson's expression was emotionless but Barnard felt his stomach lurch as Copeland, sitting out of Jackson's direct eyeline, allowed himself a very satisfied smirk.

Barnard opened his mouth to protest but Jackson waved him down before he got a word out.

'Before I suspend you from duty while this inquiry proceeds, AC Amis wanted me to question you immediately about some recent events to which Sergeant Copeland here can bear direct witness. Are you willing to consent to that in the interests of preventing what we believe is a major criminal conspiracy? It would obviously assist your defence in any subsequent proceedings.'

Barnard took a deep breath. 'What exactly does AC Amis want to know?' he asked, his own voice sounding strange to him, as if echoing in a large empty room rather than the stuffy office they were in. Jackson glanced at Copeland and indicated that he should continue.

'We are looking for Fred Bettany urgently,' Copeland said. 'We are concerned for his safety. We know you visited his house before he and his wife left. Two questions. Did you warn him that AC Amis's inquiries were coming to a successful conclusion? And do you know where he and his wife have gone?'

The questions took Barnard by surprise. He had known that ever since he arrived Copeland had been watching his movements but he had no idea he had been followed to Hampstead when he went to see Fred at home that last time. And the thought that the couple might not have had the chance to take themselves off to warmer and safer climes shook him. 'I've no idea where they've gone,' he said. 'He certainly didn't confide in me. But it was obvious when I went to talk to him that something serious had spooked him. He'd had enough and wanted to get out.'

'Did he say where he was going specifically?'

'Just abroad,' Barnard said. 'I got the impression he was in a hurry though. He didn't want to hang around.'

'Why did you go to talk to him in the first place?' Jackson snapped. 'Were you acting as a messenger boy for your friend Robertson?'

'Certainly not. I'd been trying to persuade Ray Robertson that it was a very bad idea to get involved with Reg Smith and his mob from south of the river. Ray seemed to have backed off but

I wasn't sure. I went to see Fred to try to find out what exactly was going on. And to see if he could persuade Ray to see sense.'

'That's bollocks,' Copeland said. 'You're in with Robertson up to your neck. I've seen you myself going to his gym after you went to see Bettany. And then at his mother's house. It's perfectly obvious you're working for him. If Bettany was having second thoughts about his boss, you were sent there to persuade him to stick with it and then to report back to Robertson and his friends. There's no other explanation.'

'Absolutely not true,' Barnard said. 'I didn't know until I spoke to Bettany and his wife that he'd decided to bail out. But he'd obviously made his plans. Nothing I could say was going to change his mind. And as far as I know Fred and Shirley Bettany have left the country by now, but I've no idea where they've gone. If you know anything different you need to find him fast. He was seriously worried about his own safety.'

Jackson inclined his head slightly as if to take that on board, but Copeland ploughed on. 'So what were you doing in Bethnal Green at his mother's house? Your girlfriend admits you were there. She took photographs down there that morning for Carter Price. You're his errand boy and you can do yourself a lot of good if you spell out exactly what Robertson is up to.'

'I don't know what Robertson is bloody up to,' Barnard said angrily. 'I've no idea. But if Fred Bettany's reaction was anything to go by he's got himself involved with Reg Smith's mob which I told him was a seriously bad idea. If Carter Price found out anything more he's unlikely to be able to tell us. And my bloody girlfriend has gone missing. I was just about to put out a call for her. She didn't go home last night. So if you really want answers, she's the one you need to find.'

'Has she got copies of the photographs she took for Carter Price?' Jackson asked.

'No, I don't think so. They all went to Price. I take it you haven't found any of them?'

Neither Jackson nor Copeland responded to the question.

'Are you seriously concerned for the safety of Miss O'Donnell?' Jackson asked.

Barnard nodded, his mouth dry. 'She thought someone deliberately tried to run her down as she was on the way home two nights ago. She was frightened enough to spend the night with friends and last night she didn't go home at all. Nobody knows where she is. Whoever tried to kill Carter Price would have exactly the same motive for going after Kate. To shut her up.'

'Right,' Jackson said. 'We'll put out a call for her. You, in the meantime, are suspended. We'll let you know when Mr Amis is ready to take these matters further. Your warrant card, please.'

Dry-mouthed Barnard handed over his warrant and glanced at Copeland, who was watching with a look of pure triumph in his eyes.

'DS Copeland will see you off the premises,' Jackson said.

The two sergeants walked in silence back to the CID room, where Barnard picked up his coat and hat, watched in silence by the handful of detectives who were at their desks. Copeland followed him downstairs to the main entrance.

'I'll be looking forward to seeing you in court,' Copeland said as Barnard put a hand on the swing door. Without warning Barnard swung round and punched Copeland on the mouth. There was a shout of outrage from the desk sergeant as Copeland stumbled backwards clutching bleeding lips but Barnard was quickly out of the door and heading across the road towards Regent Street. When he glanced back no one seemed to have followed him and he rubbed his stinging knuckles in satisfaction. It had made sure that it was probably the last time he saw the nick as a free man, he thought, but it was worth it.

Kate O'Donnell had woken up in a strange and rather lumpy bed that morning with a sense of deep foreboding. It took her a few moments to work out where, exactly, she was, and then the memories returned of a long journey in the Rev Dave Hamilton's somewhat dilapidated Ford, heading north, as far as she could judge, out of the city, through the suburbs and into the country where street lights became sparse and the roads narrower. They stopped eventually outside a house where lights cast what she hoped was a welcoming glow across a narrow garden between the front door and the road. Hamilton ushered her up the path to the door which was quickly opened by a grey-haired woman in an unfashionably long wool skirt and thick jumper who greeted Hamilton as an old friend.

'Another waif and stray?' the woman asked, peering at Kate in the dim light. 'At least it'll be some company for Jimmy. He's getting very bored.'

'This is May Priestley,' Hamilton said to Kate, ushering her into a hallway cluttered with a muddy-looking bicycle and cupboards and shelves overflowing with books and random papers. 'An old friend who helps me out with some of the youngsters occasionally.' May took Kate's hand and ushered her through the hall and into a living room where a teenaged boy Kate recognized was slumped on the sofa with his feet up watching a flickering black and white television.

'Hello, Jimmy,' Kate said. 'I'm very pleased to see you safe.'

The boy did little more than grunt in Kate's direction before turning back to Z Cars.

'Kate's had a nasty fright which she thinks is connected to the same criminal elements who may be looking for Jimmy, so I thought it might be good if they were together,' Hamilton said.

'I really hope I won't need to bother you long,' Kate said to May Priestley. 'If I can just make contact with someone in London who will help me I'm sure I'll be able to go back.'

'Don't worry dear,' May Priestley said, putting a comforting hand on her arm. 'Stay as long as you need to. I've known David long enough to trust his judgement. We go back a long way. If someone needs a safe haven then there's always one here.'

After waking up for the second morning running in a strange bed Kate felt that she had at least slept without the uneasy dreams which had plagued her the previous night. But as she lay gazing at the faint signs of sunlight filtering through the thin curtains and absorbed the fact that outside there was an almost perfect silence except for the monotonous cooing of a pigeon, her thoughts were overwhelmed by the predicament she was in. She was still convinced that someone had tried to kill her and might well try again. And she was deeply troubled that she had not been able to contact Harry Barnard the day before. That, she thought, was something she would have to put right today.

But it seemed that there might be more urgent problems here and now. As she got out of bed, glanced out of the window where she could see nothing except mud brown wintry fields and put on the plaid dressing gown May Priestley had thoughtfully hung on the back of the door, she heard what she could only describe as a howl of rage from somewhere in the house beneath her. She opened her bedroom door and went downstairs and into the kitchen where she found May Priestley and Jimmy Earnshaw facing each other across the breakfast table in an angry stand-off.

'Good morning,' she said quietly. 'Is everything all right?' Jimmy gave her a furious glance and spun out of the room, slamming the door behind himself while May shrugged helplessly.

'He hates it here,' she said. 'It's too quiet for him. He's a city boy and doesn't know what to do with himself.'

'I can imagine,' Kate said, thinking that for all May's kindness this was not a place where she would want to spend very long, restricted to what looked likely to be very muddy walks and the flickering TV in the corner of the living room.

'The last boy I had here had run away from his family in Essex who'd been turning him into a thief. He was a skinny little thing for his age and they discovered he could get into places grownups couldn't. But he ran off in the end. I never did hear what happened to him. He didn't go back to St Peter's, David said. I expect he's back burgling with his dad and his uncles.'

'I hope I won't be here long,' Kate said. 'If I can just contact my boyfriend.' The word still felt strange to her but it seemed the best one to use. 'He'll know what's the best thing to do.'

'Well, have some breakfast before you start chasing him up. You look a bit peaky.'

Kate managed a smile and accepted a plate of bacon and two eggs and a copious supply of toast and had to admit that after this feast she felt distinctly better. 'Can I use your phone?' she asked as she finished her second mug of tea.

'Of course you can, duck,' May said. 'It's in the hall.'

'It'll be trunk calls,' Kate said uncertainly.

'Don't you worry about that. We'll sort it out later.'

She dialled the CID office first but an anonymous voice merely told her that Barnard was not there. Then she tried his flat and to her immense relief Barnard answered quickly and his own relief was palpable even down a slightly crackly long-distance line.

'Jesus, doll, I thought the bastards who tried to kill Carter

Price had got you too and left you for dead in a back alley. Nobody seemed to know where you were.'

'I was too scared to stay at the flat,' she said, brushing her tears away. 'I couldn't get hold of you yesterday so I went to David Hamilton and he helped me get out of London. I can stay here for a bit . . .'

'Is Jimmy Earnshaw there with you? Did the Rev take you to the same place?'

'Yes, he's here and getting very bored,' Kate said. 'I'm a bit frightened he'll run off.'

'The trial should be starting soon.'

'Good,' Kate said. 'We all need this mess clearing up. But where were you yesterday? I did try to get hold of you.'

'I was a bit hung up,' Barnard said, sounding grim. 'Not to say hung out to dry. Are you really OK?'

'More or less,' she said. 'But I don't want to go back to the flat. Someone knows where I live.'

'You can come to stay with me,' Barnard said slowly. 'I think you need someone to keep an eye on you and I've suddenly got time on my hands.' He hesitated.

'Why's that?' Kate asked, instantly suspicious.

'It's a long story,' Barnard said. 'But it ended with me thumping Vic Copeland and getting suspended. It wasn't the brightest thing I've ever done. The Yard are trying to prove I'm in Ray Robertson's pocket. It's not looking good.'

'Could you come out here to fetch me?' Kate asked. 'I'm somewhere in Hertfordshire.'

Barnard hesitated. 'I'm not sure that's a good idea,' he said. 'This bastard Copeland has been following me around and I wouldn't put it past him to keep on going. The last thing I want to do is lead him to Jimmy. In fact I don't even want to know where you are myself. Talk to whoever you're staying with and see if she can get you to a station with trains to London. I'll meet you at King's Cross or Euston or wherever. I'll use the tube. He'll find it harder to follow down there.'

'It's all a bit James Bond, isn't it?' Kate said.

'It'll be safer, believe me,' Barnard said. 'This is all getting very nasty.'

SEVENTEEN

Barnard purchased a bunch of flowers from a stall outside Bart's hospital and handed them to Kate O'Donnell.

'You carry those. We're friends visiting,' he said. 'I can't blag my way in on my warrant card this time. Just keep your fingers crossed none of the same nurses are on duty.' They had travelled by underground from Barnard's flat in Highgate and Barnard was as sure as he could be that no one was following them. Vic Copeland, he thought, must be satisfied that his aim of getting Barnard suspended and probably charged was well on its way to success.

They found their way to Carter Price's ward and to Kate's surprise and Barnard's massive relief discovered that he was propped up in bed with his eyes half open in his bruised and puffy face. Kate hurried to the top of the bed, over-whelmed by a rush of emotion. She put her flowers on the bedside locker and surprised both men by kissing Price on the cheek.

'You're all right, then?' she said. 'I'm so pleased.'

'I wouldn't say that exactly,' he whispered. 'But at least I'm awake, sort of.' Price managed a tight smile before glancing at Barnard. 'The boyfriend came too,' he breathed.

'Are you OK?' Barnard asked. 'They didn't seem to think so when I dropped by yesterday.'

'Who knows?' Price said. 'For now, anyway, I suppose. Maybe next time they'll hit me even harder. I've hairline fractures of the skull, four broken ribs and they're giving me so many pain-killers I don't know whether I'm coming or going.' He tried to shift himself in the bed and winced dramatically.

'You're lucky,' Barnard said. 'Chances are they meant to finish you off.'

Price gave a grimace which might have been an attempt at a smile. 'What's worrying me is that they might try it on our Katie here too,' he said.

'I'll look after Kate,' Barnard said. 'No one else seems to be making a good job of it.'

'Do you know where our pictures are?' Kate asked, looking embarrassed at this turn of the conversation. 'I was afraid you had them with you and they took them.'

'I can't remember, pet. I can't really remember anything about it. The last thing I can recall is being in the office and then waking up here. The copper who came in to talk to me this morning says they found me half dead in an alley at the back of the *Daily Mail* building. I've no idea why I was there or where I was going.'

'This officer was from the City force, was he?' Barnard asked.

'I expect so,' Price said. 'I didn't ask him for his credentials. He said nothing seemed to have been stolen but as I'm not sure what I had with me I can't be sure, can I? They weren't after cash, it seems. My wallet's intact, but if I did take the pictures out of the office with me – and I might have done – they seem to have gone.'

'Did you usually take the pictures home for safety?' Kate asked, looking surprised.

Price nodded and winced again. 'Seemed safer,' he said, with a slight groan. 'I didn't know who I could trust when they called me off the story. Even though I knew you had the negatives, so we couldn't actually lose the story, I just didn't want anyone in the office having a shufti when I wasn't around. I wanted to find out what was really going on before showing anything else to the news desk. Obviously I wanted them to change their mind.'

Kate knew that Barnard was looking at her with a puzzled expression on his face but she refused to turn round to face him. 'So you didn't really think the story was dead,' she said. 'Not completely.'

Price spread out the hand which was not in a sling. 'I don't give up easily, pet. I still thought I could change their minds if we went a bit further,' he said.

'You obviously don't know they attacked Kate as well,' Barnard said, his voice harsh. 'You should have warned her she might be in danger.'

Price managed to nod his bandaged head. 'I didn't know I was in danger, let alone her,' he said. 'I underestimated them.'

'If you underestimated Reg Smith you're a bigger fool than I took you for,' Barnard said. 'My guess is that they intended to kill you. And if they realize you're sitting up in bed bright-eyed and bushy-tailed they may well try again. I know from other sources that there's something big being planned. You and Kate seem to have tumbled into it from another angle.'

'What I don't understand is why Mitch Graveney is involved in whatever's going on,' Price muttered. 'What's the *Globe* got to do with it, whatever it is? It makes no sense.'

'I've no idea,' Barnard said. 'But if he's involved with Smith you can bet your life it's nothing legal. If I were you I'd tell the City force what you know and ask for some protection. We just walked in off the street with a bunch of flowers. Anyone could do that.'

Price slumped back on the pillows and closed his eyes as a passing nurse approached. She cast an unfriendly eye over Kate and Barnard. 'I'm not sure Mr Price is permitted visitors yet,' she said. 'How are you feeling, Mr Price? The doctor will be back to check you over very soon.'

Barnard took the nurse's arm after she had finished checking Price's pulse and temperature and writing her results on the chart at the bottom of his bed. He wished he had his warrant card to show her but hoped that the urgency in his voice would get his message across.

'I'm very frightened that the people who attacked Carter yesterday may come back for another go if they find out he's conscious and talking,' he said quietly. 'This wasn't a robbery. There was more to it than that. I think he should be under police protection.'

'Who are you?' the nurse asked, looking astonished.

'I'm a cop,' Barnard said. 'But I'm with the Met, not the City force and I don't have the authority to do anything about this. I'm just here because of my girlfriend.' He nodded at Kate. 'She works with Mr Price. He's a crime reporter and we think he knows too much about some very unpleasant people.'

The nurse still looked startled. 'I'll talk to the ward sister,' she said. 'And the police when they come back. They said they'd be back.'

'It's serious,' Barnard said. 'Believe me.'

Harry Barnard shepherded Kate back to Highgate, took her into the kitchen and made coffee.

'Do you think Jimmy Earnshaw is safe enough where he is for the moment?' he asked.

'He's getting very bored and fed up but yes, I think so. He'll be all right if he gets all this over fairly soon.'

Barnard nodded. 'And you?' he said. 'You seem to have been a bit devious in all this. Where exactly are the negatives of these wretched pictures. I thought you said you didn't have them, that Price took everything.'

Kate flushed slightly. 'He took all the prints but I kept the negs,' she said. 'They're somewhere safe.'

Barnard groaned. 'That's the most reckless thing I ever heard,' he said. 'If these bastards really want to find them how long do you think you'd stand up to them? Five minutes? Ten minutes? And then when you'd told them they'd kill you. You'd end up buried on a building site or in a back alley. Carter Price was lucky, very lucky, to survive. You can't count on that sort of luck twice. Smith is a formidable operator and completely ruthless.'

'Maybe I should have stayed in the country,' she said. 'It was you who persuaded me to come back to London.'

'I didn't know you were sitting on information Reg Smith would obviously give an arm and a leg for,' Barnard said. He sighed and sipped his coffee. 'I think we need to talk to Ray Robertson,' he said. 'He's the only person who might know what Smith is up to. You'd better come with me. Copeland's been following me around and may still be for all I know, though he's obviously well on the way to getting what he wanted.'

'Getting you out, you mean?' Kate asked gloomily.

'In jail, if he can,' Barnard said. 'If he's found out you're in London he might try to find you to pick your brains again.'

'Maybe I should go home to Liverpool for a bit,' Kate suggested. 'If you think it's that serious.'

'Is that where the negatives are?'

Kate shook her head. 'They're safe,' she said. 'You don't need to know.'

'You're probably right,' he said. 'And maybe you should get right out of London until all this has blown over. Sooner or later either Smith's mob or Vic Copeland may work out that you're with me and come breaking the door down.'

Kate sighed. 'I don't know how I got into this situation,' she said. 'It looked like a fairly harmless assignment.'

'Price and your boss should have foreseen they might be putting you in a dodgy situation. Crooks don't like having their pictures taken.'

'I suppose not,' Kate said.

'Will you come with me to see Ray, before we decide where you should go next?' Barnard asked. 'We'll go on the underground. Less chance of being followed that way.'

But before Kate could answer Barnard's phone rang and she could see immediately that whatever the message being imparted it was not a good one.

'Do you know when?' he asked and looked even more anxious when he heard the reply. 'Thanks for letting me know,' he said before he hung up and flung himself back into his chair with an expression of total disbelief.

'That was Ruth Michelmore,' he said. 'The case against Georgie Robertson is being dropped for lack of evidence. AC Amis apparently admits now that two witnesses have disappeared – that's Hamish and Jimmy I suppose – and the arresting officer, that's me, is under suspension and he thinks the defence briefs will run rings round the prosecution in court. Georgie's getting out and she doesn't know when. Just very soon, she says. I don't bloody believe it.'

'Well, at least that's one villain who won't be looking for me any more,' Kate said faintly.

'Maybe,' Barnard said. 'God knows who he'll be looking for. I wonder if Ray even knows,' Barnard said. 'I think we'd better pay him that visit, don't you?'

They arrived at Robertson's gym in Whitechapel to find Ray closeted in his tiny office with the phone clamped to his ear, looking red-faced and furious. The door was closed but he saw them through the window coming past the almost deserted rings and equipment. He slammed the phone down and waved them in.

'Flash,' he said. 'Glad to see you. Perhaps you can tell me what the hell's going on.'

'You heard then?'

'My ma rang just now, said Georgie's getting out. No case to bloody answer. What sort of nonsense is that?'

Barnard shrugged. 'I've no idea,' he said. 'I've got my own problems. I'm suspended *pro tem*. They seem more interested in banging me up than a nutter like Georgie.'

'Yeah, I got a whisper about that,' Robertson said. 'Sorry to hear it, Harry. But Georgie? Who the hell wants him on the streets again? Except my ma of course. She's ecstatic, isn't she?'

'Do you think she could have pulled some strings?'

'Bears looking at, I suppose,' Robertson said. He was beginning to look defeated, Kate thought and she felt almost sorry for him. 'I do know Reg Smith went round to see her. She told me. She thought I was still thinking about linking up with him.'

'And you're really not?' Barnard asked, not able to disguise his continuing suspicions.

'No I'm bloody not. It looks as if he's cost me Fred Bettany already, just because I had a few discussions with him over a few drinks. No way am I getting in deep with that bastard. No chance whatsoever, however juicy his plans are, and he says he's talking Great Train Robbery juicy. But if I linked up with him he'd have me running bloody errands for him round Soho within a month. He's bad news.'

'Do you know what the juicy plans are?' Barnard asked.

'Nah,' Robertson said. 'He wasn't stupid enough to tell me that before I'd said I was in. But he was promising big money for what he said would be an easy ride. I was lucky to be asked, he said. As if I'd bloody believe him.'

'OK,' Barnard said. 'We'll just have to keep following that up. He's half killed Kate's reporter mate from the *Globe* and I'm worried now about her safety. He's a ruthless bastard.'

'Oh yes,' Ray said. 'And I should watch out for Georgie when he gets out too. I've no doubt he'll think he has a few scores to settle and you and your lovely lady friend might be top of his list. And the young lad. Is he safe?'

'Jimmy's safe for the time being,' Barnard said. 'And Kate's planning to get out of London. I'll take my chances. Do you have any idea how Georgie swung this? The case seemed cast iron to me. Even if one of the witnesses was missing there were plenty more to put him away for life.'

'Funny thing,' Robertson said. 'Reg Smith was asking me about Georgie. Seemed to think he must have been a useful man to have around. I told him he was a nutter and now they'd got him locked up they should throw away the key.'

'Well, someone's decided different,' Barnard said. 'And I'd really like to know how that happened.'

'Now what?' Kate said as they made their way from Robertson's gym back towards Whitechapel Road. Barnard glanced back towards the gym and then scanned the heavy traffic grinding east. He could see no sign that they had been followed and was beginning to think that DS Vic Copeland had been called off his tail.

'We'll go back to my place and pick up the car,' he said, turning towards the underground station. 'And then I think we might pay Ma Robertson a visit. I'm sure she'll be so excited she won't mind telling us how Georgie's case got dropped.'

'Are you sure?' Kate asked as they headed below ground again, running the last few yards as a train rumbled into the station.

'The sight of you might soften the old biddy's heart,' Barnard said lightly as the carriage doors slammed shut behind them. 'I'm not sure she'll want Georgie anywhere near us. She always seemed quite fond of me when we were kids. Though not as fond as she was of her precious baby Georgie, of course.'

Kate wondered why Barnard was so sentimental about his East End childhood. She had been brought up herself surrounded by the same sort of slum poverty and her community had been as heavily bombed – although few Londoners seemed to know

about that – but she had left Lime Street station with no regrets
and more grim than fond memories. It was time, she thought,
she moved on.

'Let's do it then,' she said resignedly. 'Though I can't see
that she's very likely to tell us anything.'

They drove across London this time at a speed Kate felt happier
with than usual, guessing that Barnard did not want to draw
any attention to themselves as he threaded his way through
busy streets to Bethnal Green. This time there were no cars
parked in Alma Street. The only sign of life was an elderly
woman standing on her doorstep chatting to the postman.
Barnard parked outside Ma Robertson's house.

'It might be a good idea if you stayed in the car,' he said.
'If anyone we don't want to see turns up hit the horn. We
can't be too careful.'

Kate nodded and then watched as he knocked on the door
which was opened quickly by a white-haired woman in a blue
patterned dress and baggy cardigan with a slash of red lipstick
across a wizened face. Ma Robertson seemed surprised to see
Harry, she thought, and looked up and down the street before
waving Barnard inside.

'You've got a nerve coming here now,' she said to him as
he stepped into the cramped living room. 'What do you want
anyway? You'd best keep out of my Georgie's way. He won't
be best pleased to see you.'

'I don't suppose he will,' Barnard said. 'I was surprised he
got the result he did.'

'I don't see why,' Dolly Robertson said. 'Everyone knows
you lot set him up.' Her face contorted with rage. 'And
Georgie's lawyer reckons his brother had a hand in it too. But
you'd know all about that, wouldn't you?'

Barnard took a deep breath at the sheer unexpectedness of
the allegation. 'You have to be joking,' he said faintly. 'Why
would he do that?'

'He wanted to keep Georgie out of the family business,
didn't he? He knew Georgie would make a better fist of it
than he's been doing lately, with his galas and social climbing
nonsense. Their father would be turning in his grave.'

'Ray might not want to work with Georgie, but he wouldn't shop him,' Barnard objected.

'You ask his brief,' Dolly said, her mouth snapping shut like a trap.

'Who is?'

'Mr Godfrey QC. As if you didn't know. He was very interested when I told him Ray had gone soft and wanted Georgie out of the way. Very interested indeed.'

Barnard could believe it. He knew Lancelot Godfrey as a lawyer who was making a lucrative life for himself working mainly for London's gangsters. He had no doubt that if he had been instrumental in getting the case against Georgie Robertson thrown out he would be very well rewarded indeed.

'Now get out of my house,' Dolly said. 'You were always a sneaky little sod when the boys were kids. It didn't surprise me when you chose to be an effing copper.'

At that moment Barnard heard his car horn sound twice and he turned to the door. When he opened it he saw a green Jaguar approaching down the narrow street and although he could not see clearly who was in it he knew without a shadow of a doubt it meant big trouble. Without a word he strode across the pavement, dropped into the driving seat of his Capri and made a racing start in the opposite direction, cutting back into the main road before the Jag had drawn to a stop outside Dolly Robertson's house. As he turned the corner he could see in his mirror Dolly coming out to greet her younger son Georgie with his arms open wide ready for a fierce embrace.

Kate, who was also looking back, said, 'That's Reg Smith he's with.'

Barnard put his foot down and accelerated away, turning the corner into Whitechapel Road on two wheels.

EIGHTEEN

They went back to Barnard's flat and sat at the breakfast bar in the kitchen drinking strong coffee.

'We need to tell Ray Robertson what his mother said,' Barnard said at length, picking up his phone, but after dialling twice he slammed it down again. 'No reply, either at the gym or the Delilah. I don't have a number for his house and I'm sure it'll be ex-directory anyway. I don't think he spends much time there.'

'Surely his mother wasn't serious,' Kate said. 'You don't really think Georgie will try to get at Ray, do you?'

'I think Georgie is capable of anything,' Barnard said. 'And his mother seems to have turned into a malevolent old bat. I guess we're on their little list too. I wasn't kidding when I said you should get out of London. I mean it. You're not safe at your flat and you're probably not safe here either. I'm sure you can square some time off with Ken Fellows, in the circumstances. Ring your mother and tell her you're coming home for a while. Ring her now.'

'She's not on the phone, la,' Kate said, laughing. 'Where I come from we use the call box at the end of the street. People like my ma don't have phones.'

Barnard did not smile. 'Find out the train times, then, and just turn up. I'm sure she'll be pleased to see you.'

Kate looked at him for a minute, her expression serious. 'I'm not sure I want to leave you on your own,' she said quietly. 'We're in this together, aren't we? I'll stay here tonight at least and then we'll see.'

Barnard put his arm round her shoulder and kissed her on the cheek. 'You're very sweet,' he said. 'But I don't want you to get hurt.'

'And I don't want you to end up in jail,' she said. 'It seems to me that if you can find out what's really going on with Georgie and Reg Smith you'll do yourself a lot of good. With what Carter Price and I discovered and what we've found out since Carter was attacked we've got a good chance of stopping something big. So let's do it.'

'You are amazing,' Barnard said. 'Are you sure?'

'I'm sure,' Kate said.

'OK, let's take a spin round to the *Globe* and see what we can dig up about Mitch Graveney,' he said. 'He's the odd one out in all this. And then we'll go and see Ray and warn him he may be in danger. I'm quite sure Georgie is capable of killing Ray if the mood takes him. And it's quite possible Ray has a pretty good idea of what's really going on. He may not have wanted to tell me before, but if he thinks Georgie's on the rampage he may be more forthcoming.'

Kate nodded. 'Let's do it,' she said again.

The *Globe* building turned a glassy face towards Fleet Street but its business end was at the back, where huge doors opened on to a back street usually packed with delivery vans during the day, ready to carry off the various editions of its sister evening paper *The Star*. When Barnard drove south from Holborn he found it difficult to park close to the building and they ended up walking towards the print shop entrance, which Barnard reckoned was a better approach than the front doors where they would be lucky to get past reception. He felt the loss of his warrant card acutely.

The huge delivery doors were fully open and dozens of men in blue overalls were milling about inside. They could see the mighty presses inside linked by roller belts to the point where the papers were tied into bundles by hand and the vans backed up, filling the air with fumes. No one seemed to even notice their arrival or, if they did, they were regarded as interested spectators rather than significant visitors.

'We're looking for Mitch Graveney,' Barnard said to one of the printers. 'I've got a message for him.'

The man glanced inside and waved in the direction of a man wearing earmuffs. 'That's Mitch,' he said. 'But he's very busy. We're about to roll.' Kate nodded, recognizing the man whose photograph she had taken several times. But before they could approach him, Graveney turned away and moved towards a separate loading bay where another van with security marking was manoeuvring into the narrow parking space.

Barnard put a hand on Kate's arm. 'Watch,' he said, as Graveney himself seemed to be watching the back doors of the van being opened and various metal boxes being unloaded. Inside the van it was possible to see more of the same. A security guard positioned by the entrance was taking a close interest in Barnard and Kate and Harry pulled her away round the corner out of sight.

'Looks like cash, for wages probably,' he said.

But before Kate could reply a klaxon sounded followed by an enormous roar which shook the building around them and even the ground beneath their feet. The presses had begun to print the next edition of the *Star*.

'Let's go and see your mate Carter Price again,' Barnard said. 'He'll know what goes on with the wages deliveries.'

'He did tell me he was paid in cash,' Kate said. 'It seemed a bit odd for someone in his position but he said because so many of the workforce were always paid that way they lumped the journalists in as well. A lot of the newspapers do it he said.'

'So a hell of a lot of cash must go in and out every week.'

'I guess so,' Kate said.

They picked up the car and drove to Ludgate Circus and cut through to Holborn and Bart's where they found Carter Price still confined to bed, but looking considerably more cheerful than the last time they had seen him.

'You're looking better,' Kate said. 'Are you feeling it?'

Price nodded, though without great certainty. 'A bit,' he said. 'I'll be here for a while though, they reckon. A fractured skull's not to be taken lightly.'

'We want to pick your brains again, in spite of the cracks,' Barnard said, slightly impatiently. 'We went down to the *Globe* this morning to see if we could get close to Mitch Graveney, but they were printing the *Star* and we couldn't get close. But what we did see was a security van pulling into the back of the building close to the print shop and we wondered how often that happened. We wondered if that was the link between Graveney and Reg Smith.'

Price gave a faint whistle. 'Jesus wept,' he said. 'You've no idea how much cash that van delivers. It goes round on a Wednesday so that people can be paid on a Thursday. But it doesn't just come to the *Globe*. It does a circuit of half a dozen papers, maybe more. There'll be hundreds of thousands of quid in that van when it starts off.'

'Does it vary its route?' Barnard asked.

'I don't know,' Price said. 'It certainly varies its time of arrival at our place so it probably does. But someone has to be told what time it's going to drive in so that the payroll staff can meet it at the back entrance. That's why Smith could have been schmoozing Mitch Graveney. He's very often in charge of the presses. He would need to know. I should have worked that out. It's not exactly the Great Train Robbery but it would be a substantial haul if anyone managed to hijack it at its first call.'

'And if the presses were running no one would hear a thing,' Kate said feelingly. 'No wonder they wear earmuffs.'

'Are you going to your boss to fill him in on all this?' Kate asked as they walked back to the car.

'Not yet,' Barnard said. 'I want to be one hundred per cent sure of the facts before I do that. I still don't understand who got Georgie off the hook and why. I can't see how even Reg Smith could swing that without some help from the law. Ruth Michelmore couldn't understand it either. The case was watertight even without the old tramp Hamish's evidence. I really don't believe his mother could have shifted the legal system like that. If she was involved she must have had some pretty powerful help.'

He swung the car east on to Holborn and skirted St Paul's.

'We'll go to see Ray again. He might have some idea who swung that for Georgie. And we need to tell him what his mother said. He won't take Georgie's threats seriously, of course. I reckon he still thinks of him as a nasty little brother whose ears he used to clip if he strayed too far out of line. He never did take on board just how vicious he was even when he was a kid.'

Kate shuddered. 'I shouldn't think he thinks that any more,

after what he was charged with,' she said. They travelled in uneasy silence until Barnard pulled up outside the Robertson's gym. Barnard glanced around but could see no sign that they had been followed. Copeland seemed to have given up on his surveillance which only told Barnard that the sergeant believed he did not need any more evidence in the case and that his goose was well and truly cooked. Looking grim he led Kate inside where they found Ray Robertson ensconced in his office as usual in a thick cloud of cigar smoke. He looked up as they worked their way between the boxing ring and training equipment but this time there was no welcoming smile.

'I tried to get you by phone,' Barnard said. 'Where were you?'

'Oh, round and about,' Robertson said airily. 'Is there any word of where my blasted brother is? I'll swing for that bastard yet.'

'Or he'll swing for you,' Barnard said quietly. 'We went to see your ma this morning. She reckons he thinks you were involved in his arrest, though how he works that out I'm not sure. Anyway, she says he's out to get you. I thought you'd better know that.'

Ray said nothing as he lit a fresh cigar. 'I've never been a grass in my life,' he said. 'You know I'd never have been involved in what Georgie was up to. Not in a million years. But I wouldn't shop him.'

'But now?' Barnard whispered, watching the mixed emotions flit across Robertson's heavy face. 'Now it's a question of survival?'

'My own kid brother,' Robertson whispered.

'He was always a maniac,' Barnard said. 'I thought we'd stopped him for good and now we seem to have to do it all over again.'

Robertson blew a cloud of smoke in their direction and seemed to come to a conclusion. 'You're right,' he said. 'I'll tell you what I know, which isn't everything, by a long chalk. But it should help. Reg Smith wanted me in on his latest scheme. I told you. I said no. That sort of heist isn't my scene. Too violent. Too risky. I reckon he was thinking of getting Georgie involved as well and when I said I wasn't interested he went for that big time.'

'Do you know what Smith is planning? What sort of heist?' Barnard asked, almost holding his breath as he waited for Robertson to break the habit of a lifetime and become a grass.

'There's a security van goes round all the newspapers around Fleet Street once a week delivering their wages. Its huge moolah, according to Reg, enough to set us all up for life. He knew I'd been spouting off about the train robbers. Thought I'd be interested. More fool me, I suppose. I should keep my big mouth shut.'

'You certainly frightened Fred Bettany,' Barnard said.

'Yeah, yeah,' Robertson said. 'He chickened out. He wouldn't believe I wouldn't go for it. Tooled up as well.'

'Guns?'

'Oh yeah. You know how Georgie would love that.' Kate saw Barnard's face harden.

'Do you know when?' he asked.

But Robertson shrugged. 'Reg didn't tell me that. The van varies its time and route, apparently, but from what he said I think he's got an inside man who's going to give him the nod. He was making a big thing of being ready at a moment's notice, like the bloody commandos he said. As if. He wouldn't have made it in the bloody Home Guard.'

Barnard glanced at Kate and she nodded. 'Mitch Graveney,' she said. 'At the *Globe*.'

Barnard leaned back in his rickety chair and looked at Robertson. 'You're in trouble, Ray,' he said. 'Reg will realize you know too much and Georgie hates your guts anyway. They'll come after you. I should get out of London for a while if poss. I'll set the wheels in motion if I can and try to stop this in its tracks, but even if I can – and I'm in the doghouse already remember – it will be much harder to keep Georgie off your back.'

'That little bastard,' Robertson snarled. 'I knew he'd be trouble the first time I saw his evil, wrinkled little face. I should have strangled him then.'

DCI Jackson put the phone down irritably. The call had come from the City of London police and had, in effect, been a complaint about interference on their patch by DS Harry

Barnard. He had turned up at Grays Inn Road station this morning, Jackson's opposite number there had complained, with some cock and bull story about a planned heist of a wages van doing the rounds of the newspaper offices.

'What the hell is going on?' DCI O'Rorke had demanded. 'We've not had a whisper. And your man didn't seem to have any evidence that was remotely credible. Do you know anything about it?'

Jackson had had to confess that he didn't, and admit that Barnard had been suspended.

'What's he trying to do?' O'Rorke asked. 'Gain some brownie points to get himself off the hook? If so I really don't want him trampling around on my ground. If anything big was going down we'd have heard about it. We're not complete fools, whatever the Met thinks.'

'I'll haul him in,' Jackson had said, his voice tight with anger. 'Find out what's going on.'

'Well, we'll keep an eye on Fleet Street but I reckon it'll be a waste of manpower I can do without. Reg Smith and Georgie Robertson are involved, he claims. As if. Georgie Robertson should still be banged up, by rights. How the hell did he get out? What is he, bloody Houdini?'

Jackson's complexion, already flushed, turned a darker shade of puce. 'You'll have to ask the Yard about that. I'm as pissed off as you are about it.'

'Right,' O'Rorke said. 'I'll leave it with you then. Get this man Barnard back under control. He's a loose cannon. I don't care how you do it, I just don't want him messing up on my patch.'

Jackson sat drumming his fingers on the desk for a moment and then picked up the phone again. Assistant Commissioner John Amis responded quickly and listened quietly while Jackson outlined the complaint from the City force. Not until Jackson had finished did he explode.

'What's he playing at?' he asked. 'We know Barnard's in Ray Robertson's pocket so this must be something he's put him up to. It must be some ploy, a distraction maybe, while they fit Georgie into whatever scheme his brother's set up for him. I'm quite sure Ray Robertson was involved in getting rid of the witnesses so the case collapsed. No doubt with Barnard's help. He knew that case inside out.'

'Barnard was heavily involved in that case,' Jackson agreed, though not without a hint of uncertainty.

'If the evidence – or in this case the witnesses – aren't there, there is no case to answer,' Amis snapped. 'Pull Barnard in. It was a mistake not to charge him straight away and get him remanded. I want him banged up. And then get Copeland working on Ray Robertson. I want him banged up for a very long time too. Do it now.' And he hung up.

Grim-faced, Jackson rang down to the CID room and asked DS Vic Copeland to come up. 'Are you still tailing Harry Barnard?' he asked as soon as the sergeant put his head round the door.

'Not now,' Copeland said. 'You didn't say you wanted me to carry on.'

'Well I want him brought in,' Jackson said. 'It looks as if he's running around for Ray Robertson, causing mayhem in the City. AC Amis wants him charged and remanded. He's got to the end of his rope and now we haul him in for good.'

NINETEEN

'We need to get out of London for a bit,' Harry Barnard said flatly. They were drinking coffee again the following morning at the breakfast bar in Barnard's flat. 'This thing isn't going to go off until there's another wages delivery due. It's not just his brother that Georgie Robertson and his mates will be looking for, it's you. If something so big is going down they won't want to leave any loose ends and you are very definitely a loose end after working with Carter Price. They've had one go at him and they won't give up easily. I hope the City force is keeping an eye on Price while he's in hospital. They'll certainly know by now that they didn't kill him, and even if they've got some of your prints they'll know there are negatives somewhere.'

'Where can we go?' Kate asked uneasily.

'How about the seaside?' Barnard asked. 'It's the wrong time of year, of course. Might be a bit chilly. But at least there'll be plenty of hotels with rooms.'

Kate sighed. 'All right,' she said. 'I'll need to go back to my place to pick up some clothes. And I'd really like to see Carter again before we go. Do you think that would be safe?'

Barnard frowned. 'I'll run you down to the hospital before you go to your place,' he said. 'I don't want to go inside but you should be OK on your own. And there's a call I want to make before we go. I contacted someone at the security company to find out how these wages drop-offs worked. Told him I worked for the City force and we wanted to increase security in the light of information received. Oddly enough he believed me. I'll just check that the next one is happening next Thursday.'

But it wasn't. When he'd finished his call Barnard looked slightly shell-shocked. 'It's Monday,' he said. 'When there's a bank holiday coming up the unions make sure everyone is paid early – on Tuesday instead of Thursday. I said I wasn't sure my boss knew that so could he make double sure that everyone was clued up. Jesus wept. Graveney must have spelt out to Smith just how ramshackle the arrangements are.'

'And when the presses are running you could march an army in there and no one would hear a thing,' Kate said. 'And Graveney seems to be in charge of them.'

They looked at each other, horrified.

'Come on,' Barnard said. 'I'll drop you off at Bart's, then at your place and we'll head off. Where do you fancy? Brighton maybe? It's the traditional place for a naughty weekend.

'Just don't tell my mother,' Kate said with a grin.

But when Kate came out of Bart's Hospital an hour later she was not smiling. She got into the Capri looking sombre. 'You won't believe this,' she said.

'Is Price OK?' Barnard asked anxiously.

'Oh yes, he's OK. Seems much better. He actually had a phone call from a contact of his. He can't chase it up, obviously. He wants us to do it.'

'Oh yes?' Barnard sounded sceptical.

'He said he asked a contact to root around in Masonic records to see if there was a connection there between Reg Smith and Mitch Graveney. And there is. They're in the same lodge in south London. But that wasn't all. The worshipful master of the lodge is John Amis. Assistant Commissioner John Amis. Is that a big enough coincidence for you?'

Barnard looked at her in astonishment. 'Jesus wept,' he said. 'I wonder just how close he is to Reg Smith.'

'Price wanted me to ring the Yard and ask him,' Kate said.

'You must be joking,' Barnard said. 'That would really be putting your head into a lion's mouth. Whether he's involved with Smith or not he wouldn't want the suggestion to get out. Come on. Let's get out of here and see exactly what, if anything, happens on Monday.'

Kate and Harry Barnard were back in Fleet Street by eight on Monday morning. Barnard parked the Capri well away from the *Globe* building, close to Holborn Circus, and they walked south to Fleet Street in silence. The area at the back of the newspaper building was already a ferment of activity with the delivery vans already waiting for the bundles of the first edition of the *Star.*

'I imagine the plan is to hijack the security van and drive it off. The other vans will let it through without any difficulty. They'll all be used to seeing it come and go. And if they do it that way it means the gang can arrive quietly without anyone noticing. On foot possibly. They won't try to bring a getaway car up into this narrow space. God knows what they've got in mind for the security guards though.'

'If they shot them you wouldn't hear anything if the presses are running,' Kate said.

Barnard nodded grimly. 'If they really have Georgie Robertson with them I wouldn't be surprised at anything.'

They stood watching the activity inside the print room from a doorway on the opposite side of the road for a few minutes.

'If we're going to call the cavalry we need a phone box,' Barnard said glancing around the street which was now lined on one side with delivery vans, most of the drivers relaxing with their *Globes* and *Mirrors* as they waited for the presses to start rolling. A hundred yards down the narrow side street he spotted the familiar red box.

'Go down to that call box,' he said. 'I'll stay here and watch. When the bad guys arrive, I'll give you a thumb's up and I want you to call DCI Jackson and ask him to get the City police down here at the double. It shouldn't take them more than five minutes – Snow Hill nick is just round the corner. They're doing this right under the bloody noses of the City police. They must be very confident. Put your call through as soon as you see me signal. Once the van's here the rest won't be far behind. They won't have much time to hijack the van before it's unloaded. Tell the DCI the robbery's in progress. Here's the number. OK?'

'Be careful. They might see you.'

'I'll be careful,' he said. 'Now go. We can't do this on our own. We're going to need help fast.' He kissed her quickly on the cheek and then pushed her away towards the phone box. She walked slowly down the pavement towards Fleet Street and the call box which she could see was empty, went inside and tried to see what was going on back at the *Globe.* Almost as soon as she had closed the door she saw the heavy security van inching past the newspaper delivery vans towards the bay where it would unload. And close behind two men strolled nonchalantly along the pavement within inches of her beyond the thick glass and she immediately recognized Georgie Robertson and Reg Smith wearing blue printers overalls as if they were innocently on their way to work. Without waiting for Barnard's signal she dialled the number he had given her and asked to be put through to DCI Jackson.

When Kate explained where she was and what she was witnessing there was a sharp intake of breath.

'Are you sure?' he asked sharply.

'One hundred per cent sure,' she said angrily. 'I know Georgie Robertson and he's within yards of a security van fully loaded with cash. You need to get someone down here before Harry Barnard tries to stop him all on his own and gets killed.'

'Right,' Jackson said crisply. 'We're on our way.'

As Robertson and Smith approached, Barnard turned away, making as if to light a cigarette in a doorway out of the wind. When they had crossed the road he glanced back and saw Kate already coming out of the call box and heading towards him. Behind him he could hear the roar of the presses starting up.

'Are the cavalry coming?' he asked Kate as they met.

'So your DCI says.'

'Good,' Barnard said. 'Well done. You can get out of the way now. Go down to Fleet Street and pick up a bus. I'll call you at the agency later when this is all over.'

'And what are you going to do?' Kate asked.

'I want to keep an eye on what's going on,' he said.

Kate put a hand on his arm. 'You mean try to stop it if the cavalry don't turn up on cue?'

'They'll need witnesses to pin these bastards down,' he said.

'Then they can have me too,' Kate said, her expression adamant. 'I owe that to Carter Price.'

Barnard sighed. 'We keep our distance? Right?'

Kate nodded and they both walked slowly back towards the

Globe where the thundering sound of the presses seemed to be shaking the very structure of the building and the vibration could be felt on the pavement through the soles of their shoes. The back of the security van could be glimpsed through the open end of its bay but it was impossible to see more until two things happened almost simultaneously. The van began to reverse slowly out of its parking place and a police squad car screamed round the corner from the direction of Holborn and slammed to a standstill across the narrow entrance, blocking the van in place. Except that whoever was driving the van now was having none of that. Instead of stopping he put his foot down and reversed hard into the side of the patrol car, pushing it across the narrow street and into the wall on the opposite side making it impossible for the officers inside to get out. The hijackers must have thought they could get away until they realized that the squad car was only the first of several and that there were more sirens blaring from the direction of Fleet Street, blocking their escape in that direction.

Men jumped out of the van on both sides, a couple heading towards Holborn, running wildly, and three into the roaring print labyrinth behind them.

'That's Smith and Georgie Robertson,' Barnard yelled.

'And Mitch Graveney,' Kate yelled back. 'He'll know his way around in there.'

'Come on or we'll lose them,' Barnard said and set off at a run into the overpowering noise of the rolling presses where newspapers were already spewing off the conveyor belts and being loaded into the first of the waiting vans. Very few men had turned towards the collision in the street outside, no doubt because they had not heard the impact or the frantic knocking on the windows of the police car from the furious officers trapped inside.

Kate and Barnard could see the fugitives, Graveney in the lead, racing up a metal stairway close to the thundering presses and then along a catwalk obviously intended to be used only when the machines were not in action. If the machine minders, all in earmuffs, even noticed what was happening they took no interest, presumably because their supervisor looked as if he was in charge.

Barnard led the way cautiously up the stairs and along the catwalk, with Kate close behind. About halfway along Georgie Robertson glanced behind and realized for the first time that they were being followed. He grabbed Graveney's arm and gestured at their pursuers and the three men stopped and began to move to block the narrow gantry. It was only then that Barnard realized that Georgie Robertson had a gun which he was pointing firmly in their direction. No one, he knew, would hear anything at all if he shot them both.

Graveney must have taken in the look of horror on Barnard's face because he spun round and knocked Robertson's arm upwards so his shot went harmlessly into the ceiling but as Robertson lunged in his direction Graveney lost his footing, teetered for a moment against the low guard rail before crashing, arms and legs flailing, into the roaring, rolling machinery below. If he screamed as he fell no one heard and it was a minute before his body arrived below, covering the morning's news with blood, and someone switched the presses off.

In that minute Robertson had moved forward and grabbed Kate, pressing his weapon against her head.

'Stay there or I'll kill her,' he said in the sudden disorienting silence which had fallen. And Barnard, dumbfounded, stayed where he was as Robertson and Smith dragged Kate onwards towards a narrow passageway and disappeared. Gripping the guard rail, his knuckles white, Barnard glanced down to where a group of men were clustered around what must surely be the body of Mitch Graveney. He was gripped by a wave of sheer fear and stayed where he was until a file of uniformed officers climbed up to the catwalk and surrounded him.

'Georgie Robertson and Reg Smith,' he said to the uniformed inspector who put a non-too-friendly hand on his arm. 'They're armed and they've got my girlfriend with them,' he said.

'Which way did they go?' the inspector asked and Barnard waved a hand towards the end of the catwalk which seemed to terminate at a door. 'This must lead into the main building. We just followed.' The inspector waved his men on towards the door but when Barnard went to follow he shook his head.

'DCI Jackson wants words with you,' he said. 'He's on his way. You wait down below and leave the rest to us.'

Barnard ran a desperate hand through his hair. 'I need . . .'

'Downstairs, sergeant,' the inspector snapped. 'Your involvement ends here.'

Kate sat in the back of Reg Smith's Bentley with Georgie Robertson's gun pressed against her ribs. They had left the catwalk above the presses and found themselves in an empty stairwell in the main part of the *Globe*'s offices. The two men had hurried her downwards to ground-floor level where they forced open a fire door and found themselves in a quiet back alley where the mayhem they had left behind them seemed to have not so far disturbed the peace. The two men had hustled her towards busier streets, Georgie with his weapon hidden in his pocket but firmly pressed into her side, where they found Smith's car parked unmolested at the kerb. Robertson pushed Kate into the back seat while Smith accelerated away.

'Stick to the plan?' Smith asked quietly.

'Oh yes,' Georgie said. 'Pity that little enterprise turned out like that. But we've still got time for lots more. I've got scores to settle, but after that we're all set, just as we planned. Even now they won't come near us while we've got this little lady with us, will they?' He leered at Kate and she shivered.

'It's a good job we covered our backs with our friend at the Yard,' Smith said.

Kate opened her mouth to speak and then thought better of it.

'It'll all come good when I've dealt with my brother,' Georgie said. 'Witnesses can disappear as you know very well. And Flash Barnard's on the skids anyway. You know that too. No one's going to believe a word he says.'

'It's not what I bloody wanted, even so,' Smith said angrily. 'You said it would all run smoothly.'

'It will, it will,' Georgie said. 'Trust me. We've got it all sewn up. That bloody poofter will do as he's told.'

Looking out of the window Kate realized that she recognized Piccadilly Circus and was not too surprised when Smith swung into the narrow streets of Soho and parked at the back of the Delilah Club.

'I'll wait here,' Smith said. 'Ready for a quick exit. You go and see your brother and take the dolly bird with you. What you do with her is up to you.' Georgie grinned, a reaction that Kate knew was very far from reassuring. He leaned across her and opened the rear door of the car and motioned for her to get out, holding on to her arm as he followed her, gun hidden under his jacket but still menacing.

'Come on sweetheart,' he said. 'We'll go and say hullo to Uncle Ray, shall we?'

Furious, Barnard did not wait for Jackson to arrive. The DCI was, he reckoned, the last person he wanted to see just now. He walked quickly away from the police activity around the *Globe* and took refuge in a phone box close to where he had parked his car what seemed like hours before but which, when he glanced at his watch, was only half an hour ago. The phone rang for a long time at the Delilah Club but eventually Ray Robertson answered it and sounded surprised to hear Barnard's voice.

'Georgie's on the loose, tooled up, and he's got Kate with him,' Barnard said. 'Have you any idea where he might hide out?' Barnard could hear the sharp intake of breath at the other end of the line.

'What happened?' Robertson asked and Barnard told him briefly.

'I never thought I'd be asking this but do you think I can get some protection. I wouldn't be surprised if he came after me. He's mad enough.'

'Call the nick,' Barnard said. 'I'm out on a limb myself, but I'll get to you as soon as I can.'

He hurried to the Capri and accelerated away hard into High Holborn where he wove through the traffic in the direction of Soho. It was a long shot, he knew, linking up with Ray Robertson but as he was excluded from the hunt for Kate it was the best he could think of and much better than doing nothing. And it might even pay dividends. The traffic was heavy around Piccadilly Circus but when he turned towards the Delilah he managed to park on the opposite side of the road and as he put his hand on the door handle he hesitated as he saw Georgie Robertson half push Kate through the doors of the club. Ray had been only too right, he thought, but at least Kate was alive. For that he gave heartfelt thanks to all the gods he did not believe in. He picked up his car radio and contacted the control room at the nick.

'Stay where you are,' the controller said crisply. 'We'll be with you in five.'

Barnard hung up, locked the car and crossed the road. He knew that reinforcements would not rush in if a hostage was being held but the hostage was Kate and he would do what he could. Now and always.

He walked quietly across the empty club where the tables were already readied for the evening's business. He could hear raised voices in the direction of Ray Robertson's office and he crept up to the door which was ajar. He could see Kate sitting in a chair facing him looking terrified as she watched Georgie Robertson waving his gun at his brother, who was slumped in his chair behind his desk with blood running down his face, from a head wound which Barnard guessed had been inflicted with the butt of the gun.

Barnard inched the door open a fraction and eventually caught Kate's eye. He put a finger to his lips and mouthed the single word: scream. Her eyes widened and she gave an almost imperceptible nod as Georgie continued to harangue his brother.

'You never, never wanted me,' he screamed. 'You did everything you could to keep me out of the business. I knew that. Ma knew that. And in the end you made sure I ended up blamed for everything and looking at a bloody life sentence. Well, if I end up in Dartmoor I may as well end up there for you too. But I won't, you know. I've got insurance now. And what you've got I'm going to have all to myself. I'm going to be the king of Soho now. Pity you won't be here to watch me.'

But as he raised the gun again in Ray Robertson's direction Kate gave the blood-curdling scream she had been saving her breath for. The distraction was enough to turn Georgie's head in her direction and that was enough to let Barnard spring on him from behind and bring him crashing to the floor. Ray Robertson found the strength to jump over his desk and stamp on his brother's hand, sending the gun sliding out of reach where Kate quickly picked it up. Twisting Georgie's arms behind his back Barnard gave Ray a crooked grin.

'You don't have any handcuffs handy, do you?' he asked.

Ray took off his tie. 'This do?' he asked.

And Barnard tied Georgie's hands securely before leaning back on his heels. 'Jesus wept,' Barnard said. 'He had me worried there for a minute.' He got to his feet and as he put his arms round Kate, Ray put a foot in the small of his brother's back to prevent his moving.

'I owe you,' Ray said briefly, pulling out a handkerchief to staunch the blood which was now running freely down his face. 'But what did he mean, he has insurance?' He prodded Georgie roughly with his foot. 'Who the hell are you working with?' he asked.

But Georgie just cursed into the carpet.

'I've an idea, but no evidence,' Barnard said.

'They talked in the car about someone at Scotland Yard,' Kate said quietly. 'A poofter who'd do as he was told.'

Georgie cursed more volubly and Barnard nodded, a cold feeling in the pit of his stomach as disconnected facts slotted into place and made sense of so much he had not understood over the last few weeks.

'You must have a very powerful lever, Georgie, to get that sort of help from the top,' he said.

'The best,' Georgie spat out. 'The very best.'

There were sounds of activity outside in the club and Barnard opened the door wide to find himself face to face with DCI Jackson, DS Vic Copeland and a couple of armed officers.

'It's all over guv,' he said putting an arm round Kate again. 'No major harm done. You don't happen to have seen Reg Smith anywhere do you? He came here with Miss O'Donnell and Georgie Robertson.'

'He was waiting outside in a Bentley,' Jackson said curtly. 'We've detained him on suspicion of armed robbery for now.' He glanced around the room, taking everything in before turning to Copeland. 'Get George Robertson back to the nick and his brother to hospital,' he said. 'I'll take preliminary statements from Sergeant Barnard and Miss O'Donnell.'

Copeland flashed a look of pure hatred in Barnard's direction but Barnard merely smiled. He guessed he would not have to put up with Copeland much longer.

'You are amazing,' Barnard said dropping a plate of steak and chips on to the table in front of her and kissing her neck as he did it. 'Most girls would have been a gibbering wreck if they'd found themselves sitting in with two feuding gangsters with murder a moment away.'

'You turned up just in time,' Kate said soberly. 'I'm sure Georgie had every intention of getting rid of me too. I'd seen and heard far too much.'

'We were very lucky,' he said, sitting down opposite her. 'I wanted to see Ray because I wanted to warn him and I thought he might know where Georgie would hide out. I'd no idea he was so obsessed with getting rid of Ray he would stop off at the Delilah before he tried to hide out. I'm surprised Reg Smith was fool enough to allow it.'

'They seemed to think they were invincible,' Kate said. 'That was my impression.'

'To an extent they were while they had John Amis behind them,' Barnard said.

'But why did he do that?'

'Smith and Graveney met him at their Masonic lodge and one of them must have discovered at some point that he was queer. Think of the scandal there'd be if a senior cop turned out to be a poofter. So that gave them a handle and I guess Reg Smith went to a lot of trouble to check out Amis's lifestyle. So when Smith wanted Georgie Robertson to replace Ray in Soho so they could run the gangs in concert together, he must have put pressure on Amis to get rid of the witnesses and somehow get me out of the way too, as I was regarded as a mate of Ray's. So Amis sent in Copeland to get rid of the pair of us and allegedly clean up Soho. But Amis was losing it himself by this point. He was linked to Nigel Wayland by now which meant Smith could put even more pressure on him. Wayland was murdered and Amis tried to pin it on Vincent Beaufort, but that didn't stick. We don't know yet whether Amis himself killed Wayland or whether Smith arranged it so that he could threaten Amis even harder. It could have worked either way. But they've found plenty of forensic evidence that Amis was at least a regular visitor at Wayland's flat in Berwick Street.'

'Has he been arrested?' Kate asked.

Barnard glanced away for a moment. 'He realized the game was up,' he said. 'He shot himself in his office yesterday, wearing full uniform and leaving a confession neatly typed out on his desk.'

Kate sighed. 'How's Ray?' she asked.

'He's OK. Sitting up in bed bossing the nurses about. His ma went to see him but he turned her away. Said he never wanted to speak to her again.'

'And Carter Price seems to be on the mend. He's already making plans to take me out to dinner.' She looked at Barnard seriously for a moment. 'I won't go,' she said. 'And what about you? Have you got your job back?'

'Apparently,' Barnard said. 'Vic Copeland's been suspended and is likely to be charged for perverting the course of justice as well as beating up Vince Beaufort. It's a pity Amis won't be in the dock with him but we can't have everything.'

'You don't do too badly,' Kate said, smiling.

'Can I have you?' Barnard asked.

'Ah,' she said enigmatically. 'We'll have to see about that, la.'